Praise for Eight Wishes

"A beautifully written, emotionally rich love story that swept me away. *Eight Wishes* is the kind of book you read for pleasure and carry with you long after. With fully realized characters, themes that hit straight to the heart, and a satisfying, soul-stirring ending, this novel is an unforgettable journey of love, loss, and second chances."

—Danny Raye

"*Eight Wishes* is a powerful, heartfelt story that dives deep into the human experience. From the very first page, I was completely hooked—I devoured it in one sitting because I simply couldn't put it down. Each chapter swept me through a range of emotions, from laughter to tears. The characters feel incredibly authentic, like people you know and care about. This moving, beautifully written novel will stay with you long after the final page."

—Tina Tower

"*Eight Wishes* is an emotional rollercoaster that completely captured my heart from beginning to end. Through Emerson's personal struggles and professional challenges, readers witness a powerful journey of self-discovery as she learns what truly matters in life, how to value herself, and the meaning of showing up for loved ones. This raw, authentic story will inspire you to examine your own life through the lens of genuine human connection."

—Allison Smith

"An emotionally resonant, feel-good novel that I would happily recommend—and can't wait to read again. Emerson's journey from control to clarity is inspiring, her social circle is full of warmth, and the ending ties everything together in the most satisfying way. *Eight Wishes* gave me that comforting, curl-up-and-unwind vibe every great chick-lit novel should."

—*Nikki B*

EIGHT WISHES

A NOVEL

CAS CALDICOTT

© 2025 Cas Caldicott
Published by Harbor and Hudson
Contact: cascaldicott@gmail.com

The moral right of the author has been asserted.

Cataloguing-in-Publication entry is available from the National Library of Australia

ISBNs:
978-0-9945610-4-6 (paperback)
978-0-9945610-5-3 (ebook)

Cover Design by Matt Roeser

For Alejandro

Who somehow convinced me that yes, I could write a novel, and no, it wouldn't be terrible, and yes, people might actually want to read it.

This book wouldn't exist without your endless supply of love, support, and gentle reminders that Netflix would still be there after I finished chapter twelve.

You're the best plot twist I never saw coming.

Table of Contents

Chapter One

I stand over the small pot of gently boiling water, watching the brown-speckled egg transform from soft-boiled to hard-boiled to what can only be described as a culinary crime scene. I've had a soft-boiled egg for breakfast every day for the last fifteen years, but today, my stomach feels like it's staging a revolution, and the egg is entirely unappealing. I flip the knob to turn off the heat and abandon ship.

I got up too early, that's the problem. I'll just lie down for twenty more minutes, and then I'll feel better. But even as I think it, I know it's a lie I'm telling myself. Going back to bed has never been my answer to any problem. Plus, I'm already dressed for the day. The last thing I want is to be wrinkled when I make my announcement. Wouldn't that be ironic? The fashion icon Emerson Bailey looks disheveled as she announces the sale of her company.

I hear the steady patter of rain on the tile of our tiny fifth-floor balcony overlooking Twelfth Street in the West Village, and I wonder if it's good luck for it to rain on the day you disclose the sale of your company, just like they say it is on your wedding day. I don't know that I need luck since the hard part is already done, but the rest feels sort of like the same thing, right? The next step, starting the next phase of my life, a huge commitment?

I thought today would be fairly easy since the papers are all signed, and the deal is done. But somehow, making the news public feels like it might be even more complicated and emotional than I thought. Instead of lying down again, I sit on the edge of the bed and wait—for what I don't know—for the day to begin, for my appetite to come back, for Jasper to wake up. As I think his name, he opens his eyes and smiles.

"Good morning, beautiful," he says sleepily. It's the way he greets me every morning, and his sweet Australian accent uttering those words always makes me melt like ice cream on hot pavement. "Happy Announce the Sale of Your Company Day."

"Thanks," I reply. He reaches out and lightly touches the back of my hand with his freckled fingers, moving them up and down. His strawberry blond hair is askew and clearly ready for a haircut.

"Also, as a bonus, Happy Day Before Your Birthday," he adds.

"Thanks," I say again, leaning toward him. He's warm and smells like the morning—that specific, impossible-to-bottle scent of sleep and safety. When I pull back, he sits up against the upholstered leather headboard and looks at me carefully.

"Are you okay?" he asks.

"I think…" I begin. Then I stop. I'm not ready, and, more than that, I'm not even sure. "I think so," I say instead, trying to sound like that was what I was going to say all along.

"Did you eat?" he asks.

It's our routine that I always get up before him, have my egg, and then I'm out the door by the time he gets up to go to the gym. Already, this day is different. I should have thrown away the egg, leaving no evidence that I might be slightly… off?

"I will. I'm just—"

"It's a huge deal," he says, not letting me finish. "You're putting your baby out into the world, letting it spread its wings without you."

I feel acid come up my throat and swallow it away. For the tenth time this week, I tell myself I shouldn't have eaten that sushi the other day. But even as I think it, I know it's a ridiculous excuse. A diversion.

"Are you sure you're okay?" Jasper asks again, narrowing his eyes in what I think of as his laser-beam vision, trying to see inside me. Luckily, he can't. I'm good at many things, and keeping a force field around me is one of my superpowers.

"Yes," I say, clearing my throat and sitting up straighter. "You're right. It's a big day. It's normal to feel anxious."

He looks at me one more time before deciding that he will believe me. He will take my explanation at face value instead of questioning it like he sometimes does. He knows by now that never gets him anywhere anyway. The harder he pushes, the higher my walls get. We are both aware of my tendency to do that, and I'm working on it for me and for Jasper. I can almost see Jasper choosing to give me a break, to trust that I am telling him the truth. The acid in my throat comes up a little higher.

Jasper and I have been together for almost ten years. A little over a year ago, we decided to live together out of one apartment instead of two. It was time to take that step, and it's been good. Maybe it's even been great. I like coming home to him every night. I like knowing he'll be there, not having to coordinate our schedules, no longer having to decide which apartment we'll sleep in on any given night. My biggest concern was work and the possibility that I would be distracted or that he'd get mad if I wanted to work at night, which I almost always did. I worried he'd push back when I had my phone on all night in case someone in Tokyo or Sydney needed me. Mostly, he didn't. He knew what he was getting himself into. He joked more than once that I loved my business more than I loved him, even though I reassured him that wasn't true, at least most of the time. But none of that is going to matter anymore. Everything is going to change today. Literally everything.

"Bathroom's free?" Jasper asks with raised eyebrows.

"All yours," I say. I watch as he goes in and closes the door. Then he opens it and sticks his head out.

"Oh, I've got something for you," Jasper says, standing naked in the doorway. "Don't go anywhere."

"Okay," I say slowly.

"Let me shower, and I'll be right out," he says, closing the door. I listen for the click.

I'm not great with surprises. I like to give them, at least in theory—and, as it stands, I might be holding on to a doozy—but receiving them feeds into my anxiety over needing to control essentially everything in my life.

Once I hear the shower running, I let out a long, slow breath. *Get it together, Emerson,* I chant to myself. *You can do this!* I hear him humming in the bathroom; it's a familiar tune, one he's been writing for a few weeks. And then I know what I have to do. I have to get out of here. Whatever he has for me can wait, I'm sure of it. I take the pad of paper that says IDEAS off Jasper's bedside table and scribble *Sorry, I got a call and had to go in. See you later! I love you! E.* I place it on his pillow. I take one last look at myself in the mirror in the foyer. I arrange my six necklaces— all of which we sell—so they aren't twisted and push my long hair over my shoulder, then bring it back forward to frame my face. I notice that the blue hue of the skin under my eyes matches the blue of my irises a little too much these days. I lean in closer, wishing I had time for an under-eye mask. I tap the spot below each eye, realize there isn't much I can do right now, and head out the door, pulling it gently behind me.

I grab my phone and call Billie as I step into the elevator. She answers on the first ring, and I can hear one of her seven-year-old twins in the background screaming "Pancakes!" Except it sounds more like a crisis than breakfast should call for, like they're shouting "fire!" or "help!"

"Pancakes?" I ask, laughing.

"They are very popular around here," Billie says. "And apparently, they aren't being made fast enough."

"I won't keep you," I say as the elevator reaches the lobby, and I step out. "We can talk later."

"No, it's okay," Billie says, though the demand for pancakes has not eased; the word continues to be shouted in the background as if pancakes are both the problem and the solution to all of life's troubles.

"It's coming," I hear Billie say to someone. "I'm back. Waiting two minutes for breakfast never killed anyone, and I've been wondering about you. Anything… new?"

"Nope," I say, coming out onto Twelfth Street and admiring a small cherry blossom tree that is almost in full bloom. I should have called an Uber, but in my rush to escape Jasper's surprise, I didn't, so I hail a cab. I get in and sit back.

"So, what's the plan?" Billie asks.

"I was hoping you could tell me."

Another call comes through, and I pull my phone away from my ear to see who it is. Jasper. Shoot.

"I'm so sorry. I have to take this," I say. "Can I call you back when I get to the office? I'll have about twenty minutes before the meeting."

"Ooh, the big meeting," Billie says. "Don't eat that raw," she shouts, then to me, "Sorry. Focus on that. We can discuss the other thing later."

"Take care of the munchkins. I'll call you soon."

I hit the end and accept button.

"Hi," I say to Jasper.

"You ran out on me."

"Oh, come on. You know I had to get going, and I hate surprises."

"I know," he says with a forced laugh. I can almost hear him shaking his head at me through the phone. "I shouldn't have warned you. I should have just shown you—or played it for you. You'd think I would know that by now."

I look out the window as we head uptown on Sixth Avenue.

"So, dinner tonight?" Jasper says when I don't say anything. "Bad Roman at six. It was the only time I could get."

It feels like an eternity between now and then, but this is what I've been working toward. This is the end of one race.

"Yes! Bad Roman. I can't wait to have the garlic babka and the chilled artichokes," I say convincingly, hoping that by 6 p.m. my favorite dishes won't make me want to hurl.

"And the meatballs," he adds. "By then, the news will be out. You will no longer be the owner of your company. We'll celebrate."

As we drive north, I spot the T-Mobile store that took over a clothing shop my oldest friend, Luna, and I loved. It was small and personal, in a way most stores aren't anymore. Really, it felt like an extension of my closet in the best possible way. Luna and I still miss it. On many weekends, the two of us would basically play dress up there, just like you see in a 2000s makeover movie scene. And then suddenly, the memory of the first time I got Luna dressed to go out so many years ago pops into my head. I know I'm being extra sentimental because of the announcement today. Once I started dressing her, I couldn't stop, and I went from my closet to my mother's closet to Luna's overnight bag, and by the time I was finished, she looked perfect.

"You should charge other people for this," she'd said, laughing.

"And I should charge you double," I said, pretending to sound harsh. Before I had a chance to say just kidding, Luna rolled her eyes dramatically—she has always been an expert eye roller.

At the time, I had brushed her off. Obviously, we were joking. But then I started writing about clothes and styling principles and began the blog, which I called Style Me Saturday. And that took off, like crazy, and I got question after question after question: Can you wear navy and black together? Can you wear tights in the summer? Is it true I can't wear white in the winter? And I answered every single one. Then, one day, Luna was out of town and had a last-minute event. She asked if I could assemble an outfit for her and ship it. I did. And, while I didn't know it in the moment, StyleShop was born. I started offering a virtual styling service across the U.S. and then Canada, which involved shipping the perfect outfit for whatever the customer needed: a date, a wedding, or a high school reunion. I started slowly and eventually hired a few of my friends to be stylists and buyers. They scouted stores across the country. It quickly became clear that my apartment wasn't big enough, so we finally rented an office in New York. It was a good thing because the demand continued to swell. We could barely keep up. Still, I loved every minute of it.

But in the last few years, as we expanded globally, I found myself so removed from why I started the business. I began it because I loved being creative and loved the challenge of finding the perfect outfit to make our clients' day, night, or vacation memorable. As the business grew, it became more about managing the team, the finances, and the logistics. While I had a great leadership team in place, the role of the CEO was no longer the one I wanted—working seventy-hour weeks with zero creativity coming out of my bones. I knew something had to change.

We were discussing options when The Red Dress approached us. They have a similar model, though they focus more on enhancing the everyday wardrobe than styling for a particular event. They are the number one leader in online personal styling, followed closely by us, and I've always had a great relationship with their CEO. They offered a crazy amount of money to absorb us into their company, with the caveat that they would keep our name and work out of our current location. How could I say no? It made all the business sense in the world, but I do wonder how much I'll miss it. Then I shake it off. I will be thirty-nine tomorrow and can't continue like this forever. There is more to life than my career. There has to be. Right?

"Yes, we'll celebrate," I say. I know that's what he wants to hear.

"So, the announcement meeting with the team and then the interview with *Forbes*?" he asks.

"That's the plan," I say as the cab pulls up to my building on Forty-Second Street between Fifth and Sixth. Our office is on the fifteenth floor. I have a view of Bryant Park. I pay and get out, thinking this is the last time I will stand here like this, the owner of StyleShop.

"Love you, good luck!" Jasper says.

"Thanks, babe, love you, too." I wait and let him end the call.

Suddenly, I am so hungry that getting food seems more important than anything. I spot a pretzel cart, something I would generally walk by without a thought, and march to it like a woman possessed. I get a pretzel with mustard and an ice-cold can of Coke. I eat it in two minutes. I down the Coke even though I haven't had a soda in over five years, and it is the best thing I've tasted all year.

The good thing about wondering if you're pregnant before you planned to be is that it blurs everything around you. I barely remember how I got to our conference room, with my team sitting around the table, smiling at me expectantly. I am not a crier, but as I look out at everyone and then down at my speech, I think I might start. Except now it seems that announcing the sale might not even be the most important thing I do today, and that knowledge makes me feel like there's a scrim between me and my emotions.

"Seventeen years ago, I stood in my bedroom with my best friend, Luna. I took her look from utterly dull to precisely fabulous—my words, not hers," I say. I hear some laughter, followed by confused looks exchanged between the eight members of my leadership team as my tone becomes more serious. I won't make them wait too long for it. I wrote an extensive speech, laying out each step of my journey, but now, standing here, I don't think I will use it. I put it on the table in front of me and feel inspired to go with my heart.

"Fashion has been my life, from raiding my mother's closet when she was away on set to auditing my friends' outfits and making them swap clothing items in the bathrooms at school. It's often been a lifeline and always been at the center of who I am and how I show up in the world. You all know that," I say, pausing to let it sink in a bit. "I have loved every second of this journey, starting and growing StyleShop. I've loved our customers and the lives we get to change every day, but the biggest gift has been welcoming all of you into the company and into my life and each other's lives. While other organizations wave their 'we're a team, not a family' corporate speak around Wall Street, I truly believe that we've become a family. But businesses expand and priorities change. When I was approached about the possibility of selling" —I pause, and I hear the quiet gasps in the room—"I took a clear look ahead to the next decade of StyleShop and the vision we've created together, and I had a moment of truth. If we want to continue to be leaders in the industry, we will need a much deeper level of support and resources. And so, after much thought, I said yes to The Red Dress's proposal to acquire StyleShop."

Short, simple, to the point. I assure everyone that their jobs are safe and that I will stay on for a year to help the company with the transition. Our incredible president, Maddi, will take over as CEO when I exit in twelve months. We've been working together on this over the last year, and she's the best person for the job, plus the team absolutely adores her. I don't let myself think that a year might be longer than I have to offer right now. I'll deal with that when and if I have to. And then everyone is hugging me, saying they are happy for me, for the company. I take it all in, and I absorb it.

When I return to my desk, I wait while the email goes out to the rest of the staff, followed by a press release announcing the sale. I check my phone. *Forbes* confirmed the interview; a reporter will be here this afternoon at 3 p.m. Jasper sent a text with question marks and then clapping emojis when I didn't answer. He really does always give me the benefit of the doubt.

My dear friend Ryder sent a balloon and heart emojis and a text saying *Heya! Anything happening today?* Followed by a winky emoji, and *I love ya guts!* It makes me laugh. Of course, he knows I am announcing the sale today, but he also knows how nervous I was. He is always my cheerleader; I couldn't have done this without him.

Luna sent a congratulations text. I send a note saying, *This is all because of you, you know that, right?* She writes back immediately. *I know! Let me know when my truckload of cash is arriving!* That is followed by a laughing, crying emoji and a heart, which is followed by a GIF of Kim Kardashian fanning herself with one-hundred-dollar bills.

And, finally, three missed calls from Billie. She's the one I really want to talk to. She is my only friend who has kids. As a mom who got pregnant in her late thirties, I know she gets it.

"Hey, sorry," I say when she answers. "One announcement down."

"Good for you, and congrats!" she says. Billie and I met last year through a mutual friend. At first, I thought we wouldn't have much in common since she has young twin boys, but I immediately liked her. When she said at the time that she was desperate for 'me' time, and I suggested we meet for coffee, she said, "Hell no, what about goat yoga?" I've loved her ever since.

"And I ate carbs and drank a non-diet soda before nine a.m.," I add.

"Hmmm," Billie says.

"It could still be just a coincidence, right?"

"Do you want me to bring you a test?" Billie asks. "Think of it as an early birthday present." I can practically hear her smirking through the phone. I can tell she's having fun with this, but I know she really cares.

I have tests in my drawer left over from one time when I missed my period and thought I might be pregnant—back when it was the last thing I wanted. I wasn't, and I never mentioned it to Jasper. Even though we haven't officially started trying yet, it is what I'm supposed to want, part of the grand plan. Everyone tells me (including my mother on the regular) that if you want to be a mother, you better get around to it before you turn forty. So that is what we are doing. The plan was to sell StyleShop, take a significant step back from work, and, once things settled, try to conceive. Then, next on the to-do list, we'll get married. I am nothing if not a planner.

"So sweet of you," I say with a Luna eye roll. "But no thanks. I have a few tests here. I'll take one."

"Do you want me to come and sit with you while you do it?"

"Thank you, but no."

"Plllleeeaaasseee," she says like it's the most crucial thing in the world, "keep me posted."

"Nah. I think I'll keep it a secret for a while."

"If you do, I'll wait at your door and throw pancake batter at you," Billie giggles.

"Hon, I'll call you back."

I grab the box, put it in my bag, and walk to the bathroom. When I get there, I check the date to ensure it's still good, and then I pee on the stick. I left my phone on my desk, so I count the minutes off in my head. And then, there they are—two bright pink lines. Huh. I have another test. I could take it to make sure, but I don't have to. I am not surprised at all.

"So what is it?" Billie asks when I call her back. She is half-chuckling, but I think she's just nervous. "One line or two?"

I'm silent for a moment, then I whisper, "Two lines.

Positive."

"That was so fast," Billie says after a few seconds. "And so easy. It took years to conceive the boys."

"I'm sorry I didn't know you then. I'm sorry it was so hard."

"No, that's not what I mean. My point is, this is good," Billie says. "I never expected anything less from you. You say you will do something, and you do it."

"Well, yeah, but this is ahead of plan. I thought I'd have a little more time to get used to the idea."

"Even better," Billie says. "You overachieved, as usual. And getting used to the idea is a myth."

"I don't know how to be a mother," I say, more to myself than to Billie. And I'm not kidding or exaggerating. My own mother has been less than, well, motherly.

"We've talked about this. You can do anything you set your mind to. That is an undisputed fact. And I will be there every step of the way. You're good."

My assistant comes to my door and indicates *Forbes* is here and waiting in the conference room.

"Gotta go," I say. "Thanks, Billie. I'm so grateful for you."

"Same," Billie says.

I was glad when *Forbes* reached out last month to do an interview after I was named one of the forty under forty (just barely in my case) women to watch. I'd put it off and was relieved when they agreed to do it today. I think they'll be glad, too, since there is much more of a story now with the sale than they expected.

"Emerson Bailey," the reporter says, putting out her hand. She looks about my age with light brown hair cut into a bob and the brightest green eyes I have ever seen. "Pleased to meet you. I'm Cynthia Reid."

"I appreciate you coming in today."

"Well, we just got the news," she says. "We thought you would never sell."

I laugh, trying to relax and remembering our laughing meditation at last year's corporate retreat. It works. I will give myself this moment to be proud of what we have all achieved. I'll sort everything else out later.

"I thought that for a long time, too," I begin. "But we don't always know what's around the corner."

I sit back and take in the view of Bryant Park below. Colleagues walk by, and when they see me through the glass wall, they wave or give me a discreet thumbs-up. I smile back nervously.

"So, how is your team taking the news?" Cynthia asks.

"So far, so good," I say because it seems to be true. The email went out to everyone. Right after the sentence that said The Red Dress had acquired us came the sentence everyone worried about: *Nobody will be laid off in the foreseeable future.* It was the best I could do. In our negotiations, they agreed to stick to that for at least six months, but the foreseeable future sounds better than half a year, so that's how we wrote it. If I have anything to do with it, everyone will stick around until at least the end of my transition year.

I enjoy the interview. I always do. Cynthia asks all the usual questions: What was the moment I knew I wanted to be in the fashion world? (Styling Luna!) Did I play with Barbie dolls when I was little, dressing them? (No!) Did I have a strong female role model at home? (Not really, not in the way you mean.) When did I know that I had made it, that the company was no longer surviving day to day but thriving, a true success? (That holiday season when we generated double the expected revenue.) She then dives deeper and does a good job taking the information you can find about me online and putting a twist on it, getting me to open up and talk.

"You've been so generous with your time," Cynthia says. "And I know there's a lot going on today, but I have two final questions."

"Shoot."

"It's been reported that The Red Dress bought your company for two hundred million dollars," she says slowly. "Why sell now when you're on top?"

"This company has been everything to me, but in the same way you raise a child and plan to send them off to college, sometimes you reach the point when you have done everything you can to build something, and now you need more support, some new ideas. Think of it this way. Your kid excels at math or any particular subject, but you have already taught them all you can. With that knowledge, you bring in the big guns, the best tutor you can find, so they can do well, move on to the next level, and continue to grow."

Cynthia nods like she agrees with what I'm saying. I'm not sure I believe it, as it's all so new and fresh. But it's what I've been telling myself for the last year, and it should make for a good quote when the article appears.

"So," she says. "What's next for you?"

I sit up straight. I had this answer prepared—I knew it was coming. *What's next for me? Well, of course, I'll oversee the transition and always remain in fashion in one way or another. There is always someone who needs styling, right?!* Then I would smile, sit back, let Cynthia nod, and finish taking her notes. But she is looking at me in a way I didn't expect, like she knows me and senses I am keeping a secret. And would it be so bad to tell her what's really going on instead of the stock reply, the expected response? Would it be so bad if everyone out there knew I was much more nuanced than that? In addition to wanting a successful career, I also want a family. What is it that Billie says, 'The company isn't going to love you back'?

I stand as though the interview is over, and Cynthia looks startled. She sits up straighter and raises her eyebrows as though asking if I'm dodging the question. I nod toward her, almost a challenge, and she asks the question again as I hoped she would.

"So, Emerson Bailey," she says, a small smile on her face. "What's next for you?"

"I'm pregnant," I say loudly and clearly, putting it into the universe.

As soon as it's out of my mouth, I want to put it back in, rewind thirty seconds, rethink it, and make the more logical choice. Cynthia looks surprised and then pleased. She knew I would share something, but I bet she didn't see this coming.

"Wow," she says as I begin to panic, calculating that Cynthia Reid from *Forbes* is the second person I have told about my recent discovery, and I know that is not the proper order. I also know I don't have much time before she puts it out there. A quick hit on one of the social media sites: *Emerson Bailey, CEO and Founder of StyleShop is moving on to her next creation—a human being!* I could backtrack, tell her I'm not thinking clearly, that that was meant to be off the record. That would buy me some time, but I would be lying. I knew what I was doing.

"Well, that's an exciting next chapter. I wish you all the very best," she concludes, and I believe her. Why shouldn't I? She's so lovely, I consider asking her to give me an hour, maybe two, before she announces anything. She might agree that it isn't too much to ask for, but it would make me look unprofessional and wishy-washy after such a great interview, and I don't want to do that. I don't want to appear unstable. I don't want it to look like anything I said was less than fully thought through and honest, but maybe not this transparent.

I quickly thank her, run to my office, and avoid as many people as possible as I walk to the elevator. I have to be at Bad Roman in less than an hour, but more than that, I have to get to Jasper before someone else tells him. I try to hail a cab, but they are all full, so I walk up Sixth Avenue, past 30 Rockefeller Plaza and Radio City Music Hall, past Fifty-Seventh Street, to Central Park South and then Columbus Circle. Every block or so, I call Jasper, but it just goes to voicemail. My only hope is that he is totally unplugged, working on a song in the studio, and he'll realize what time it is at the last second and run, not having a chance to check anything.

When I got in the elevator at my office, I felt overwhelmed and slightly out of sorts, maybe even a little guilty, especially after being reminded of what Billie had been through to conceive her twins. But by the time I enter Bad Roman, I believe—or at least I've convinced myself—that I have executed the most perfect trajectory of events possible. I did it efficiently, effectively, and productively—and with style. I succeeded at something that is never a given and often difficult, but I basically just had to think it, and now it is true. How much luckier could I be? I smile to myself and touch my belly for a second.

I see Jasper waiting at the end of the bar. There is a crowd. He wasn't kidding about how hard it was to get a reservation. I try to find a way to get through the large group of people waiting to speak to the host. At that moment, my phone blows up—*ping, ping, ping*. I will myself to not look, but it doesn't stop. I see Jasper free his phone from the charger and look at the screen.

"Wait!" I call louder than I mean to. I push through the group, almost knocking over a little kid. I turn slightly to make sure he has his footing. His mother glares at me. I mumble sorry along with my best please-don't-hurt-me face and turn back toward Jasper. But it's too late. He looks up from his phone screen. His eyes are wide open, his eyebrows raised, and his jaw is dropped open in what might be considered a perfect O.

"I'm sorry," I say when I reach him. "I'm so sorry."

"Is this true?" He looks back down at his phone and reads, "Emerson Bailey announces sale of StyleShop and baby on the way."

"I never should have—" I begin.

"Is it true?" Jasper asks again, reaching gently for my wrist. His hand feels warm and comforting.

"Yes," I say, exhaling and moving closer to him. "I tried to call you. You didn't answer."

"My phone ran out of juice. They had a charger here. It just came back to life."

"I don't know what I was thinking. Are you mad?"

"Mad?" he asks, like that is the last thing that occurred to him.

"That I told *Forbes* before I told you?" I ask, stopping short of holding my breath.

He puts his arms around me and begins to laugh quietly at first, and then loud rolling chuckles.

"I'm not mad. I'm thrilled. And honestly, if I had to guess how I would learn one day that you are going to have our baby, I would say *Forbes* is a pretty good bet. I know you, Emerson. You're awesome, and I love you. I wouldn't change a thing."

I lean into him, and he picks up his water glass and hands it to me. Then he reaches across the bar, picks up the one the bartender just put in front of me, and holds it up for a toast.

"To our next chapter, to becoming a family," he says, holding my eyes with his and clinking his water glass with mine. "To an early happy birthday and a wonderful year ahead. Here's to us."

"Here's to us," I say, and we drink.

It isn't until I'm lying in bed later that night that I remember you are never supposed to toast with water in your glass. It is said to bring bad luck.

Chapter Two

One year later

I have three minutes to eat my soft-boiled egg before I'm out the door early this morning to catch my Uber. I've always had this quirky little hack of eating before breakfast meetings—because who wants to talk business with food on their face or, worse, tucked between their teeth like unwanted guests at a party? But today, I feel like the world is spinning half a rotation too fast. I take one bite of the egg and decide I'll grab something when I'm with Maddi. It's not like I'm trying to impress her. Plus, we're meeting at Angelina Paris, which is basically heaven if heaven smelled like butter and chocolate.

I pause at the mirror in the foyer, as I always do—a ritual that feels both comforting and torturous. I immediately regret cutting my hair so short a month ago. But I needed a change, didn't I? That's what women do when their lives implode: they cut their hair. It still falls well below my chin, but I miss the length. I miss being able to pull it over my shoulder and let it cascade down the front of my floral, V-neck, flutter-sleeve top like a security blanket. Just as I decide I'll let it grow—because isn't that what I have now? Time?—my phone pings with the two-minute warning for my Uber, mercifully saving me from having to acknowledge that soon I'll have all the time in the world to obsess over my hair. I shut the front door quietly and rush to the elevator and down to the street where my car awaits.

"Good morning, Emerson?" the driver calls over his shoulder as I throw myself into the backseat like I'm diving for cover. He has a British accent, which—ever since my Harry Potter phase that never actually ended—makes me feel slightly calmer, as if Hogwarts might still send me an owl any day now.

"That's me," I say, strapping in and settling back for what will be my last official drive to the office. *Stop being so dramatic*, I scold myself internally. It's not like this day was a surprise attack. And it's not even like I've been going to the office every day. I haven't. I've been working remotely most days, at least lately. But there's something about the last time that feels like standing at the edge of a cliff with no safety net.

We head to Angelina Paris, just south of the office. I walk in and notice someone waving from the corner of my eye. It's Maddi, already seated, probably having arrived before the doors even opened. She looks as effortlessly chic as always in a short, black, high-waisted skirt with boots and a flowing white Milano silk blouse that perfectly complements the restaurant's checkerboard marble floor.

"Did you match with this place on purpose?" I ask, leaning in for a hug. She has what appears to be black coffee in front of her instead of their signature hot chocolate that basically tastes like melted candy bars. "Aren't you having something a little more exciting than that?"

"Are you kidding me? I had to unbutton my skirt as soon as I saw those people eating bagels at the table next to us," she jokes with a self-deprecating laugh that makes me smile despite my mood.

"Ha, I'll be right back," I say, joining the line. My phone pings, and I scroll through messages while waiting. *Hey Girl! Happy almost the age that we shall never mention! P.S. Good luck today*, from Ryder. *Enjoy the last day of your thirties and StyleShop*, from Billie. I see typing bubbles and know she's still writing. *I can't wait to celebrate with you!* I heart both messages and scroll back to make sure I haven't missed anything. Luna has been suspiciously quiet lately. She's usually so obsessed with birthdays and normally the first person to message me. I figure she must be pretending to forget so she can surprise me with something, knowing it will absolutely terrify me because I hate surprises almost as much as I hate turning forty.

"Can I help you?" a young woman asks from behind the counter. She looks about twelve, though she's probably around twenty-two, and for some inexplicable reason, that hits me like a truck. Wasn't I just that young? How can I possibly be heading into my fifth decade on this planet? I reach for my hair, wanting to pull it around to the front as a shield, and then remember I can't.

Out of professional habit, I immediately notice the safe, expected uniform they make employees wear: a white collared shirt and white apron, like she's back there baking instead of taking orders. It's the kind of thing you'd see in the gift shop after the Ratatouille ride at Disney World's Epcot. My mind automatically begins sketching a new uniform for her—a light blue tweed bow dress with chrome buttons and a signature arctic blue bow positioned near the breastbone. When I realize I've been staring too long at this poor girl while mentally redesigning her workplace attire, I nod toward the counter.

"Thanks," I say. "I'll have the chocolate croissant and your hot chocolate."

When in Rome, right?

"Sure thing," the poorly dressed twelve-year-old says.

"Actually, make that two croissants," I add, because if there was ever a day to double-carb, it's the day before you turn forty and lose your company baby. "And you know what? Throw in another hot chocolate."

"Never a bad decision," she says with a wink that makes me wonder if she can see my existential crisis written all over my face.

Maddi's eyes widen as I approach the table carrying actual food. I place a pastry at my seat and one in front of her, then go back for the drinks. I settle into the chair across from her.

"Thank God," she says, leaning forward with a conspiratorial laugh. "I'm starving. And the hot chocolate at the next table smelled so good, I was contemplating a heist."

"I know! And I am, too, actually."

We both take enormous bites of our croissants, and the buttery bliss is as perfectly flaky as every croissant dreams of being. Then we sip the warm hot chocolate, simultaneously wiping our upper lips as though we're looking in a mirror. I take another bite, savoring it.

"So," I say as I chew, not giving a single damn about the crumbs that might be decorating my face like confetti. "We're here. It's official."

"You've been happy with the way things have been going this year, right?" she asks, then shifts uncomfortably in her seat. "I mean, at StyleShop?" she clarifies quickly. I know she's worried I'll think she's referring to my year in general, which, as she well knows, has been about as pleasant as stepping on a Lego in the dark. But this part has been happy. Mostly.

"Absolutely. You are the best person for the job," I say, and I mean it with every fiber of my being. "I am very happy."

I can see her relax a bit as she takes another bite. It's kind of her to care about my opinion, because she doesn't have to. I'm in no position to make any important changes now—not that I want to.

"What's on your agenda today? Anything I can help with?" she asks. "Don't forget your farewell lunch with the team at one."

I nod as I look around the café, which is now fully bustling with people who all seem to have a purpose. Everyone I notice looks engaged and happy, like they're living life to the fullest and going someplace important. I'm going someplace too… today. But tomorrow? I snap out of it and lean in, making sure I have Maddi's attention.

"We've done it," I say, purposely shifting my thinking away from the void that awaits me. "I will walk away at the end of the day knowing we executed this transition pretty perfectly. Are you happy with how everything has played out? Is this what you thought it would be?"

Maddi is nodding before I even finish my sentence, like a bobblehead in a hurricane.

"I've certainly been pushed out of my comfort zone over the past twelve months, and for that, I'm grateful to you. And yes, I am very happy," she says, putting the last of her croissant in her mouth like it might escape if she doesn't.

"And thankfully, we were able to negotiate that the team was safe this whole year, which was no small feat, but the year is up, and layoffs are imminent," I add, the words feeling heavier than they should.

"Yeah, about that. I know it's all part of the job, but dealing with layoffs is my least favorite part. I can't stand it, sitting across from them, seeing the exact moment they realize their lives are going to change. I mean, I know there are other places they can go, and they are all talented, and we have a plan ready to support them and ensure they will find a place to land, but still…" Her voice trails off, laden with guilt.

"I can relate," I say, nodding again.

"I'm going to wait until after lunch to tell them," Maddi says. "That way, everyone will still be in good spirits when you address them for the last time."

Her words—*address them for the last time*—echo in my ears like a gong.

"I'll do it," I say, without really thinking it through, like jumping off a diving board before checking if there's water in the pool. "I'll tell them."

Maddi looks at me with a furrowed brow. Incongruously, it occurs to me in that moment that I should ask who does her eyebrows. At a second glance, it looks like threading.

"Why?" she asks suspiciously. "Why would anyone do that if they don't have to?"

"Because… I don't mind," I say, persuading myself with each word. "I mean, I mind, but I feel like it's my responsibility. If I hadn't moved forward with the sale, they wouldn't be losing their jobs. Also, I don't have to face them every day anymore. You do."

Maddi has the look of someone who just dropped a seventy-pound backpack on the ground and is now floating three inches above the floor.

"You're a gift, thank you," she says as her cheekbones rise with her warm smile.

"Don't mention it," I say, trying to match her smile, though mine feels slightly plastered on, like I'm posing for a driver's license photo.

My phone pings again, and I pull it out to see who it is.

Lady, I'm so proud of you. Soak it up today—it's from Luna. I smile and then double-check who the message is from because in the two decades I've known Luna, the words *proud of you* have never escaped her mouth. I wait for her typical cynical message or inappropriate GIF to follow, but there is nothing.

"Shall we, Ms. CEO?" I ask.

"We shall," Maddi says, positively gleaming, like she's about to take the ride of a lifetime.

Once we're outside, she loops her arm through mine, and for a second, I have the sense she's about to start skipping and singing that we're off to see the wizard. I imagine a yellow brick road appearing in front of us that will lead us to our office building, or maybe it will lead us to Oz if we're lucky. I think of Dorothy and the Tin Man, the Scarecrow and the Lion, and all the wishes they had. Of all of them, I realize now, I am firmly in Dorothy's camp. I just want to go home. But at this point, what does that even mean? Another year at the company? I don't think so. That's the only part that has gone fairly smoothly. Overall, the team and I have done an even better job than I had hoped in leading StyleShop through this transition.

"We're here!" Maddi exclaims as the elevator doors open on our floor, her voice bursting with excitement that I wish I could bottle and save for later.

"Yes, we are," I whisper bravely with a deep inhale as I take my first step on the floor for the last time.

Everyone I run into hugs me or shakes my hand as I walk toward my office. It was left empty all this time, but I know people have been using it for meetings and calls, and Maddi will move in once I'm out, which I pretty much am now. I have only one framed photo left on the desk, taken by Ryder at my apartment. In the picture, I am packing our very first style box with the first rendition of the StyleShop logo (stickers printed from Kinko's, because nothing says 'legitimate business' like office supply store stickers). My grin takes up my entire face. I allow myself to be transported back to that day for just a moment, and I contemplate the past nearly twenty years and how this company has changed my life and the lives of our team and, most importantly, our customers. I place the photo in my moving day box along with the essentials I've kept in my top drawer: toothbrushes, toothpaste, chewing gum, a handful of lipsticks, Sour Patch Kids, and an almost empty bottle of Advil. I've slowly been taking things home piece by piece for the last twelve months, and this is the last of it. I had asked Maddi to send in the employees being laid off, and one by one, they come. I don't expect the conversations to go well, but they are even harder than I anticipated, like trying to rip off a Band-Aid that's been superglued to your skin. Still, it is the least I can do for Maddi, for everyone.

We get through them with some tears, a little pushback, and I leave everyone with the promise that I will always have their back if they need me, that I'm ready to give them a reference at the drop of a hat, as they are all terrific at what they do. At one, I head down the hall to the conference room for the farewell lunch. There are balloons and flowers, and my favorite Don Dom pizza from Motorino. We eat and toast and laugh, and then I take my spot at the head of the conference table for the last time. Everyone begins to quiet down; I hear a bunch of hushing noises move through the group like a wave.

"So, this is the end of a chapter," I say, standing tall. I have prepared for this moment for the last twelve months, rehearsed it in my shower, in front of my mirror, in my dreams. "I am leaving you in fantastic hands with Maddi as our new CEO. It has been a wonderful journey with the best people I could ever have wished for. Thank you all for showing up every day, committed to transforming lives across the globe. And as I close this door as your CEO, I'm excited to open up a new one as your customer. I look forward to getting my first StyleShop delivery!"

Everyone claps and cheers. People take turns hugging me, then head back to the food table. Someone turns up the music, a balloon pops, and suddenly, without even thinking it through, I am running to the bathroom like I've been shot out of a cannon. I get there, close the stall door behind me, pray no one else is in here, and start sobbing—all-out, full-body, mascara-destroying sobbing. I feel like my insides are coming out through my eyes, like I have absolutely no control over myself.

I didn't see this coming. I felt fine all morning. I didn't even feel the prick of a tear. I come out of the stall—I can't stay in there all day, tempting as it is—and stand with my back against the entry door. The last thing I need is someone seeing me falling apart during the final hours. My goal—what I want, what I intend, and what I plan to do—is to walk out of here with my head held high. I don't want anyone to think I have any regrets or doubts about moving on or the future of the company. Hoping beyond hope that nobody will come in, I stop barricading the door and go to the sink. I run the water cold and splash my face, but I am still crying so hard I feel like I am walking through a waterfall. I grab paper towels and go into a stall again, locking it. I put the seat cover down and sit, letting myself cry all out for another three minutes. I hear someone come in, and I remain quiet as a mouse. They pee, flush, wash their hands, and leave quickly.

"Get it together, woman," I say out loud to myself as I take deep breaths. "You've got this, breathe."

Slowly, I'm able to stop crying, but my breathing is ragged like I've just run a marathon in stilettos. I head back to the sink. I look awful, like I've been through a car wash with the windows down. I splash water on my face again, trying to figure out what happened and why I'm losing it now, but every time I go down that road, I can feel the prick behind my eyes, and I will it away. I'll unpack it later. Actually, I probably won't. What's important now is getting out of here and saving face. Would it be so bad to slip out and not do another round of goodbyes?

The door opens, and Maddi comes in. She almost doesn't realize it's me, which is both good and bad, and then she does a double-take.

"Are you okay?" she asks, gently putting her hand on my shoulder. I stand up straighter, as if good posture might convince us both that I'm fine.

"Yes," I say, like I believe it. "I'm just going to miss this place."

She looks at me, her eyes soft with understanding.

"It's a lot," she says. "These past twelve months have been a lot for you. I probably should have said more about that at breakfast. I just didn't want to, I don't know, bring up anything you might not want to talk about."

"Thank you for that, and they have," I say truthfully, but I can't think about it all now. I just want to go home and pull the covers over my head for about a year.

"Here," she says, reaching into her bag and handing me a silver square a little larger than a condom. "It does wonders."

I take it and slowly turn it over in my hand. It says CalmGlow. I open it, pull out the wipe, and brush my face slowly. It feels cool, and in a matter of seconds, the blotches begin to disappear like magic.

"What's in this?" I ask, amazed.

"Green tea, coconut oil, cucumber extract, lavender oil, chamomile… oh, and a little aloe," she rattles off without taking a breath, like she's been waiting for someone to ask.

I examine my face in the mirror again, recognizing my old self coming back to life. "This is magic," I whisper.

"You think? I'm so glad," Maddi says gleefully. "It's something I've been working on for a while."

"Wait, this is your product?" I ask, suddenly interested.

"It is," she says proudly.

"You aren't going to—" I begin, my business brain clicking into gear despite my emotional meltdown.

"No!" she says, cutting me off. "I am fully committed to StyleShop, like fully."

I smile and nod. Honestly, it is not really my problem anymore. But I believe her, for now at least.

I look at myself again in the mirror, and it's like the waterworks never happened. It's actually kind of miraculous.

"Can I take a few of those with me?" I ask.

Maddi digs back into her big shoulder bag and pulls out a small stack of the wipes. She hands them to me.

"Just in case," she says, smiling warmly.

"Thank you," I say, taking them, wondering where these were the past six months of my life when I needed them most, when crying was my main form of exercise.

I am itching to get home, and I also want to avoid it. But really, it is the only place to go at this point.

"I'm going to sneak out," I tell her. "I've had enough goodbyes for today."

Maddi leans in for a hug. "You're one of a kind, Emerson."

"Right back at you," I say, meaning it.

Unapologetically, after quickly stuffing everything left in my office into a large tote bag, I walk right to the elevator, eyes on my target, and head down to the lobby. I cross the street and walk through Bryant Park. I decide to walk home, which will probably take over an hour, but luckily I'm wearing flats, the tote bag is fairly light and sits comfortably on my shoulder, and my thinking is that I will be so tired when I get there that I'll just collapse on the couch and maybe never get up again.

It's almost five by the time I get back to my building. Maybe I'll skip dinner. Perhaps I'll go right to sleep. It is at that moment that I see Ryder sitting in my lobby on one of the plush dark purple benches, his head against the wall, his raven-black hair in stark contrast to the white wall behind him, his eyes closed, a cooler on the floor below him and the game Cards Against Humanity next to him. For a second, I imagine him in his former incarnation, before I knew him, when he was what I can only imagine was a fabulous dancer. He doesn't talk about it much, but I know he was injured and that ended his career. I stand in front of him now, my feet throbbing, eclipsing some of the bright light from the lobby chandelier, and he opens his eyes. I smile for the first time in hours.

"Took you long enough. I thought you were going to be home by four today," he says drowsily, waking up from his nap. He looks up at me with his usual sparkle in his brown eyes, smoothing his well-groomed beard with one hand while reaching for the cooler with the other.

"If I'd known you were here, I would have taken a cab," I say, my feet silently screaming at me.

"You walked?" he says, shocked, as if I'd told him I swam across the Hudson.

"I did, in a lame attempt to numb my brain," I say, exhausted, letting the tote bag fall off my shoulder and placing it on the floor in front of me. It was heavier than I realized.

"What are you doing here? Why didn't you tell me you were coming?"

"Ah, because I know you, Emerson Bailey. And I knew you would say no," he says, laughing. "Honestly, I wanted to be with you on the last day of your thirties, and my Bumble date canceled." He rushes through that last part like he's trying to sneak it past me. "And it was your last day at StyleShop. How was it, by the way?"

"Yeah, good." I shrug. "As good as it could have been. What did you bring?" I ask to change the subject before he can dig deeper.

"Sushi," he says, pointing toward the cooler. "From Blue Ribbon," he sings with a shimmy that makes me wonder how I ever doubted he was once a dancer.

"You know how to make a girl swoon."

He mimics putting his fingers down his throat. "Making girls swoon has never been on my bucket list." He laughs. "And... I have a game!" My turn to mime putting fingers down my throat.

He follows me to the elevator, and we head upstairs. As always, I am comforted by his presence, which is a cross between a cuddly bear and the head of a fancy wellness hotel. I open the door to the quiet apartment.

"Eat first or play?"

To be honest, neither sounds too appealing, but I know he

isn't going to leave me alone, and maybe that's exactly what I need right now.

"You decide while I quickly use the bathroom," he gently commands.

I haven't fully turned on the lights yet, and as he heads down the hall, I hear him crash into something.

"Shit, ouch," he yelps. "Can a guy have some light back here or night vision glasses?"

I jump to flip the switch, and I see he tripped over the folded stroller that was leaning against the wall. It must have slipped during the day. Last night, I finally moved some of the baby gear out of the nursery, but I didn't get too far with it. When Ryder sees what it is, he mutters, "Sorry," and I know that will be that. He won't mention it again, and I love him fiercely for knowing when to let sleeping dogs lie.

He comes back and unpacks the sushi quietly. It is so much more than two people can possibly eat, and I wouldn't expect anything less from Ryder. His middle name is Extra, and I love him for it. He digs right in, using the tiny plastic cups to mix his soy sauce and wasabi. I go through the motions, pretending to study the pieces before using my chopsticks to put a few pieces on my plate, and he doesn't question me when I barely eat anything. Then he points to the game, raising his eyebrows like a cartoon villain.

"I think I've had enough activities for one day," I say, feeling like I have about a two percent charge left on my brain and body.

"A movie then?" he eagerly asks.

I shake my head. "Will you be mad at me if we call it a night?" I ask. "I just want to sleep."

"No, no, you don't. Sleep is overrated," he says compellingly, starting to pack up. "Tomorrow is a big day.

Tomorrow, my best friend Emerson Bailey turns"—he pauses when I give him a look of *don't you dare*—"the number we do not mention. We will celebrate from dawn to midnight!" he declares with an annoying amount of enthusiasm.

I half smile and award him an A+ for effort in my mind. If I'm being honest, there isn't much to celebrate, but at the same time, I know he won't stand for that kind of talk.

I muster out, "We will," leaning in convincingly for a hug. "Can we maybe start a little later than dawn, though?"

"I will be at your beck and call," he says, which I know is a reference to *Pretty Woman*, but I don't pick up the thread and ask if I am his beck-and-call girl. He looks at me for one beat longer than someone might think is normal, but he lets me off the hook.

"I love you," he says, looking me directly in my eyes, and I feel his warmth and worry.

"I love you more," I say to him, accepting his hug good night.

Once Ryder is gone, I get into bed and check my email, which is part of my unhealthy nighttime routine. There isn't much, which initially is a shock, but in that moment, I'm reminded that I'm unemployed. I go to my personal email inbox, and as I'm scrolling through the spam, one comes in from Jasper, and I practically jump. We haven't talked in weeks. I close my eyes tightly, wishing it away, then open them. It's still there, like a pebble in my shoe. I click on the email. It is a reminder of a group reservation for tomorrow night at Buddakan. We had planned it for my birthday months ago, after everything happened and before it was all over. I had occasionally wondered what happened to the reservation and if anyone was still planning to come, but had been too busy wrapping up at work to give it any real attention. That's the story I was telling myself anyway. Twelve people, tomorrow night at 7 p.m.—cocktails and then dinner. At first, it seems like there isn't any message with it, like it is just the forwarded reservation from OpenTable, but then I see it—he did write something.

"I reminded everyone about the dinner. Hope it goes well tomorrow," he wrote. "I'm sorry I can't be there."

I think back to one year ago today—announcing the sale, telling that reporter from *Forbes* about the pregnancy, and running to meet Jasper at Bad Roman to celebrate our next chapter. We had no idea what was in store for us. I guess nobody ever does. Almost every day for at least the last few months, I've thought about that toast, along with all the what-ifs. What if we had waited for a proper cocktail to salute our future? Does that sort of thing really matter? Can it really doom a family, a couple, or a person? What if I hadn't rushed to tell anyone and I had just sat calmly with it for a little while? What if I hadn't worked so hard those next few months? What if, what if, what if?

I think about writing back to Jasper, maybe saying thank you or asking whom exactly he reminded about the dinner, but I don't. I close my email and place my phone on the charger. I reach into my nightstand drawer and find my sleep edible, which I would usually cut in half, but I pop the whole thing in my mouth. I need this day to be done. I need this year to be done. I turn off my light, and just as I fall asleep, I feel that I'm missing something or that I forgot to do something. Then I remind myself there is nothing to do and nobody is waiting for me. What a shitty way to begin my forties.

Chapter Three

Seven Months Ago…

"You will feel weightless, like you're floating," the young woman promised as she ushered me into their 'heavenly suite', adorned with lavender sprigs draped across every conceivable surface. The place reminded me more of a Lush store than a relaxation haven—a botanical explosion that assaulted my senses with purple tranquility. Definitely not how I would've decorated or dressed their massage therapists (in those tissue-paper-thin, dated, buff brown tunics) if it were up to me, but I reminded myself it wasn't. I was the customer. *Relax, Emerson,* I chanted internally. *You can't be in charge of everything.*

When Luna and Billie gave me the joint prenatal gift a week ago, I had been skeptical. When I looked at the website and saw their slogan, 'You may almost forget you are pregnant', my suspicion morphed into full-blown doubt. But they were so excited about it, and Billie promised she had a friend who had gone recently and loved it so much.

"If I ever get pregnant again, send me to this place and then kill me," Billie had said, laughing with that full-body cackle of hers.

I had barely seen either of them in the last month as I was tasked with spearheading the integration of our inventory process with The Red Dress's system. The relief I felt announcing the sale of the company seemed like a distant memory, a mirage shimmering on the horizon of my stress-soaked life. Five months later, my shoulders were riding high up near my ears again, and the long, deep breaths I had managed to master had reverted back to old habits—those short, shallow gasps that left me feeling like I was drowning. There was a term for it: air hunger. I was literally hungry for air 24/7. That couldn't be good for anyone, not to mention a nearly six-month pregnant person. Oh, and how could I forget? My old friend, the seventy-hour workweek, was back. Not exactly what I had expected after selling the company.

But there was a light at the end of the tunnel—the first day of fall, just one day away. For the last seven years, Jasper and I created a tradition where we would go up to Warwick in the Hudson Valley for apple picking and then come home to make our own apple cider and watch a Hallmark holiday movie. It was ridiculously simple, yet somehow a highlight for both of us that we looked forward to annually. No email, no calls, no work talk. Just us, apples, and the kind of cheese-ball romance that makes you roll your eyes and melt simultaneously.

"Ouch," I yelped as the aesthetician dug her knuckles into my right shoulder like she was mining for diamonds.

"Deep breaths," she commanded as she worked her way into what felt like every uncooperative muscle in my upper body. I certainly was not feeling like I was floating or weightless, and I felt more pregnant than ever, like I was hauling around a watermelon that had opinions. But slowly, I began to relax. I don't know if it was the abundance of lavender assaulting my nostrils or the release of tension I gradually witnessed in my body, but something was working. It was possible I had not felt that relaxed since the week after the announcement of the sale.

Over the last five months, I'd been asking myself if I made the right decision selling StyleShop, replaying the announcement over and over in my head like a movie I couldn't decide if I liked. One day, I was proud, thrilled, and excited for the next chapter, quickly followed by days of regret and anxiety about this unpredictable journey I'd embarked on. I'd devoted approximately eighty percent of my life to this business over the past seventeen years, but never stopped loving it. Whether it was physically or emotionally healthy or not (spoiler: it wasn't), there was no denying that I had experienced many fulfilling stretches watching StyleShop grow. The company had undoubtedly given me some of the most euphoric moments of my life to date. I had long wondered where I would find that same joy and excitement again, or if I ever would.

I knew all of that contributed to the dip I felt after announcing the sale, along with the constant questioning. But five months into that decision, the deal became old news, and it was while I was an employee of StyleShop, setting the business up for success when I finally left, I had discovered this completely new side of myself. Knowing that I was building a family with Jasper became my new eighty percent, the new headline in my life—Mamma coming through—and I had fallen head over heels in love with this tiny being inside of me (even if he or she didn't follow my intended timeline).

Perhaps I had been pushing harder than I should have. Miss 'I Can Do It All' proudly wore her crown and cape nonstop daily despite the fact that I was supposed to be taking a step back. I was eating all three meals at the office, and one night last week,

I came home to find Jasper slow dancing in the kitchen with a life-size cardboard cutout of me from our winter promotion. A cardboard version of me was getting more intimacy than the real thing. Over the past two weeks, he had gently suggested I slow down, and I intended to, but I hadn't been listening. Not yet anyway. I finally decided to put on the brakes when I saw him with the cardboard version of myself and started doing most of my work from home.

"Let's move to the float tank," the woman said, pulling me out of my thoughts. "It is lukewarm, the perfect temperature, and has the ideal amount of Epsom salts for an expectant woman."

I would have preferred to stay where I was, but she hadn't steered me wrong yet. I got up, a little woozy, and followed her into the room next door, where there was what looked like a big egg, or a spaceship designed by someone who'd watched too many sci-fi movies from the '70s.

"I'll leave you to it," she said, disappearing from the room with a flutter of her paper tunic.

I eased into the small warm pool and decided she was right—it was worth moving to the next room for this. I closed my eyes and tried to clear my mind. By the time Billie picked me up, I was fully relaxed. My whole body felt like jelly, like I might slide through the car seat if not for my seatbelt.

"Don't talk," Billie said gently, ushering me toward her car. "Go home and rest. I've texted Jasper and told him to keep you well hydrated and calm for as long as you can."

As she dropped me off, I leaned over and hugged her, my growing belly between us like a third friend joining the embrace.

"Thank you," I said. "It was exactly what I needed."

At about four in the morning, I began to feel it, but it was still a part of my dreams, the woman pushing on me, massaging me, but this time she was working on my abdomen, and she was pushing harder than felt right. But I trusted her, so I didn't say anything. And then I was awake, at home, not at the spa, and I reached down to feel my lower left side. It was a strange feeling, crampy and uncomfortable, but not so bad. I managed to go back to sleep.

"Are you okay?" Jasper asked me as the sunlight hit my face through the bedroom window. "You're moaning."

"I think so," I said, startled, a little out of sorts. I pushed myself up to sitting, still surprised that there was so much more of me than there used to be.

"Okay, great, because it's our big day!" Jasper said cheerily, like a five-year-old presented with a pint of ice cream and permission to eat the whole thing. "Apple orchard, here we come."

I smiled, began to get up, and then I had to lie back down. There was a heaviness I didn't recognize, and I felt strange, like a swirling in my veins, an awareness of my heart beating too fast, too strong. I settled back into bed and pulled the comforter up to my chin like armor.

"I just need a minute," I mustered out.

"Let me run out to get some pastries and coffee. I'll be back in fifteen."

As soon as I heard the front door close, I went to the bathroom. I felt like I was going to boil over, like my skin wasn't going to be able to contain my insides, like my body was staging a coup against itself. It was the strangest feeling. I hadn't been pregnant before, so I figured this could all be very normal—just another delightful surprise in the nine-month carnival ride I'd signed up for. I went over everything that had happened the day before—the massage had been gentle enough, especially anywhere near my belly, the water had not been hot, and I hadn't even been in the float tank for too long. And then I remembered that a few nights before, I'd had this same feeling, but it passed within a minute or two. And then again, when I had to deal with the one person at The Red Dress who I didn't see eye to eye with, who questioned every one of my decisions on the holiday promotion for quarter four.

I sat down to pee, stood up, and saw the blood. It could have been spotting, possibly, but it felt a little heavier than that. Still, I knew that could be totally fine. I knew it didn't necessarily mean anything bad. I waited to feel the baby move, to reassure me, but he or she must have been sleeping. I couldn't feel any movement. I went to the kitchen, found some orange juice, and drank it, hoping the sugar would kick in and get the baby moving. I waited for three minutes, but still nothing. That's when I was overcome with such a sharp shot of pain in my belly that I had to ease myself down onto the floor. I reached up onto the counter to grab my phone, glad I had thought to bring it with me from the bedroom, and I did something I almost never did. I called my mother.

"How are you, darling?" she cooed into the phone. Normally, I would be annoyed by her attempt to pretend everything was so good between us that we could address each other casually, and that my calling so early on a Saturday morning didn't strike her as odd.

"Well," I said, knowing I could still choose not to involve her. I could tell her I was fine and make an excuse, but frankly, my anxiety was rising fast. "I'm having a bit of abdominal pain, and I can almost feel my blood moving through me. It's so strange, and my heart is beating extremely quickly. And I think it's just spotting, but I saw a little blood this morning."

"Where's Jasper?" she asked, not alarmed or at least not clearly alarmed. It was just an ask, like she was inquiring about the weather.

"He went out to get coffee and breakfast."

"When he gets back, I would go see someone, dear," she said, her voice steady. "Actually, it's the weekend, so, you know what, I would just go to the ER."

"The ER?" I yelled into the phone. Leave it to my mother to jump to the worst conclusion. But there was something that made me think she was right, a primitive knowledge that something was very, very wrong. I managed to get back to bed, and when Jasper got home, I told him how I was feeling, and off we went. My blood pressure was through the roof, like it was trying to break some sort of medical record.

When we arrived, they could still find the baby's heartbeat. It was slower than they would have liked, but it was there. They admitted me and gave me medication to bring my blood pressure down. Jasper repeatedly reassured me that it would all be okay and that our baby was as strong as their mother. When my blood pressure didn't come down as quickly as they had hoped and the baby's heartbeat became fainter, they started talking about delivery, a C-section, since labor would just elevate my blood pressure further.

I was twenty-four weeks pregnant. The chances of the baby's survival were fifty percent. If only I had been one more week along, the chances would have increased by twenty to thirty percent. One week. Seven days. One hundred and sixty-eight hours standing between us and much better odds.

"I can't do this," I said to Jasper, defeated already. "Any of it."

"We have no choice," he said gently. "And you can."

But Jasper was wrong. I couldn't do anything. I couldn't get my blood pressure down. I couldn't make the baby's heartbeat stronger. I couldn't keep our baby alive. We lost her before they even decided to deliver her. She was a girl. We named her Evelyn, little Evie.

The doctors assured me that it wasn't because of anything I had done. It wasn't the massage or the float tank. It wasn't my working, though Jasper and I both knew the stress of the last few months certainly hadn't helped. But nobody said it. Once it was over and they had extracted Evie from my body, Jasper and I sat together and cried.

"I loved her," I told him. "I hadn't expected to, but I did." I hadn't expected to, but she had become the center of my universe, a tiny constellation of possibilities.

"I did, too," he said as tears streamed down both cheeks.

He went home that night. It had been an awful, stressful day, and we both needed to sleep. He didn't want to, but I told him to go, to come back in the morning when I would be able to go home. I dreaded the moment when I would wake up and remember. I wanted to be alone for that. I wanted to absorb the first shock wave of grief without witnesses.

"I love you," he said. "We will get through this."

I believed him. That night, though, something happened to me. My blood pressure was back to normal. I was out of danger, but I was empty, I was alone, and I had failed at what some might say was the first important task of my life. Looking back, I think in the same way the Grinch's heart grew three sizes after his Christmas revelation, my heart shrank when we lost Evie, collapsing in on itself like a dying star.

Jasper came back to get me the next day with apples and fresh apple cider that Billie had brought over to the apartment. He kissed me on the cheek; I was nice and polite, but I wasn't there. I didn't deserve this love and attention. This love was for other people, people who could carry a baby to term, whose bodies did what they were supposed to do. I was crushed. I had checked out—how else was I going to be able to say goodbye to my baby, to the life we had so carefully planned that had seemed, well, to have a life of its own?

I didn't think Jasper could really understand. He said all the right things—that we would try again, that our time would come. That this just wasn't meant to be right now. That another child was circling our orbit. Then we were in the elevator exiting the hospital. I was in the wheelchair, my belly still big but, of course, empty, with no baby in my arms. On another floor, a young man stepped in and looked at us, somehow missing the total haze of grief around us and somehow missing the memo that you should never, ever assume.

"Congratulations!" he cooed.

For what, I had no idea. He must have thought we were pregnant and going for tests. Maybe he thought we were bringing home our bundle of joy.

"Thank you," Jasper whispered.

I glared at him. Why would he do that? Why would he give that man a break from feeling bad at our expense, at my expense? When Jasper put his hand over mine, I pushed him away. And when we reached the lobby and the doors began to open, I cried out, "Our baby is dead."

The man looked like he had been punched. Jasper's cheeks turned red, and he looked away. I would venture to say that after that, nothing was ever the same between us. The moment stretched between us like an unbridgeable canyon, and I wasn't sure either of us knew how to build a bridge across the emptiness.

Chapter Four

Today…

At 1 p.m., I look in the mirror at the disaster that is me—physically, emotionally, existentially—and accept that I need the kind of intervention usually reserved for reality TV makeovers. I open the Glamsquad app, frantically booking hair and makeup for this afternoon, while a chorus of my inner critics chants *self-indulgent* in perfect harmony.

So far, I've accomplished exactly nothing with this day—my fortieth birthday. I didn't even emerge from my cocoon of blankets until nearly eleven, which for me is like normal people sleeping until next Tuesday. When was the last time I slept past 8 a.m.? My memory files return zero results. I blame last night's whole edible instead of my usual half, but that's just the excuse my brain is offering up like a sad party favor. Some delusional part of me hoped I'd wake up today to someone jumping out of my closet shouting, "JUST KIDDING!" and revealing that the last twelve months had been an elaborate prank show, and my life would revert to its previous programming. That wish evaporated when I woke up exactly as I have these past few months: alone and without a business to use as a relationship substitute.

There's no other word for my morning but lazy. I puttered around my apartment with only my thoughts for company—a dangerous duo—replaying the horror movie that was the last year of my life, director's cut with extra scenes of humiliation.

I should have planned this day better, but really, I didn't plan at all. I just kept pushing it away like vegetables on a five-year-old's dinner plate. And while I'm physically alone, I'm not completely abandoned. I've received the obligatory birthday emails, the social media drive-bys from 'friends' (people I wouldn't recognize at Target), and then the few text messages that make warmth spread through my chest like good whiskey. Billie's video of her boys competing over who could say "happy birthday" the most times in thirty seconds, and Ryder in a blonde wig performing his best Marilyn Monroe "Happy Birthday, Mrs. President"—a performance that would definitely go viral for all the wrong reasons.

Then there's Mom's annual photo message: us on her fortieth birthday when I visited her TV set. I look like I was dressed by wolves (that's the tradition), but she looks like she just stepped off a magazine cover (also tradition), with the caption: *Darling, this was me at 40, and now it's your turn.* Thanks for the reminder, Mom. No pressure.

My phone pings, yanking me back to reality. And there it is. The message I wait for every birthday: a text from Aunt Pearl, who upgraded from fax to text just two years ago when she scored an old Nokia 5110 from the Salvation Army ("They don't make phones like fortresses anymore, Emerson!").

Sweetheart, I'm not going to pretend that today won't be hard, but I also know that moments of joy will visit you if only fleeting. Each day in my morning prayer, I thank our creator that I was chosen to have you in my world. Lovely, I can't tell you how proud I am of the person you have evolved into. And while I know the evolution of Emerson isn't done, I hope you take a breath today to acknowledge your growth. Through becoming more of you, you're giving gifts to the world every day. I love you, sweetheart, and I can't wait to wrap my arms around you tightly soon.

Aunt Pearl always knows exactly what to say. I wipe away two perfectly symmetrical tears. She wanted so badly to be here tonight, but she's recovering from the flu. I understand, of course. Though understanding doesn't make her absence hurt any less.

My alarm blares, startling me like a cat in a cucumber video. This is standard operating procedure. I'm a set-an-alarm-for-everything-yet-provide-zero-context-in-the-name type of girl, leaving present me to decode past me's cryptic intentions. What am I supposed to be doing right now? After a moment of existential pondering, I decide it's time to shower and wash my hair, aiming for that perfect level of dampness for what I hope will be a complete transformation.

And sweet merciful heavens, it is. When I look in the mirror after my Glamsquad guru Belle has worked her magic, tears immediately spring to my eyes. What's reflected back at me—at least for this moment—is the old Emerson. The person I used to be… before.

"Oh, sweetheart," Belle says, gathering her supplies, leaving a trail of glitter and confetti like some kind of glamorous Hansel and Gretel. Her tone echoes my aunt's and threatens to burst my emotional dam, but I resist. Crying in front of her isn't ideal, especially with a face full of makeup that probably costs more than my monthly coffee budget.

"Take deep breaths," she instructs, demonstrating: one breath in, one breath out.

I follow her lead, desperate not to mess this up. I liked the old me. I can't remember the last time she visited, and I don't want to wash her away with an ill-timed emotional breakdown.

After about thirty seconds, I regain control. For a moment, I feared a replay of yesterday's office bathroom meltdown, but the crisis was averted. I still have a stack of Maddi's makeup wipes in my bag just in case. My Daily Quote app informed me this morning that I am stronger today than I was yesterday. So hopefully those wipes can remain unused, like my gym membership.

At least that killed an hour, I think after seeing Belle out and wandering back to the kitchen. I glance at the clock: 6:07 p.m. — time to get ready! How did three hours disappear? It feels like a birthday gift, another part of Belle's magic — the swift passage of unwanted time. What a relief, because today was shaping up to be a long day's journey into self-pity, and the combination of solitude, self-flagellation, and highlight reels of last year's greatest disasters was making me feel less 'forty and fabulous' and more 'forty and falling apart'. But now I'm feeling almost spectacular, maybe even ready to face an evening with my crew.

I slip into my Ieena gold, metallic, tiered gown by Mac Dougal, one of my favorites from StyleShop's spring collection. I step into Jimmy Choo gold, liquid metal leather sandals, a StyleShop distribution exclusive that I'd been embarrassingly proud to secure at an unprecedented price for our customers. I check the mirror one final time before summoning my Uber. I'm actually smiling — a fact that shouldn't feel like spotting a unicorn in Central Park but somehow does.

I notice the tiny purple bottle of Calming Chaos that Belle pressed into my hand before leaving — *Happy birthday, sweetheart,* she'd said — and place two drops behind each ear, closing my eyes momentarily. After a few beats, I look once more in the mirror by the door.

"Through becoming more of you, you're giving gifts to the world every day," I whisper, channeling Aunt Pearl's wisdom, letting myself believe it for just this moment before walking to the elevator.

I feel a flicker of disappointment crossing the empty lobby. Jasper would usually head down early while I finished up, sweet-talking the Uber driver into waiting beyond the two-minute grace period, timing the door opening to perfection, then escorting me to the car like I was someone worth waiting for. I had also thought Luna might be plotting something—she's been suspiciously brief in her texts lately and hasn't called or done anything unexpected, which is, well, unexpected for her. I'd better stay alert at dinner—I bet she has something planned. She always does.

The Uber arrives at 7:12, perfectly fashionably late. I settle back, close my eyes, and let it carry me toward my birthday party—and whatever awaits me there.

Chapter Five

I step inside Buddakan, channeling Carrie Bradshaw from *Sex and the City* with every ounce of confidence I can muster. Steadying myself at the top of the stairs, I try to ignore the ache in my chest where Jasper should be. Even though things weren't great when we officially made these plans, I still thought he'd be here with me for this milestone.

The restaurant unfolds below like a scene from someone else's life—chandeliers twinkling overhead, the grand staircase before me, and that long table waiting at the bottom. There's an empty seat at the head, decorated like a queen's throne with classic gold and black balloons. Next to it stands a blown-up photo of four-year-old me drowning in my mom's pearls and her blood-red fascinator hat, holding up a blue polka dot dress to reveal high heels swallowing my tiny feet. I look impossibly proud and, surprisingly, happy—despite happiness not being the general theme of my childhood. I wonder where they unearthed that photo. My mother barely took pictures, let alone preserved them.

My eyes drift to the chair beside mine, where Ryder has claimed his spot—thank God it's not my mother. He's somehow squeezed his ridiculous mirror ball-esque jacket from prom into the evening (he'd already given me the complete outfit rundown earlier this week to ensure we wouldn't clash).

When his eyes meet mine, he dramatically gasps, placing his hands over his heart with a slight head tilt that's pure theater. I'm taking this as a sign he welcomes back the old Emerson, even if it's just for tonight. He acknowledges I'm not ready to face the entire group yet and turns his attention to Billie beside him.

She looks like she stepped straight off a 1950s film set—blonde locks gently swept to one side, complementing her single-shoulder black dress that hugs her body in all the right places. I'd asked if she wanted to bring her husband, but she declined. One of the most fascinating things I learned about her during our first friend date at goat yoga was that she and her husband—thirty years her senior—have an open relationship.

"We love each other," she'd explained with a dramatic wave. "And we also love other people, but just for a night." Then she'd winked like she was sharing the secret to eternal happiness.

"You can actually make that work?" I'd asked, assuming her casual mention gave me permission to dive in.

"We do and have for ten years," she'd answered, like I'd just asked her favorite color instead of her entire relationship philosophy.

I try catching her eyes now, finally ready to join the party, but she's deep in conversation with Ryder. I scan the rest of the table—my college roommate, two beloved StyleShop veterans from the early days, and at the far end, as distant from me as possible, sits Luna.

I wonder if her position was intentional or if she just arrived last—unlikely, since she's been late exactly once in our nearly two-decade friendship. She looks… burdened? Distracted? Her shoulders seem heavy, and everything about her posture screams that she'd rather be anywhere else. I've been wondering on and off this past week if I've done something to upset her. She also looks pale, though that could be intentional—maybe she's experimenting with some Victorian-era snow-white skin aesthetic. Weird.

On Luna's other side sits my mother, chatting with my college roommate, Margaret.

I take a deep breath and step into view, lifting my skirt slightly as I place my gold-sandaled foot on the first stair. Ryder spots me moving carefully downward and starts clapping, then stands proudly.

"For she's a jolly good fellow," he sings, way louder than appropriate for a restaurant with other patrons. But everyone joins in, clapping along, and I grip the railing tighter. What an entrance that would make—tumbling down the stairs while they serenade me. Instead, I stand tall, flash my brightest smile, and make it safely to the bottom step.

Ryder rushes over with a hug, followed by Billie, then everyone else. Luna hangs back, waiting until the crowd thins before offering a loose embrace. I pull her in tighter. She resists briefly, then surrenders, leaning against me momentarily.

She's impossibly thin—always fit, but this feels different. I must have missed her latest fad diet. The scent of Marlboro Gold clings to her, and I try holding my breath, but the smell alone unlocks a vault of childhood memories. My mother smoked constantly when I was little—one of the few distinct memories I have from our limited time together. As Luna pulls away, I lean in, my lips nearly touching her ear.

"Hey, are we okay?" I whisper.

She pulls back, looking startled—or maybe caught off-guard—but quickly flashes her winning smile and squeezes my hand.

"We're fucking fantastic, babes," she says, meeting my eyes for the briefest moment before turning away. Before I can pull her back, Ryder appears, grinning as he gestures toward a server holding a tray with twelve shot glasses of añejo tequila—my favorite blend of sweet and oaky flavors.

"One for everyone," he announces. "But the birthday girl goes first."

He hands me a shot, which I accept, but my mind lingers on Luna. When I glance her way, she's back in her chair, talking and laughing with Billie, who's squatting beside her. Maybe I imagined the tension. She seems like herself now—stressed, possibly about her upcoming gallery show, but otherwise fine.

I raise my glass. "To forty!" I shout, channeling my inner Ryder with enthusiasm I hope seems genuine.

"To forty," everyone echoes.

I throw my head back dramatically, downing the shot in one go. The burn spreads through my chest and stings my eyes. Looking up, I see everyone experiencing various stages of the same sensation.

"More!" Ryder demands.

"I haven't even sat down yet," I laugh.

Two tequila shots in, I begin to feel the warmth spread through me. Three, and I'm pleasantly buzzing. Food arrives in waves: edamame dumplings, lobster spring rolls, Peking duck salad, tea-smoked ribs. When the spicy peanut noodles and ginger scallion chicken appear, I know without a doubt that Jasper arranged this menu. It's literally all my favorites.

The question nagging at me: When did he do this? Months ago, when we made the reservation, or just yesterday? For a fleeting second, I want to call him. I haven't spent a birthday without talking to him in ten years. The past nine birthdays were with him. Last year, we stayed in bed all day, avoiding the press, celebrating our new chapter and what we knew was coming. We ordered this exact selection—minus the lobster spring rolls—from Buddakan, declaring it so good we should have my birthday dinner there next year.

I close my eyes as the memory washes over me.

"We'll be parents by then," Jasper had said, eyes wide with wonder.

I'd nodded, still unsure how I felt about it all.

"Can you bring a baby out to dinner?" he'd wondered aloud.

"I'm sure you can," I replied. "But we'll get a babysitter. And order the lobster spring rolls. My only regret today is that we didn't get them."

"I'll order them now," he'd said, jumping up for his phone.

"No, no." I laughed. "We have to have something to look forward to."

"We have so much to look forward to," he'd insisted, clutching my hands like they were his lifeline.

"Earth to Emerson," Ryder yells in my ear, yanking me back to reality. "Is the tequila getting to you?"

I glance around, relieved to see everyone engaged in their own conversations rather than staring at my emotional time travel.

"I think so," I say, leaning toward him. "That and everything else."

Ryder meets me halfway, resting his forehead against mine. I push forward, letting him shoulder my weight for a moment. He pulls away slowly, clears his throat, and stands.

"Can I have everyone's attention?" he calls. When nobody responds, he clears his throat again—much louder—stands on his chair, and practically shouts: "Can I please have everyone's attention?!"

The entire restaurant goes silent, all eyes on us.

"Oh, sorry," Ryder says, suddenly flustered. "I just meant our table. Please, everyone else, carry on. Talk amongst yourselves. Everyone but this group."

His rare moment of embarrassment makes me smile. He waits for the ambient noise to resume.

"Wow, I can really command a room," he says with a flourish, already recovering. "Now feels like a good time for anyone who wants to say a few words about our birthday girl. You can all relax, as I'll go first. And, of course, we're going to double the fun. You'll notice four shots and two cocktails have been placed beside Emerson."

He nods toward me. I look to my right and, sure enough, there are four shots and two tropical-looking drinks that appeared as if by magic.

"We're playing a drinking game," Ryder announces, focusing on me. "Anytime someone says 'Emerson', she must take a drink—either a shot or a sip from one of the cocktails, her choice. Pace yourself, but do drink. Every time you forget, you'll owe two shots. Ready?"

Do I have a choice? I wonder silently. But I nod anyway, enjoying the pleasant buzz that's quieted the thoughts swirling in my head these past months. The trick will be not getting so drunk I forget where I am. I don't think Ryder would abandon me on a curb, but I'm acutely aware of Jasper's absence—he would always have my back and get me home safely if I overindulged.

"My dear Emerson Bailey," Ryder begins, still standing. He pauses while I take a small sip of the cocktail—heavy on pineapple and lime, definitely a Matador. I mentally high-five whoever made this, grateful we're sticking with tequila. At this point, my only goal is to avoid mixed liquors.

Ryder smiles. "You are my best friend, my ray of sunshine. Sometimes they say it's always darkest before dawn." He pauses. "And you, my friend, have been there, done that, and are now seeing the dawn, the light, the hope."

Another pause—is he crying? He quickly wipes his left eye and straightens his posture.

"Emerson Bailey," he says again, earning laughs from everyone. This time I down a shot, met with enthusiastic applause. "I wish you a year of happiness, every wish coming true, friends and family, and most importantly, finding love and the path to true fulfillment." He extends his arm, and I blow him a kiss. "Emerson Bailey," he repeats, prompting more laughter. I take a tiny sip of the cocktail.

Billie stands next, smiling warmly.

"Although ours is a newer friendship, from the moment we met, I knew we'd be in each other's lives forever," she says, looking directly at me with a slight head-duck and wide smile. "And I'll give you a break. Let's call you E.B. for now."

Everyone laughs again, and I'm enveloped in a blanket of warmth. At first, I attribute it to the tequila, but I know it's something else entirely. In this moment, everything feels right— like I'm exactly where I'm supposed to be, with these people, in this body, in this life, experiencing it all: the good, the bad, and everything between.

"You are my support, my confidante, my adventure partner, and I want to be all those things for you. I am all those things for you. Happy birthday, Emerson." She pauses while I sip. "My kids love you, my husband loves you, and I love you."

Everyone applauds. My mother rises next, and I brace

myself. This could go in so many directions.

She raises her glass with practiced grace. "Darling," she begins, "it's so nice to see those dark circles under your eyes ever so slightly lighter, which is the first of forty things I love about you."

My instinct is to cringe, but everyone laughs, so maybe it's not as awful as it sounds to my ears? She proceeds to repeat my name obsessively, as if her mission is to intoxicate me, forcing sip after sip as she lists more of her forty beloved traits—my thick hair, fashion sense, listening abilities. I let her continue, wondering if anyone might doze off, but her animation prevents that. Around numbers thirty-two and thirty-three—my surprising love of pickled herring and ability to name all fifty states, things I didn't know she knew about me—I realize she's putting on a show. When she reaches forty—my talent for whistling—she takes an exaggerated bow, waiting for applause. The crowd obliges.

Margaret, my college roommate, stands next. She traveled from Philadelphia for this, and I'm grateful, though it feels like she belongs to a different lifetime. I think she feels it too.

"Happy birthday, she whom I will not name," she says simply. "I am grateful for our years of friendship."

Finally, Luna's turn arrives. She starts to stand but reconsiders. She raises her still-full glass instead.

"Let's be honest. We all know I'm your very best friend," she says with a grin as Billie and Ryder toast the OG bestie. *There's my spirited Luna,* I think happily. "Nearly twenty years doing life together, side by side. God, have we dealt with some real shit or what?"

She pauses, her normally buoyant tone shifting momentarily—something probably only I notice.

"But we've also celebrated the incredible occasions life has gifted us," she continues. "I'm grateful for you. Words can't express how thankful I am to have the one and only Emerson Bailey in my life. I love you."

She takes a long sip, and as our eyes meet, I swear I see tears trailing down her left cheek before she quickly wipes them away.

We wait for Luna's usual chaotic encore. Typically, she'd be the party's heartbeat—creating an impromptu dance in my honor or surprising everyone with an unexpected guest (like the stripper she brought to my thirty-seventh birthday breakfast). But she seems finished. She turns to her left, indicating that the next person should begin.

My heart sinks. She must be angry with me about something, though I can't imagine what.

By the time the toasts conclude, I've progressed from pleasantly buzzed to legitimately drunk, slurring my words. The food has disappeared, a cake with what looked like a hundred candles has come and gone, and we've attempted a sloppy, rowdy version of 'Happy Birthday'.

"Let's go dancing!" I spontaneously suggest.

"Let's!" Ryder agrees enthusiastically, as if he'd telepathically planted the idea.

After debating venues, we somehow agree on the Mirage in Brooklyn.

"Wait, weren't people abducted from there?" Billie asks, concerned.

"Yes, but just one, and he survived," Ryder answers like it's a selling point. "It's the hottest place right now. At least on TikTok."

A dark thought crosses my mind: Would it be so bad if I was

abducted? I don't have much going on. Would anyone miss me? That's when I realize I've crossed a dangerous threshold in my drinking journey. I need to slow down—or stop altogether. I know myself; it only gets darker and more incoherent from here.

"For your records," a server says, presenting a silver tray with a long receipt. Panic strikes—I hadn't considered the bill or tipping after inviting everyone here. I would have walked out without thinking about it. How embarrassing.

I examine the total: $2,489.00. I'm not sure if that's excessive or reasonable when I notice 'PAID IN FULL (including gratuity)' printed at the bottom. I scan the table. Ryder? No way—he's not one to part with that kind of money without demanding credit. My mother? She'd be the typical choice if we had a typical mother-daughter relationship, which we definitely don't.

"Sorry, I think there's been a mistake. It says it's been paid for," I tell the server, holding out the check.

"Yes, ma'am. It was prepaid yesterday over the phone," he confirms with a smile. "By a gentleman," he adds.

That eliminates my aunt, unless she deliberately tried to throw me off track by having someone else call—which isn't her style. Confusion clouds my thoughts, and my brain feels increasingly disconnected. None of this makes sense, but I'm determined to solve the mystery. If only I could think clearly.

"Come on!" Ryder calls. "I've ordered three Uber Black SUVs—enough room for everyone. Follow me."

I turn to find Luna beside me. Her color looks slightly improved. I wish I'd sat next to her tonight, even if she hadn't wanted me to. Why did I just accept the seating arrangement without question?

"Hey," I say. "Come in my Uber. I don't feel like I've talked to you enough tonight."

"I'm heading home," she replies matter-of-factly. "I'm beat. But I'll see you tomorrow at brunch."

In an effort to stay busy, and after my mother insisted it was "only right" to provide multiple meals for out-of-town guests (though there were only two, including her), I hastily organized brunch at Jack's Wife Freda on Carmine Street.

"Please come?" I beg, tugging her arm toward the stairs. "It's my one and only fortieth birthday," I whisper, shamelessly applying guilt.

Something unrecognizable flashes across her face, then vanishes.

"Babes, you don't need me to have a good time," she says kindly. "I've been fighting a bug all week, nothing serious. I just want to be well for tomorrow."

So I hadn't imagined it after all. "At least take one of the Ubers," I insist.

"No, that's okay," she refuses, and before I can protest further, she's ascending the stairs and disappearing.

I want to chase her, to make her stay, but my head is spinning, and those lobster spring rolls are threatening a reappearance. I let her go, closing my eyes and willing myself to feel better. I don't want to disappoint Ryder, but it's inevitable. I approach him, and he wraps an arm around me.

"I drank too much," I admit slowly.

"No, you drank just the right amount," he encourages.

"I want to go home," I confess.

"No!" he protests, reminding me of a toddler on the verge of meltdown.

"Why don't you come to my place after? I'll make up the couch," I offer, trying to escape without hurting his feelings.

I watch him recalibrate his expectations.

"Are you sure?" he asks, hand on my shoulder.

"Thank you for making my birthday great. I'll tell the doorman you're coming later," I say, leaning against him.

"Okay," he concedes. "But only if Mr. Right Now doesn't fall into my arms at the Mirage."

"Do not bring a man back to my apartment," I warn, half-joking as I playfully punch his arm. "As the birthday girl, I decree that if I'm not having sex tonight, nobody is."

"If you came to the club…" he hints, letting the suggestion hang.

"Another time," I promise.

"Take one of the Ubers," he says. "I'll figure out the rest. Thank you for a fabulous dinner."

I experience about three seconds of regret when I arrive at my empty apartment. It's 11:45 p.m. on my fortieth birthday. I have fifteen minutes left, and I'm spending them fighting nausea while hunting for extra bedding for Ryder, who probably won't even show up.

Once the pillow is located and my stomach settles, I know exactly what to do with these final birthday minutes. I gather the pile of baby gear Ryder tripped over yesterday—a stroller, a bag of unopened blankets, and a travel crib. I sling the bag over my shoulder and lift the rest, surprised by how light and manageable it is. Why didn't I do this sooner? I don't let myself answer that question.

I carry everything down the hall and prop it against my neighbor's door. They're expecting a baby—they shared the news excitedly in the elevator recently. They can believe it appeared through some benevolent fairy godmother. Walking back to my apartment, I already feel lighter. In the bathroom, I no longer need to navigate around these reminders.

With nothing left to do, I crawl into bed and wait for midnight before officially ending this day. Just as sleep begins to claim me, a thought hits with such force that I bolt upright, heart racing wildly: *Could Jasper have paid for dinner?*

Chapter Six

I wake up on the first day of my fifth decade feeling unexpectedly hopeful, which seems almost offensive given how much tequila I consumed last night. The apartment is so quiet that I assume Ryder never returned. I check my phone—no texts—then wander into the living room and stop short. The sheets and blanket are folded, but in a completely different place from where I left them.

I must be remembering wrong. Or maybe tequila has finally achieved what years of therapy couldn't: selective memory erasure.

I shuffle toward the kitchen where, stuck to the fridge, is a note: *Wish granted. I was sexless last night. Think of it as a birthday present. I love you. Had to run. See you at brunch.*

I smile, grateful I wasn't totally alone. But brunch. The word lands like a thud. Seeing my mother again today feels like volunteering for a second root canal. I can't imagine what more she'll add to her Top 40 Greatest Hits of Emerson's Shortcomings after last night's performance. Plus, my head is pounding with the kind of hangover that makes you swear off alcohol forever (or at least until happy hour).

I locate some Tylenol, swallow it dry, and jump in the shower, carefully avoiding my hair. I don't want to break whatever magical spell Belle cast on me last night—the one that transformed me from 'woman who has clearly given up' to 'woman who might actually have her life together'. When I get out, there's a text from Luna: *Babes, I'm still a little under the weather and won't make brunch. Let's catch up next week so I can give you your present. It was too big to bring last night.*

I sit on the bed, reading her message over and over, feeling like a detective trying to decipher a code. Something feels off, but I can't quite place it. I'll get through brunch first, then shift my attention to mending whatever I've broken with Luna.

As I walk out, remnants of the old Emerson reflect back at me from the mirror—mostly just the outline of my blowout— and I silently thank Belle. I add a few drops of the oil she gave me, resisting the urge to pour the entire bottle over my head. I need all the strength I can get to make it through a more intimate brunch where my mother will no doubt star as the lead, and I'll revert to my usual role: Best Supporting Daughter (Always Nominated, Never Winning).

***

It's an easy walk to the restaurant, and we've been gifted with one of those perfect late spring mornings that make you believe in second chances. Instead of enjoying it, though, something nags at me the entire time.

I'm fairly sure Jasper paid for the meal last night. No one else owned up to it, which makes sense—he was always good at stepping in silently when needed. But why would he do that? We've been done for months.

He's certainly been a constant presence in my mind lately, particularly in the week leading up to both my birthday and my final days at StyleShop. I've been freeze-framing on all the moments where I was less than pleasant toward him. Not that he was always great to me toward the end, though to his credit, he tried for a long time.

But when I finally exposed him to the full contents of my mind—everything I'd been holding onto and obsessing over— namely that I didn't know how we would ever escape our grief if we just kept pretending we could still be happy together, he didn't fight me. He knew I was right. He was kind, saying over and over that he wished me happiness.

There was just that one moment after he'd packed the last of his things and walked toward the door. He turned back to look at me.

"I thought you were stronger than this, Emerson. I thought you would fight for us," he'd said, void of emotion. He just looked me in the eyes while being wedged between his two suitcases and the door.

At the time, I was stunned and couldn't assemble any response. I proceeded to think he was being ridiculous and dramatic, but now I've begun to see it differently. It was like a parent saying they weren't mad at you, but that they were disappointed in you. He was disappointed in me. I had let him down. I had led him to believe I was something I wasn't, someone capable of things I clearly wasn't capable of.

I take out my phone and find his contact information, which was always at the very top of my contacts, but has now moved way down since we haven't talked in so long. My finger hovers over his number. What would I even say? *Hi! It's Emerson. Thanks so much for taking care of dinner last night! Sorry again that I ruined your life.*

And really, I don't take all the blame. Do I even take half of the blame?

No, better to leave it as is. Maybe he didn't pay. Maybe someone else did. I decide to go with that theory—it's my birthday weekend, after all. I deserve the gift of convenient delusion.

***

When I get to the restaurant, Ryder is out front on his phone. He's talking loudly, gesturing wildly with his hands as he speaks, and he doesn't see me coming.

"Come on," he says, sounding frustrated. "You have to. This has gone on for way too long."

I come up behind him and touch him on the back. He jumps, then puts his hand to his chest and breathes dramatically in and out. Ryder is nothing if not expressive—the human equivalent of an exclamation point.

"I have to go," he says into the phone. Then to me, "What the hell?"

"Who was that?" I ask, ignoring his fake anger. "One of your many men from the past week?" I tease.

"Something like that," Ryder says, but he doesn't look at me when he says it. He doesn't make playful faces or amusing hand gestures the way he usually does when he talks about his Mr. Right Now dalliances. "Let's go in," he adds, before I have a chance to question him further.

But the line is long to check in, and I feel antsy. In the end, not too many people are even coming. Luna canceled, and my college friend Margaret had to head back to Philadelphia, and a bunch of people said they drank too much and are just going to lie low today. After all, it is a last-minute, optional meal due to my mother's demands, which she called "strong encouragement". So I think it's just going to be Ryder, Billie, and my mother. As I think that, my phone pings.

Sorry, I was walking out of the house when one of the boys threw up. No brunch for me. I'll make it up to you, I promise.

"Billie's out," I say.

Ryder nods, but he seems distracted, like his body is here, but his mind is stuck in the phone call I interrupted.

"Really, who was that?" I ask again.

He looks at me.

"It was Luna," he says, still not meeting my eyes.

"Yeah, she texted saying she's under the weather," I say, keeping my eyes on his face. "She was odd last night, right? Is there something going on with her? Is she upset with me for some reason?"

He shakes his head.

"It's not for me to say," he mumbles. Ryder almost never mumbles. Ryder has exactly two volumes: Loud and Louder.

"What is going on?" I ask, becoming alarmed. "She's been giving me zero energy vibes, and I think she's the palest and thinnest I've ever seen her. She's not, I don't know, she's not herself. She's distant, and I feel like she's purposely staying as far away from me as possible, even when we're in the same room. I don't know what I've done."

I see Ryder wanting to burst into telling me everything, but he just nods, remaining uncharacteristically quiet. He looks off to the side, pretending he's trying to gauge how long the line is.

"We have a reservation, right?"

"Don't change the subject," I say firmly. "And we do, but now I think there are only three of us. It was originally for nine. They are going to hate us with the fire of a thousand suns."

"Let me go talk to someone," Ryder says. "It's under Bailey?"

"I'm going to head out, actually," I say, surprising even myself.

"What?"

"I'm so sorry," I say, feeling like a caged animal. "I have to get to Luna."

Ryder nods so somberly that I know I'm making the right decision.

"You can handle my dearest mommy, right?" I pull a credit card out of my pocket and hand it to him. "My treat. Think of it as payment for dealing with my mother. Although I know you secretly love hearing all her on-set drama stories, so I'm confident it may end up being your best brunch in months," I say as lightheartedly as I can. I still don't want to believe something is as wrong as it seems it might be. He gives me a quick hug, and then I back out of the crowded restaurant.

Once I'm outside, I squint into the bright sun. From a distance of almost two blocks, I can see my mother coming toward the restaurant. She's talking on her phone and doesn't see me. I head the other way and turn right as soon as I can, feeling like a character in a heist movie making a getaway. Ryder will explain.

Once I'm definitely out of sight, I hail a cab and give the driver Luna's address. I don't text her or call her. I don't want to give her the chance to tell me not to come or make up some reason why I shouldn't. And then I am on her stoop, and I have to ring her apartment. I can't just walk in. I know she could pretend I'm not here, or she could ignore me. I take a deep breath and then I buzz.

"Hello?" she calls. She sounds okay.

"It's me," I say.

There is a hesitation.

"Em, I'm really not feeling well. You don't want to catch this, trust me. Let me call you tomorrow."

"I don't believe you, Luna. And I don't care about catching something. Please."

Another hesitation, and then she buzzes me in without another word.

I take the stairs two at a time to the third floor. There is an elevator, but waiting for it just seems like it would be frustrating and increase my anxiety. I have to keep moving. As I come around to the top of the stairs, I see Luna standing with her door open. She looks even worse than she did last night, and as I get closer, I realize it's because she wasn't expecting me, so she didn't put on any makeup or choose clothes that don't hang off her. She is so pale it is startling.

"Hi!" I say, leaning in for a hug, trying to act like this is any other day.

"Hi," she says, accepting my hug and hugging back. "Come in."

Inside, her apartment looks tidy enough. Her television is on, but it's on mute, and it looks like she's watching a movie, maybe one of the Terminators. I think she must have been lying on her couch; her pillow is tucked at one end, and there is an unfolded fleece blanket I imagined she threw off when she heard the buzzer. There are a number of prescription bottles on the table next to the couch, and my heart sinks. It takes all my energy to resist the urge to go see what they are and then Google them.

This whole time, I've been thinking that I've done something to hurt her, but in that moment, it becomes clear this is something far worse than friends being upset with each other. This is something medical, something serious.

"Can I get you anything?" Luna asks, ever the hostess.

"No, can I get you anything?" I ask back.

"No, I'm all good, thanks," she says, but I know she's lying.

"Lu, what is going on?" I ask, taking a seat on the couch and motioning for her to come sit next to me. When she does, I put the fleece blanket over both of us. It is soft and warm. She leans against me, and for the first time in a long time, I don't think she wishes I weren't here. For the first time in a long time, it feels like she is actually here with me.

"Are you sick?" I ask directly. "Sicker than just being under the weather?"

"Do you really want to know?" she says, her tough, confident demeanor nowhere to be found at the moment.

"Of course I want to know."

"You won't once I tell you."

"Luna, what is going on?" I stop short of saying that she's scaring me. I don't want her to shut down again, and I now know for certain this is way more about her than it is about me, and I'd better start acting like it.

Luna takes a deep breath and then coughs. She does not sound good—too many cigarettes, too many late nights, too much everything.

"Can I give you your birthday present first?" she asks.

I want to say no, but I nod.

She pushes herself up to stand, which appears to take some effort, and enters the other room. She comes back with a large, flat, wrapped gift. When she hands it to me, it is heavier than I expected. I settle it on my lap.

"I didn't want to burden you with it last night," Luna says, but the word 'burden' seems to have multiple meanings in that sentence.

"We said no gifts, remember?" I say, hearing the *we* of it, meaning when we planned it, Jasper and I. I said I wanted to gather everyone, but that I didn't want people to go to any trouble. In the save-the-date note, we stated that no gifts were needed and included a link to the five charities we support, in case anyone wanted to make a donation. Somehow, that leads me back to Ryder and how I left him at the restaurant. He can charm anyone, but I hope my mother isn't making it hard for him. I glance at my phone. I'm surprised I haven't heard from her.

"Okay, then think of it as less of a gift and more of a token of acknowledging how fucking brilliant I am," Luna says, jumping back into old Luna for a split second. She laughs, and it feels good for a few moments, until she starts to cough.

I begin to unwrap it, and I immediately know what it is. Her original Heather Galler painting, which I always thought of as a farm with colorful rows of circles and squares that look like crops to me, a red barn at the far-right corner, and trees and sunshine at the top. I have loved it since she got it and put it up in her kitchen. It is the centerpiece of her art collection. She has been approached twice to sell it, once for what I thought was a lot of money, and she said no both times. I have joked more than once that she should leave it to me in her will. Why did I do that?

"I can't accept this," I say, feeling the prick of tears.

"Yes, you can."

I don't want to make this about me, I really don't, but this is the worst possible thing. It has to be so bad, so final. I look at her.

"I have an aggressive form of lung cancer, stage four," Luna says, looking at her lap as she talks. "I have four to nine fucking months left."

I know I am not hearing her words properly. Her tone is her usual tough tone. She can't possibly be saying what I think she's saying.

"Sorry," she whispers then. "Not the birthday present I meant to give you."

Luna reaches for a cigarette and lights it.

"Should you…?" I begin but don't finish.

"It won't make a difference now."

"Oh, Luna, I knew something was wrong." But how long ago did I realize something was off? A couple of weeks? When she didn't do enough for my birthday? God, I'm horrible.

"How long have you known?" I ask.

"I found out for sure at the end of February."

"But it's April," I say dumbly.

Luna shrugs.

"What… happened?" I ask.

"I was dragging for months, longer even," she says like she's told this story before. "I was coughing. I had pain in my chest. At first, the doctor dismissed it, but I kept going back. Eventually, he took me seriously, probably because by then I was coughing up blood. One thing led to another."

"Why didn't you tell me?" I ask, trying to think of what I was doing in February and how I could have missed this. But, of course, I know exactly what I was doing then. I was grieving and feeling sorry for myself.

"You know," Luna says slowly. "You had a lot going on."

"But…" I protest.

"You did," she insists. "It wasn't very long after you lost the baby. You and Jasper had just broken up. I just couldn't. I didn't think you had it in you to, I don't know, to care for someone else."

Again, I remind myself this isn't about me. It isn't about defending myself or making myself feel better, but what she says hits hard. Everyone has things going on all the time. Granted, what I went through was not your average setback, but still, what kind of friend am I if my oldest friend, the one who I have become an adult with, the one who always keeps me straight and set me on my path to StyleShop, who nursed me as best she could when we lost baby Evie, despite the fact that she was dealing with her own horrible situation, can't come to me when she is sick?

And then something else comes to mind. I am a teenager, and I have just learned my father has died. I can barely breathe. I call my best friend Luna. I'm crying so hard I can't talk. One of the kindest things my mother has ever done for me, maybe the only thing that required some selfless forethought, was to call Luna before I did, so she knew; she didn't have to understand what I was saying. She came right over with a bag of Twizzlers, my favorite candy, which she put on my dresser. She sat with me on my bed; she didn't make me talk. Hours went by. When my mother finally said it was time to go to sleep, and I was so terrified—I didn't want to sleep and wake up and remember— Luna asked if she could sleep over, like she understood without my having to tell her any of it. She did, and I slept, and when I woke up, she was already awake and holding my hand. It was such an awful moment, realizing that the day before had not been a nightmare but instead was my new reality. But having her there made it possible not to curl up in a ball and give up. Having her there made it possible to survive the greatest loss of my life. When she left later that day, she pointed to the candy.

"You don't have to eat that," she said. "But I brought it because one day, I promise, you will want to again. And it will taste just as good as it always did."

I don't know why that had such a huge impact on me, but it did. It was like she was telling me my life wasn't over, despite the fact that it felt like it was. Now I look at Luna. Who is going to hold my hand if she can't? Who is going to promise me that all the good things in life aren't gone? She was my rock then. Who is going to be my rock now?

And then it hits me—four to nine months to live? To live? To be alive on this earth? To be able to speak and sit next to loved ones and exist in this world? Luna sees it on my face.

"I know," she says.

She moves away from me and settles on the other side of the couch, stopping just short of fully lying down.

"I need to rest," she says.

How I hold it together between tucking her in and getting her a glass of water, packing up the painting—which she insists I take now because she doesn't want to go through this again— and leaving her apartment, I will never know. But I do. And then, not until I am down all the stairs, down her stoop, and around the corner do I let myself sink to the ground and cry.

"Are you okay, miss?" a man with an Irish accent asks. "Can I call someone?"

"No, no," I say, pushing myself up to stand. "I'm okay. I just got some bad news."

"I'm sorry to hear that," he says, moving on. "Glad you're okay."

I walk blindly south, the painting getting heavier and heavier in my arms. I keep shifting it and feel relief for a few minutes, and then the aching sets in again. I deserve any pain I'm feeling.

***

It's late afternoon by the time I finally get home, and I realize I haven't eaten all day. I unpack the painting and lean it up against the outer wall of my living room, near the balcony. My shoulders are sore, and I have red marks up and down my forearms. To make things worse, I feel vaguely nauseated from my hangover and from the news I just got. I have the panicked feeling that if I don't eat something, I will get all-out sick, but I don't know what to eat. So I heat up some frozen boiled chicken and broccoli that I have in the freezer. I eat it, barely tasting it, and then I just sit there. I think about calling Luna, but what if she's asleep? I consider calling Ryder, but now I think he must be leaving me alone for this very reason. Same with my mother, too.

I go about my usual Sunday afternoon routine as best I can, preparing for the week ahead, and then I get to the email part, checking work first, as I always do. I wait for it to load, thinking this is taking so long. And then it hits me at the same time as I get an error message saying, 'Server not found'. This is it—I am officially no longer an employee of StyleShop.

I move to my personal email because I have to do something. There are a few birthday greetings, some promotions for sales, and one thanking me for my donation to the cancer center that supported my father before he died. I think again of Luna and the candy and her incredible force of love and friendship. The email is the first thing I have encountered all day that makes me feel like I am doing anything good. Even before I earned any money to speak of, I would give them a donation each year around my birthday, which increased as I started generating an income. They were so good to my father when he was sick. I think of him, pale, weak, still making jokes, still worrying about whether I had eaten or done my schoolwork. I was only eighteen when he died. It hits me that I have now lived more years without him than I did with him.

He was the best father, always making me his priority when my mother was away, too busy chasing her career. An audition or her sick daughter at home? What do you think she chose? But not Daddy. He never made me feel like the obstacle or the thing in his way. He always made me feel like I was his number one.

I am all-out crying now, trying not to think about how I can picture Luna's next few months all too clearly. Somehow, it looks like I am going to lose my other favorite person to the same fate. As I let that sink in, telling myself all I can do is pray for a miracle, I notice a familiar name in my inbox. It's an email from Gerald Finn, my father's good friend from his college days. The subject line reads *Hello, Hello, and a Question.* It's like my thinking about my father conjured him up. I click on the email.

Emmy, it has been just over a year since I sent my last email to you about your sale. I think of your father often, and I never mean for so much time to go by in between our conversations. I hope this finds you well. Any chance you might be willing to come in to talk about the possibility of you consulting on one of our projects? I could really use your help and expertise. I know it's a long shot — I know you are busy. At the very least, let's meet for coffee and catch up. My treat. I'll look forward to hearing from you. Gerry

My first thought is no, I didn't leave StyleShop so I could pick up a consulting gig working for someone else. My second thought is, what am I going to do tomorrow, and the day after that, and the day after that? I write back to Gerald.

Gerry, it is so nice to hear from you. I was just thinking about my dad. You must have read my mind. I would love to see you, and I am very open to hearing more about the project and what sort of consulting you are looking for. As luck would have it, I am no longer quite as busy as I once was. Please let me know when you would like to meet. I will look forward to seeing you. Emmy

I am very rarely bored, but when I am, I create something to do. My days have always been so full, sometimes too full to even think or do everything I had planned to do. I am nothing if not a chronic over-scheduler and overachiever. Jasper would often laugh and say, "You were born without the relax gene." I sometimes wished for downtime, so I could do… I don't even know what. Read? Watch movies? Bake?

And then an idea strikes me. I go to my closet and pull down a box I put away after losing Evie. I open it, and at the top is my sketchbook. I flick through the pages, looking at my different designs from over the years. Some I like better than others now, but looking through it and having it in my hand gives me a tangible hit of dopamine. I sit down and study my last design—a dress not too different from the one I wore last night. I find a pencil and make some adjustments. And then as quickly as the good feeling came on, it is gone, and I just feel empty and alone. What am I doing? Going backwards? I close the sketchbook and put it back in the box. I put the box back in the closet.

It's only 9 p.m., but I decide to go to bed. For the second night in three days, I have the sense that I just want this day to be over with. Maybe tomorrow will be better. And then I think of Luna, and I know tomorrow won't be better. I open the drawer to look for my edible and remember I'm out; that whole one I took two nights ago was my last one. I'm starting to regret my goal of beginning this new decade without sleep support. Now I am completely on my own. I am considering the vodka in my freezer or finding another way to knock myself out when my phone pings. It's a message from Ryder.

Brunch was fine. I know how to handle your mother, hehe. Did she spill the tea on all the diva demands from the big Hollywood actor in her last film or what?!

There are subsequent pings, and three photos come in from last night—one of the entire table with everyone smiling, one of me with Billie, Ryder, and Luna in the background, and one of me doing a shot and everyone around me cheering.

Thanks, you're the best, I text back. It doesn't feel like enough, but I mean it. I'm not totally alone. Ryder will make sure of that. I expect him to write something more. He knows I know about Luna now. But I guess there is nothing to say. *Love you,* I text. He texts back a string of hearts in every color.

I spend a lot of time looking at the pictures Ryder sent, really looking at people's faces. Despite everything, these are the people who have stood by me. Have I done enough for them? Have I been a good enough friend? I think of Luna and how she didn't think she could confide in me or lean on me, and I know something has to change. In that moment, I vow to do better.

Chapter Seven

A sign reading SWEAT IS FAT CRYING glares at me from the wall. My first thought is that this place could use a PR intervention. I mean, who actually sweats harder because fat is supposedly weeping? But I remind myself I'm not here to rescue anyone from their misguided motivational tactics; I'm here for me. Just me on the elliptical, attempting to resurrect my fitness routine from the dead.

I thought easing back in would be the smart approach, but I'm quickly learning there's no gentle on-ramp to exercise after a three-week-and-two-day hiatus. You just have to dive into the deep end of discomfort and hope you remember how to swim.

And I am swimming! Well, flailing might be more accurate. But I'm here, which is something. Between my birthday and *gestures vaguely at the universe*, I haven't felt like working out. For once, I embraced the break instead of mentally flogging myself for it.

I've officially said goodbye to my once-sacred morning routine—the one I used to evangelize about with cult-like enthusiasm. If I'm being honest, if I see one more soft-boiled egg, I might commit a crime against poultry.

This morning, I banished my egg pot to the cabinet netherworld and dusted off the Vitamix. A smoothie felt revolutionary—cooler, fresher, less… eggy.

Now I'm second-guessing that protein-light choice as I battle this elliptical machine that suddenly feels like alien technology. I mentally add 'buy protein powder' to my endless to-do list, which is growing faster than my anxiety in social situations.

There's something both brutal and freeing about knowing that nobody is monitoring my mornings anymore. There was a time when someone would have noticed my abandonment of My Perfect Morning™ playbook—two hours of precision-timed egg consumption and calculated calorie burning. Jasper would have noticed. Or someone at work. Someone who might have asked if I was okay, and I could have said, "I'm totally fine. Just dismantling my self-imposed prison of routine and trying to actually live, even if that means gaining seven pounds in my gym-avoiding spree."

But now? No explanations needed. It makes me wonder why I ever felt I owed anyone an explanation in the first place.

As I play the mental game of 'don't feel guilty, you magnificent disaster, you're doing your best', I try to distract myself with the TVs mounted at every conceivable angle. Each one is locked on *Hello America*, like we're in some dystopian future where Roslyn Harlow is our benevolent overlord. I scan for a remote—some way to assert control over my viewing destiny—but there's nothing. I've always been a *Wake Up* person.

To add insult to injury, the volume is set to that special level where you can tell people are talking but can't make out what they're saying over the symphony of ellipticals and treadmills. And someone has committed the cardinal sin of forgetting to turn on closed captions. Had I known I'd be trapped in this silent

TV purgatory, I would have brought my phone and earbuds to escape into a podcast, but I deliberately left them in my locker, thinking 'unplugging' might be good for me. File that under 'Ideas That Seemed Smart Five Minutes Ago'.

Now I'm bored, inexplicably exhausted, and without anything to distract me from both conditions. I strain to hear what's happening as Roslyn Harlow welcomes a woman in a flowing skirt and cowboy boots, guitar in hand. They chat inaudibly for a minute before Roslyn exits, leaving the woman to perform. She looks so familiar that it's actually painful not knowing where I've seen her. Like having a word stuck on the tip of your tongue, except the word is a person.

Then, as if the gym gods have taken pity on me, all the machines seem to pause at once, creating one blessed moment of quiet where the music can finally be heard.

"But the echoes linger, a prisoner of the night, dreams untold, waiting for the dawn's first light," the woman sings, casually strumming her guitar.

Something shifts inside me, and I stand straighter, finding a new rhythm on the machine. Step, step, step, step.

"I'm breaking free from the shadows that bind, emerging into daylight, leaving the past behind."

Have I heard this before? It's as if I know exactly where the melody will go before she even sings it. I could almost finish her lines. It's the strangest sensation—like déjà vu, but for my ears. I tell myself I'm being ridiculous; if she's on *Hello America*, this song is probably inescapable right now, playing in every coffee shop and department store in the USA.

She continues to strum and sing, and I lean forward like proximity might help me understand this nagging familiarity. And then it's over, and Robin Roberts returns, clapping enthusiastically. She hugs the singer, and I almost—almost—have the artist's name, but then she's gone, replaced by an ad for Fitness4You.

I'm not at Fitness4You. I'm at Elevate—so much better, except for their strange vendetta against fat and apparent belief that it has tear ducts. I think, *Okay, I'm doing it, I'm back.* For five heroic minutes, I focus exclusively on the exercise, pushing a little harder and feeling my muscles file a formal complaint. When I can't stand it anymore, I grab a towel, slow down, and retreat to the locker room.

I feel surprisingly good as I shower, singing quietly to myself. Maybe I don't need to immediately return to my previous drill-sergeant approach. Every other day seems reasonable for now, before building back to my six-day-a-week routine. Why set myself up for failure with impossible expectations? I'm pleased with this flash of self-compassion. Still singing, I dry my hair and dress in a skirt and blazer for my meeting with Gerald.

"I'm breaking free from the shadows that bind, emerging into daylight, leaving the past behind."

It's catchy, I'll give it that. And then I nearly drop my hair dryer as realization hits me like a cold shower. Jasper. It's Jasper's song. I should have known. I did know, somewhere underneath all my carefully constructed distractions.

How many times did I hear him working through it? Playing with different lyrics and bridges, appearing in whatever room I was in to ask if I thought there were too many shadows and echoes. Me, barely listening, barely caring when he asked, knowing he would figure it out—he always did.

I return the blow dryer to its holder, slip my feet into my flats, and slowly ease my earbuds into my ears. I find the song on Apple Music (ah, Kaci Sands, of course), and press play. I sit on the bench in the empty locker room and just… listen.

"In the quiet corner where the shadows play, a heart concealed, lost in shades of gray," Kaci sings. I let it play through to the end. "No more hiding in the corner, no more fear, I'll rise above the darkness, crystal clear. With every step, a liberation song, I'll dance in the light where I truly belong."

When it's over, I check the time. I have just under an hour to reach Gerald's office. No problem. I press play again and listen one more time.

Jasper is so good. I mean, I knew he was, but when was the last time I actually listened to one of his songs and gave it my full attention? I honestly can't remember. His playing and lyric-workshopping were the constant soundtrack of our life together. Stopping to fully appreciate each iteration would have been like pausing to contemplate every siren that wailed past our window, wondering where it was going and who needed saving. I tell myself it would have been impossible, exhausting even. But now I wonder—was that true? Or was it just more convenient to believe it was?

And then I'm transported back to a night right before everything changed. Before I knew I was pregnant. Before I announced the company sale. Before that surreal day with the *Forbes* interview. Before I lost something I hadn't known how desperately I wanted. Before the avalanche of things I never saw coming buried me alive.

I had just gotten home from work and was in the kitchen. I'd hung my coat but left my scarf and hat on because an email demanded immediate attention. Jasper was home, but I didn't even call out to him. I was too focused. The email concerned our spring line—another company had snatched up the inventory from a dress shop we wanted to work with. At the time, it felt catastrophic, like we were failing our customers before we'd even begun.

As I was writing back to Maddi, an email arrived from the dress shop, saying they'd work with us after all, if only we increased our order and committed to the next two seasons. Something felt off. I was standing there, phone in hand, caught between conflicting emails, when Jasper bounced into the kitchen, cheeks flushed from working, hair adorably disheveled.

"Hey," he said, breathless. "I'm so glad you're home."

"Uh-huh," I replied, barely glancing up from my screen. Maddi was obsessed with these dresses; she couldn't fathom why I was hesitating. She'd sent photos of a yellow cotton spring dress she insisted would be "the talk of the town." According to her, missing out would be a professional tragedy of Shakespearean proportions. I was studying the dress, wondering if we could find something similar elsewhere, and trying to pinpoint why this dress company triggered my internal alarm system.

"You are not going to believe this," Jasper said. "My agent called, and Disney is looking for a song for their next movie. It's animated, a retelling of *Cinderella* with an urban spin. It sounds really good. Anyway, can I play what I have for you so far?"

"Now?" I asked, finally looking up from my phone with what I'm sure was the facial equivalent of a heavy sigh.

"Well, they want the concept by tomorrow. One of the songwriters pulled out last minute," he explained.

"Um, let me just finish this one thing, and then I'll listen, okay?" I said, attention already recaptured by my phone.

"Sure, great," he said. "It's supposed to touch on a fairy-tale theme without actually saying it, so I'm thinking some moonlight, some stars. I have it. I actually think it's good. I would just, I don't know… you have such a good ear."

"Sure, babe. I'll be right in."

He nodded and retreated to the living room. I could hear him on his guitar, singing, "beneath the moonlit spell, where stars align, a symphony of magic, a dance divine." He cleared his throat. "Beneath a moonlit sky—no, spell."

I could hear him, but I was barely listening. I was emailing Maddi, asking if she could investigate whether other companies had negative experiences with this dress shop.

Always the stickler! she wrote back immediately, and I smiled. I knew that was our secret sauce. We were always careful, more careful than necessary.

"Butterflies whisper in the secret grove, as we unravel the mystique, the purest treasure of love. Every touch, a spell; every kiss, a rhyme."

Somewhere in the distant universe outside my email, I heard Jasper repeating "spell". I thought maybe his second attempt— "sky"—had been better. I was going to go tell him that. Any second now.

My phone rang. Maddi.

"Hey," I said, my voice lowered as if that would somehow make my distraction less obvious.

"You're right," she said, disappointment evident. "I spoke to Hendrick. He said they ordered from this shop last year, and they were slow to deliver. He said they're unreliable. How did you know?"

"Just a feeling. No, that's not true. It was something about their email, pushing us to commit before we really knew how they operated."

"Em?" Jasper called from the next room.

"You should write a book!" Maddi exclaimed simultaneously.

"What?" I responded, confused by the conversational whiplash.

"Are you coming?" Jasper asked, thinking my question was for him, but I was talking to Maddi.

"You should write a book," she repeated, now with the confidence of someone suggesting you try breathing oxygen. "It's the obvious next step."

"Coming!" I called to Jasper. Then to Maddi, "I'm flattered, really, but a writer I am not."

"Well, people could learn a lot from you. You should consider it."

"That means a lot. If I ever do, I'll dedicate it to you."

Maddi laughed. "Have a great night. See you tomorrow."

By the time we hung up, three new emails had materialized, including one from the dress shop owner we were now trying to avoid. I had questions multiplying like rabbits, but I forced myself to place my phone on the counter and go to Jasper.

He was on the couch, guitar in hand, leaning over to write something on paper. When he heard me approaching, he repositioned, ready to play, but when he saw my face, he set his guitar aside.

"Everything okay?" he asked.

"Yeah." I settled onto the love seat across from him. "Work stuff. We almost made a bad deal, but we caught it. I think it's the right move."

"You always know."

"Maddi thinks I should write a book." I laughed. "Nobody's ever suggested that before."

"Maybe you should," he said, standing to place his guitar on its stand before joining me. "I'd read it."

My phone started ringing in the kitchen. It stopped, then immediately began again.

"You should get that," he said, releasing me, though I can see now he never really had me. I was never there.

What a shame, I think. What I wouldn't give to listen to that song he was working on now. In my mind, I rewrite the scene. I put my phone on silent. I leave it in the kitchen. I go to Jasper and his guitar. I curl my legs under myself on the couch, showing him I'm fully present, ready to listen.

And he begins to play.

Chapter Eight

Today…

As I get out of my Uber and walk toward the door of Gerald's office building, I hear a chorus of voices in my head, like the world's most unwelcome Greek tragedy. Billie telling her husband, *Emerson's not a good listener* after I asked him for the third time where he went to college. Ryder saying, *You're a doer, not a listener.* Luna deciding not to tell me about the worst thing that has ever happened to her. My aunt saying, *You're a talker, a fixer. Nowhere on your report card did it ever say, good listener.*

And Jasper—oh god, Jasper—easing his guitar to the side so he could give me his full attention, instead of me giving mine to him.

How odd that this chorus is happening now—I barely acknowledged any of it the first time around, at least not in any meaningful way. Which is exactly the problem, isn't it?

I push through the revolving door and step inside. I'm hit hard by the corporate smell—floor polish, perfume, and stress accompanied by the mechanical odor of a lot of elevators working at once. It's like Eau de Career Ambition with notes of existential dread.

I'm surprised by the nostalgia I feel at being in this overly corporate setting. I mean, sure, we had to walk through a lobby not too different from this to get to StyleShop, but once you were up there, it was like nothing you'd ever seen before. I'm pretty sure there isn't a single office in this building that's as spectacular as ours is—was. I can almost taste the lack of creativity here, like biting into a cardboard sandwich.

I'm about to check in at the main desk when I see Gerald standing near the elevator bank, smiling. When he sees I've spotted him, he waves and walks over. He looks the same as he has for years, tall with gray hair and a mustache. His pot belly might be slightly more pronounced than the last time I saw him, as if he's been storing extra snacks in there for the winter.

"Emmy!"

"Gerry!"

I lean in for a hug, and I have to close my eyes for a second. It is the closest I can get to hugging my dad.

"You look so grown up," he says when we each take a step back.

I laugh. "I am grown up," I say, resisting the urge to check if I've suddenly sprouted a briefcase and sensible shoes.

"Surprises me every time," he says. "Do you want to come up? Or should we go to a coffee shop?"

"Let's go up," I say. I hadn't expected to, but I feel like I'm satisfying some sort of craving I didn't even realize I had by being here. Like when you suddenly need pickles at 2 a.m. and nothing else will do.

"Let's," he says, and I follow him to the desk, where he signs me in and leads me toward the elevator that says floors 20–40. We are pleasantly quiet while we wait for the elevator to come and while it takes us up to the thirty-seventh floor. I feel like I've stepped back into my old skin. My posture improves, and my mind clears. Corporate Emerson reporting for duty.

We head down the hall to his office. I'm reminded of how nice it is, big and airy with floor-to-ceiling windows, and I feel immediately bad that I was so snarky a few minutes ago. Pot, meet kettle. He sits in a chair at a table by the window, not at his desk, and I choose the chair next to him. I scoot it back slightly so I can face him without having to awkwardly turn my head like an owl with a neck sprain.

"So, the sale is completely done, and you're out, is that right?" he asks.

Jump right in, won't you? But I say, "Yes, I can't believe it. I went in for my last day. It felt… weird."

"I hear you did quite well," he says warmly.

"I guess I did," I say, no reason to be modest with Gerald. If anyone is rooting for me, he is. The man has witnessed every phase of my life, including that regrettable period where I thought crimped hair and platform sneakers were the height of sophistication.

"Your father would be so proud of you," Gerald says, surprising me.

I look to the side and then back at him, hoping the prick of tears I feel isn't evident. I can feel one threatening to spill out, but wiping it now would be too obvious. Then I think, *Who am I fooling anyway?* and I wipe it away while smiling.

"I think he would be, too." It feels so good to be honest. I didn't realize how much I needed this.

"Do you know what I miss the most about your dad?"

"Tell me."

"I miss our Monday night tennis games and then going out after for a big burger at the bar around the corner," Gerald says with a smile. "I loved being home with my family, but that, that always felt like a vacation, or like I was being given a gift. We kept it up for years until he couldn't do it anymore, and then we still went for that damn burger until he couldn't do that anymore."

"My dad loved that, too. Especially those burgers!"

We say the same things every time we're together, and I wouldn't change any of it. Our little ritual, our shared liturgy of grief.

Gerald clears his throat.

"So, I asked you to come for a few reasons," he says. "The first is the project, which I'll tell you about shortly, and the second is that I am finally retiring."

"What?" I say, shocked. Gerald is ten years older than my dad would have been—I know that—but still, I thought he would work forever. I sit back in the chair, my mind racing, thinking, *I don't know if I can take any more shifts in my world order,* and also, *did I just retire?* It feels like it. Like we're both part of some generational changing of the guard, except I'm about two decades too young for my part.

"Well," he says, "it's time."

"Good for you," I manage to say.

"I do worry about what I'll do with my time. How I'll fill my days."

I am almost at a loss for words. It feels like he's using some sort of reverse psychology to see if I'm okay, if I will be able to fill my days. But that's ridiculous. Not everything is about me. The voices screaming, *I'm not a good listener,* pass through my mind again. Maybe that's because I am always thinking that the things people say have to do with me. But that's not a bad thing, right? Isn't that empathy? Or am I confused about that? Is there a self-help book called *So You Think Everything's About You: A*

Narcissist's Guide to Pretending to Care?

I force myself to stop the chatter in my head and focus on Gerald.

"Do you have any hobbies?" I ask, even though it sounds silly to my own ears. *Do I have any hobbies?* Then, *There you go again, Emerson.* "Or things you wished you could do when you were busy working?"

"Strangely enough, no," he says, and we both laugh. "You know what I'm thinking of doing? I'm almost embarrassed to even say, since I am clearly not in the best shape, but I'm thinking of getting back into tennis. I haven't played in years. Well, at least, not much since your dad died."

"That's a good idea. A really good one."

"Plus, Lucille is going to finally leave me if I don't take her on a proper vacation." He chuckles. "Do you know we have never truly gone away and been away? I mean, we've traveled, sure, but I never, ever, in all our years, fully unplugged, even before that was something we said. I always went on vacations, saying I was fully reachable, which often translated to working for much of it. It felt right in the moment, and it certainly got me where I wanted to be." He stops and sweeps his hand around his spacious office. "But, well, you can't do it all, can you? You have to make choices. But now, well, I'm thinking she deserves something great, something where we are truly away, where she has my full undivided attention."

For a split second, I see Jasper on a beach in St. Croix on one of our trips, walking beside me, reaching for my hand, but I'm too busy thinking about our spring sweater line to be fully present with him. I remember it so well. I told him to hold that thought, and I ran back to the room to send a few emails. By the time I found him again, he was three piña coladas in at the bar, staring at the ocean like it held all the answers to why he married a workaholic. I shake the image away.

"So enough about me," Gerald says. "Let me tell you about the project. We've come up with a new design for the logo and everything that comes with it, sort of a parting gesture and a new life for the company, as I take my departure. I wondered if you could advise us on the social media aspects of it all, making a splash online?"

I nod again. I can do that, though it feels like something I would have delegated to someone else at StyleShop. I wonder if I am ever going to stop thinking that way—that I miss using my CEO brain—and then I remind myself that there must still be a good use for it. I have to give myself time. Rome wasn't built in a day, and personalities don't change overnight, no matter how many mid-life crises you stack on top of each other.

Gerald and I talk about some basic ideas, and I tell him I'll get back to him with a more detailed report.

"One other thing," he says slowly. "We have an open spot on our board. We are always looking for smart, important people to fill positions. I thought of you right away. It isn't much of a time commitment, and we could really use your insight and, I'd be lying if I didn't add—your connections."

I wasn't expecting that, but taking a board position was something I thought I might do at some point once I sold the company. And it's hard to say no to Gerald.

"Sure," I say, instead of my usual, *Can I have a little time to think about it?* "I would be happy to."

"Really? I haven't even told you how much it pays. I figured you'd take some convincing."

There is something very nice about being known so well. I smile.

"Well, that is probably true of the old me," I tell him. "I'm trying something new."

There is a knock on the open door, and we both look up. A well-dressed woman is standing there, smiling.

"I'm sorry to interrupt," she says. "Gerald, you have your noon meeting coming up. I just wanted to remind you."

"I thought that was tomorrow." He looks at me. "I'm so sorry, I thought we might have lunch together."

I pat him on the hand again and stand up. "That's okay," I say. As nice as it was being here, I am also happy to go. Who knows what he'll get me to sign up for if we have another hour together? I could end up on the board of twelve companies and chairing three charity galas by dessert. "I'll get started on that report, and I'll be in touch in a day or two."

"Much appreciated." He stands up and leans in for a hug. "Hang in there, Emmy." It is at that moment that I suspect he is doing this—involving me and giving me things to do—more for me than for him or the benefit of his company. He is such a smart man.

"Thanks, Gerry," I say as I hug him back. "For everything."

He steps back and smiles.

"You know where you're going?" the woman asks Gerald, and he nods.

"Bye," I say with a wave, and then I'm out the door and walking down the hall toward the elevator. I feel someone come up next to me.

"Hiya." It's the woman from Gerald's office.

"Oh hey," I say, thinking maybe I forgot something, but that doesn't seem to be the case.

"I'm Sally, by the way."

"I'm Emerson," I say, offering her my hand.

"Oh yes, I know," she says, which isn't creepy at all.

I keep expecting her to veer off toward one office or another, but she doesn't. She just keeps walking with me. At the elevator, I stop and push the down button. She stands with me. I smile and try not to look weirded out. It's possible she also has to go down to the lobby. The door opens and I step in. Sally follows. We are the only ones in the elevator. As soon as the door closes, she lets out a low whistle.

"He didn't see us, did he?" she says.

"Who?"

"Gerald!" she says like I should know.

"Oh, no, I don't think so. But why would that matter?"

"I want to talk to you. Top secret."

We are almost there. It is a superfast elevator. Like my thoughts right now, racing at warp speed.

"About the board?"

"The board?" Sally says. "No, not about the board. About Gerald! I need your help."

The door opens, and we step out into the sunny lobby.

"Do you have a sec?" she asks, pointing to a few low couches surrounded by a jungle of potted plants.

"Sure." I really have more than a second. I have the whole rest of the day, but since I don't yet know what she wants, I decide to keep that information to myself in case I need an excuse to leave.

We sit. She smiles at me.

"You've known Gerald a long time, right?" she asks.

"I have, yes. Since I was pretty young, he and my father were best friends."

"Did he tell you he's retiring?"

"He did." I'm still not sure where she's going with all of this.

"I'm in charge of his retirement present, and, well, I am totally stumped."

"Oh." I laugh. "I had no idea why you wanted to talk to me."

"Sorry! I didn't mean to be so cryptic. Do you think you could help me come up with a good idea? Something he'll love, something that will surprise him, something personal. In other words, not a gold watch."

I laugh again. "Definitely not a gold watch," I agree. "Unless maybe it comes with a time machine so he can go back and take all those vacations he missed."

"I've thought of making a donation in his name or getting him a chair with the company's logo on it, but does he want to be reminded every day that he is no longer here? Nothing seems right."

"What's your budget?" I ask.

"Oh, the sky's the limit. I mean, not a million dollars, but he's been president of this company for over twenty years. They want his gift to be very memorable." She says the words *very memorable* in an overexaggerated way.

In my head, I go back over all the retirement gifts I have heard of or helped to give over the years: gardening supplies, fruit trees, golf lessons. Billie told me that when her mother retired from her position as president of a community college, she was given a puppy. It seems they're never quite good enough at the best of times and misguided at the worst, no matter how hard people try. And then something occurs to me.

"I have an idea, but it will be expensive," I say, wondering if the company would even consider my suggestion.

"What's your idea?" she asks, but then she grabs my arm, pulling me down, and ducks. *Gerald*, she mouths. Thank goodness for the forest of plants around us because he does not even look our way. "That was close."

It occurs to me we could have gone somewhere else, but I don't say it. I'm too busy feeling like I'm in a bad spy movie. All we need are trench coats and dark sunglasses.

"My idea," I say, "is to send him on a trip. A wonderful vacation with Lucille."

I can see that is not what Sally thought I would say. She makes a "huh" sound, like she isn't sure.

"He told me he has never gone on a proper vacation," I continue. "That he always worked, even if he went away." I'm internally priding myself on the fact that I actually listened to him, and now that will come in handy. *See*, I want to tell all my doubting friends, *I am a good listener. I can listen! Someone give me a gold star!*

"That's true," Sally says.

"So how about an amazing, wonderful, work-free vacation?"

Sally nods, and I can see she's warming up to the idea.

"Where to?" she asks.

"Well, we would have to think about that," I reply.

"I like this," she says, nodding faster now. "This is personal, surprising. There's a chance he'll love it. It checks all the boxes. Yes, perfect. But not a monthlong trip, right? Not like a cruise around the world or anything. That might, um, not be in the budget."

"Do you think Gerald would want to be away for a month?" I ask.

She pauses and then shakes her head. "I knew you would help," she says. "You know Gerald better than any of us. He is surprisingly quiet, you know. He doesn't share much."

We sit there in silence for a few seconds, and I wonder if she's ready to let me go.

"Could you, do you think…" she stammers. "Would you plan the trip?"

"Plan it?"

"Well, yeah, I mean choose a destination, maybe a hotel, or hotels depending, you know, a place where there would be things for them to do, things he likes…" she says, her voice trailing off.

I have never left a meeting that had nothing to do with my actual work with so many assignments before. But sure, why not? I love doing research, and who doesn't like to find a nice hotel? Now I wish I had asked him more questions. Like, does he get seasick? Is he allergic to coconuts? Does Lucille secretly hate him, and the only reason she's stuck around this long is that he's never home?

"Yes, of course," I agree. "I have a few ideas. Let me do some research, and I'll get back to you soon, in a few days?"

"Perfect." Sally smiles. "Tomorrow would be ideal. We have to move on this fast but take your time!"

I laugh again. "Tomorrow then."

At least now I know what I'll be doing for the rest of the day. Nothing like planning someone else's perfect getaway to make you forget about your own life falling apart.

Chapter Nine

I push back out through the revolving doors into the bright sunshine of the city, and I feel a pop. It's not just the usual pressure change that happens when you escape the hermetically sealed environment of a big office building—this time, it feels different. It feels like a release, like the universe is exhaling along with me. I turn and walk across the small plaza toward Madison Avenue just as my phone buzzes in my pocket. I pull it out and see it's Ryder.

"Hey you," I say, bracing myself for his signature snark.

"Hi, Emerson." There's something off about his tone—a seriousness that makes my stomach twist. Ryder only calls me Emerson in that somber way when he's about to make me do tequila shots or deliver bad news. I decide I'm overthinking it and ignore the warning bells.

"As always, your timing is impeccable," I say, beginning my walk south. "How do you do that? Do you actually have a crystal ball in front of you watching all my moves?"

"Well," he says, sounding a bit more like himself, "I knew your meeting with Gerald was at eleven, so I figured thirty-five minutes of talking, maybe a little walking around the corporate environment, and maybe a cup of coffee in the lobby before you said goodbye to it all, and then you'd be out. Did I miss anything?"

"No, you mostly got it. And there were a few extras."

This is where Ryder would normally jump in with something like, *Oooh, I need a few extras,* complete with eyebrow waggling I can hear through the phone. I wait, but he doesn't say anything. I pull my phone away from my ear to make sure the call didn't drop. The screen confirms we're still connected.

"Are you okay?" I ask.

"Me? Sure! I'm always okay," he says with forced brightness. "I'm better than okay. I'm on fire today."

"Okay, good, because you sound a little funny. Hey, I've been wanting to tell you something."

I hadn't planned this conversation, but for some reason, I feel compelled to tell him now, and I know he'll be glad to hear it. I almost never talk about the baby or my grief to anyone. It has become one of those taboo subjects that everyone tiptoes around, which, I think, is how many devastating events are handled. But I also know it probably isn't the healthiest approach.

"You know that, um, equipment you tripped over on your way to the bathroom the night before my birthday? Well, I gave it away, finally. It is out of my apartment. You will never trip on it again. My neighbors are having a baby, so I put it all in front of their door like an unexplained gift. It is all brand-new, so I figured they'd be glad to have it," I say in a rush.

As I say the words *all brand-new,* tears well up in my eyes, and I remember why I never talk about this. My throat tightens like I've swallowed something jagged. Again, Ryder is uncharacteristically quiet. I would expect a huge response from him about my confession. I would expect him to praise me gently and then suggest we get together to talk about it more, to coax me into admitting there is more to give away, like the drawers full of onesies and burp cloths I haven't looked at since I washed and folded them so long ago.

After that, he would probably say something about being emotionally exhausted and having to take the rest of the day off. With that in mind, he would add, we should go to a spa together for some important self-care. But Ryder says nothing. What is going on?

"Ryder? Did you hear me?"

"Em, that's great. Really, really great. I know that couldn't have been easy for you."

Now it's my turn to be quiet. He knows that couldn't have been easy for me?

"Well, I should hop," he says. When I still don't say anything, he adds, "But you know I love you."

I squint my eyes and stop short of gritting my teeth. I probably shouldn't have answered. The sense of freedom I felt walking away from Gerald's building is long gone, replaced by a creeping unease. Then I realize Ryder would never be mean or uncaring toward me. There must really be something going on with him.

"I love you, too," I call out quickly, but I'm not even sure he hears me.

He must have been in a place where he couldn't talk freely. That's the only explanation I can come up with. Maybe he stopped by his office to pick something up and felt like people were listening. He rarely goes in since he usually sees clients on-site, making people's homes both elegant and cozy simultaneously—his phrase, not mine. One drunken night, we spent a lot of time trying to come up with a word that combined elegant and cozy—cogant? elecoz?—and decided there wasn't a suitable choice.

Or maybe he was at an appointment of some sort, but really, I can't think of an appointment that he wouldn't tell me about. He tells me everything — about the hot dental hygienist Paul who always flirts with him, about his therapist who always gives him one life lesson each session that he stores away (*Can you believe how lucky I am? My shrink gives me actual practical advice!*), and his primary care doctor who tells him at each appointment that he should consider going vegan (*If I wanted to be a vegan, I would move to Portland!*).

I think back to the first time we met, literally the first time I laid eyes on him. We were redoing a few offices at StyleShop, including mine, and our usual person didn't have an opening for six months. We didn't want to wait, so I asked around for recs, and someone told me about Ryder.

Apparently, interior design was his second profession, coming off a successful career as a dancer, I was told, and he was supposed to be one of the best in the business. We had talked on the phone, and from his tone and unusual accent (which I found out later was put on), he'd led me to believe he was older than he was. I'll never forget when he stepped off the elevator—a young, gorgeous Asian man with thick black hair and the most open face I had ever seen. My first instinct after saying hello was that he was a poser who puts on a fake accent when setting up initial meetings with possible clients. But then I watched him look around the office. I saw his eyes twinkle, and he turned to me and took my hand.

"This place is awesome," he said. "I will give you the best-looking office in all of New York City."

I felt like I knew him already. It was that feeling that I had met him before, though I knew I hadn't. Maybe I had known him in another life. I invited him into my office to talk details, and we ended up telling each other our life stories. That night, he came out for drinks and met Jasper for the first time. By the next day, it seemed he was already my best friend.

I begin my walk south, thinking he'll call me back any second to explain. I decide I'll stop for a slice of pizza on the way to delay my walk home. That way, I can meet him if he wants to. Thinking of my favorite slice shop reminds me of Roberta's Pizza on Park, one of Ryder's favorites, though I'm not entirely sure why. I call him back. It rings and rings, eventually going to voicemail.

"Hey, where are you?" I say. "If I've called you three thousand times during the course of our friendship, I think you have not picked up maybe five of those times, and it was never good. Are you okay? I'm getting worried now. I'm heading to Roberta's. Yes, you heard me right, Roberta's. Your holy grail of pizza. Please come and meet me. Maybe twenty minutes? All the cool kids will be there. I know you never want to miss a cool kid convention."

I am starting to sound crazy. I am an inch away from begging him to come. I change course slightly to head toward Roberta's. If Ryder gets the message, I know he'll meet me there. He once told me he would happily slay a dragon to get his hands on a Roberta's margherita. I keep checking my phone, but he doesn't call, and he is nowhere to be found when I get there. I call one more time. It goes right to voicemail.

"Hi again," I say, trying to sound more upbeat and less borderline hysterical. "I forgot to say it will be my treat. I'll head in and order. Please come if you can get here in the next twenty or thirty. I don't mind waiting."

I go in and order too much. Ryder never shows, and I end up

leaving enough pizza for at least three other people on the table. The whole way home, I worry about Ryder. He never ignores me, and it is starting to feel scarily like Luna. I tell myself nine different ways that this is not that. I need something to distract myself until I can talk to him.

And then I know exactly what I'll do. I change into my favorite cropped toile BedHead pajamas from Neiman Marcus—never mind that it isn't even three in the afternoon yet—and I get to work. I pull out my rainbow Post-it notes and my favorite notepads and colored markers, the ones I always used when we brainstormed at StyleShop. Just having them within my sight line makes me want to do something creative and important.

Where would Gerald like to go on his trip? I think of everything we discussed and write each word on a different Post-it note with a different color marker—tennis, hamburgers, Tivoli poster (which I noticed on his office wall), and talks with my dad. As I write the last words—*talks with my dad*—in green letters on a bright blue sticky note, I am transported back to being twelve years old.

Dad and I were at a diner, and it must have been a weekend morning. My mother was probably off somewhere trying to be a star because it was just the two of us. It was almost always just the two of us. We were talking about something, probably a movie I had seen, and in walked Gerald. I remember being a little disappointed initially because I had been enjoying my father's full attention. Of course, we invited Gerald to sit with us. He eased into the booth next to Dad and immediately wanted to know all about me: what was I learning in school, had I read anything good lately, had I seen any movies?

I remember thinking I'd been wrong to initially not want

Gerald to impinge on our time. He just made it better. Now, I had the full attention of two men who loved me. Eventually, I was just happy to eat my eggs and let them talk. It was comfortable and easy, and I liked listening to them.

I close my eyes because something is coming to the surface, and I will it into my mind. That day, they talked a lot about finding their happy place. That was it. My father had mentioned he needed to go home and do work, and Gerald agreed he did, too. Why did we all work so hard, they wondered out loud, and why was the quality of life better in some other countries where the work/life balance was more thought out and embraced?

"Maybe I'll move," Gerald suggested, and my twelve-year-old self had initially believed him. "What are the countries where they say the people are happiest? Denmark? Finland?"

"Ha," Dad laughed. "Good idea. Maybe we'll come, too."

When I looked up with what were probably wide eyes, he winked at me.

They went on that way for a while, talking about snow and fireplaces, four-day workweeks, weekends that were really weekends, and free healthcare. Finally, Gerald mused, "But you probably can't get our burger over there."

"Probably not," Dad agreed.

"And what about all the smells, the noise, the people, the magic? Can you get that in Denmark or Finland?" Gerald continued.

"I don't think so."

Then Gerald added, "Plus, I love my doctor."

"Yeah, so do I," Dad replied.

Pretty quickly, I knew they were talking about New York City and that this was their happy place, and they were never really going to go anywhere.

But now I think, that's it!

I Google 'Happiest Places on Earth'. Finland comes up over and over again. Denmark also comes up, and I think again of his poster of Tivoli. I keep searching, Googling tennis (with Gerald in mind) and spas (with Lucille in mind) and beef and burgers, and by the time I look up, not only have I managed to not worry about Ryder for a long time—or think about anything else for that matter—but I have a perfectly tailored vacation for Gerald and Lucille.

I am just getting ready to email Sally when my phone rings. I look at the clock. It is almost 7 p.m., and I have been sitting in the same place, barely thinking of anything else, for four hours. Maybe I should go into the travel business. I am glad to see Ryder is finally calling me back.

"Where were you?" I ask. "You missed some damn good pizza."

There's no response, and I wonder if he called me by mistake.

"Ryder?"

"I'm here." He sounds drunk—not fun, tipsy Ryder, but sad, hollow, drunk Ryder.

"Ryder, where are you?"

"I'm here," he says again, even more slurry and belligerent this time. "I told you, I am right here."

"Here, as in at my apartment?" I ask, standing up, ready to call down to the doorman.

"Not there. Here."

"Have you been drinking?" Clearly, Ryder is a huge partyer when the time is right, but I have not known him to be an afternoon drinker, unless, of course, there is some sort of cocktail party or something. "Was there an event?"

"No event," Ryder says, sounding uncharacteristically defeated. "In fact, the opposite of an event, if you are asking about my day. It was an anti-event. Is that a thing? An anti-event?"

"I don't think so," I say gently. "Where are you exactly?"

"Here. Out."

"Can I come meet you?" I would have to change out of my pajamas, obviously, but that's okay. I figure my pajama situation is going to be fluid now.

"I am not fit to be met," he says.

"Ryder, come on. You're really worrying me. What happened? Did something happen?"

"Things happen every day."

"Yes, but did something specific happen to you that upset you and led you to drink?" I say as clearly as I can.

"I am drinking," he says slowly. "To drown my sorrows because I no longer am who I once was."

"Of course you are," I say, but I have no idea what he's talking about.

"Did you know," he whispers conspiratorially, "that they gave my role to someone else?"

I nod, but of course, he can't see me. That is what he's been dreading, but he also knew he wasn't going back to the dance company, and eventually they would come back around to his favorite production—the one that made him famous, he always says with a flourish. With his injury, there was no way he was coming back. That's why he pivoted and got into interior design, which, of course, I am so grateful for. Not because he lost one of his dreams—I would do anything to give that back to him—but because that new career led him to me. I honestly and literally can't imagine life without him.

His most recent MRI showed that his injury was not healing as everyone had hoped. It was sort of the last hope dashed—that and the fact that Ryder is no longer a spring chicken. Not long after we first met, he said to me that every second not dancing was a wasted second, but he never says things like that anymore.

I realize now we don't talk about it enough—or maybe at all. It runs through my mind that this is his version of my not talking about the baby. I think we are both a little too good at deflecting our true feelings. The thing is, I didn't actually think he was still sad about this. I thought he had accepted it and moved on. I was so clearly in denial.

"Oh, Ryder, I'm so sorry. Tell me everything. Did you run into someone?"

He's quiet again, and I worry he is going to say something hostile, like why should he or what's wrong with me wanting to put him through that, but he doesn't.

"I went in to pick up a check," he begins softly. "You know how they had me do the curtains at the dance studio? I didn't really have to pick up the check, of course. I mean, they could've mailed it to me, but I hadn't been in for so long. I... I don't know, I craved it. At first, I was so happy to be there, the smells, the music coming from the different rooms leading up to the main practice hall, which is my favorite place in the world—except, of course, Buddakan on your birthday."

I let out a much louder sigh than I mean to. I am just so incredibly relieved to hear him in there, somewhere beneath the sadness.

"Thanks," I say. "Keep talking."

"I've had this fantasy," he continues, "that I would get there, and somehow the air or the energy or some kind of magic would heal me. I would no longer be injured. I would walk in and dance, surprise everyone, and I'd be back."

"Oh, sweetie."

"Needless to say, that didn't happen. Agnes at the desk just handed me my check. She smiled and said the curtains were fabulous, but she didn't act like it was anything unusual to see me there. She didn't make me feel... I don't know, special or anything. Then I was leaving, and I heard it—coming from the main practice hall—the music to my number. I'd read they were bringing it back this season, but I was still totally shocked. And I still had this damn fantasy that if I just tried, I would somehow be able to overcome the stiffness and pain. I mean, I wasn't even thinking about the damage I could do. I was smiling, actually smiling, as I walked down that hall. Can you imagine?"

He stops for a second, and it occurs to me he is sounding less slurry. I hear a loud car horn behind him and a siren in the distance, and I wonder again where he is.

"I mean, yes, I can imagine," I say, to encourage him to keep talking. I put the phone on speaker and begin to get dressed. I have to get to him. That is the only logical thing to do.

"So I come up to the door, which is closed, and I take a deep breath, I push it open, and I'm ready to say some stupid thing like, *Baby, I'm back*, which A, was a total lie and B, was completely untrue. I mean, I was there, but I wasn't back, I was as not back as a person could be. But before I can say anything, I see they are in full rehearsal mode, and I can barely bring myself to say this out loud. There was a young guy, tall and built, and God, he was handsome, dancing my dance. He was doing it all, and to make things even worse, he was good. And that's when I knew."

"When you knew what?" I'm dressed now. I look for my purse and keys.

"That it's over," he says softly. "That I'm finished."

"Ryder." I stop what I'm doing and focus on our conversation, but honestly I feel like I'm in uncharted territory. Ryder has never really indicated that he believed he would dance again, at least not in a really long time. "Can we get together? To talk? I had no idea you were thinking all these thoughts."

"And every day that goes by," Ryder says, ignoring what I just said and acting as though he is having a conversation with himself, "I get older and older."

"Please, let me come meet you," I say, trying again. "We can, I don't know, get a snack, get ice cream, or I'd even eat more pizza. I just want to see you."

"Do you know what the worst part is?" He continues to ignore me completely.

"What?"

"He was seventeen. I asked Agnes on the way out."

"Please, where are you?"

"And he had this gorgeous head of blond hair that moved with him perfectly."

"Ryder," I say more forcefully now. "I am walking out. I am coming to meet you. Where are you?"

"Just got home. Going to bed. Tomorrow, I'll be another day older."

"I don't want to make this about me or anything, but you are sort of scaring me."

"No need to be scared," he says. "Satine will comfort me."

Satine is Ryder's adorable French bulldog. She is small for a Frenchie, gray with lots of spots, and one white patch and one black patch. It's like she is the perfect palette for a dog. And I swear she has a human face. When she looks at you, you feel like she is really looking at you, that she's seeing you. If any dog could comfort someone in this state, I am confident it is Satine.

My instinct is to tell him to stop feeling sorry for himself, but maybe that's not the right thing to say. Maybe it's okay for him to feel sorry for himself for a little while. Maybe that's better than pretending.

"Can I come to you?" I try one more time. "I would love to see Satine."

"No, I'll be okay. I'll try to find a different attitude tomorrow."

That makes me smile. "Okay," I say reluctantly. "I'm here if you change your mind. You can call anytime—day or night—you know that."

"The one good thing is that at least you're older than I am. I'm not the oldest person in the room when I'm with you."

"Ha ha," I say, relieved again to see a glimpse of his usual self. "I'll call you first thing in the morning if I'm not too old to figure out how to work the phone."

"Good night, my dearest friend."

"Good night, my dearest friend," I say back.

"No matter how old you are." I can hear the tiniest smile in his voice.

Once the call ends, I look around. These days without StyleShop feel so amorphous, like I'm floating in some liminal space between my old life and whatever comes next. I make half a turkey sandwich with avocado, eat it standing up with a tiny can of pineapple juice (vegetables and fruit!), and change back into my pajamas.

I email Sally with the itinerary for Gerald's trip, complete with a price list and a lengthy explanation of why I chose the places and why I think it would be the perfect retirement gift for him. I might as well aim high. I really have nothing personal to lose.

I begin to clean up all the Post-it notes and markers, and as I do, I have a thought that leads to what I hope is the best idea. I get back into position and bring out a new stack of blank sticky notes and notebooks, and I get to work for the second time today. When I'm finished, I send Ryder an email: *I'm kidnapping you on Wednesday. I will not take no for an answer. I'll call tomorrow with the details. I promise you will thank me for it.*

I pull off a red Post-it note and use a black marker to write RYDER'S PERFECT DAY in all caps. I stick it to the top of my pile of notes, and I go to sleep, thinking I haven't felt this accomplished or excited in a long time.

Chapter Ten

I told Ryder to meet me on the corner of Fifty-first and Broadway at 11 a.m. I didn't share anything else except that he should expect to be out all day, so he'd need to make arrangements for Satine. Right now, I'm standing in line at Ellen's Stardust Diner—arguably the most touristy spot in New York City and also, I believe, one of the most hopeful places on earth. It's a '50s-style diner serving acceptable food while the servers belt out Broadway songs with professional-level talent that would make a casting director weep.

There's this scene in *New Year's Eve* that takes place here, and once, when I watched it with Ryder, he said he was interested in going but thought "no self-respecting New Yorker would be caught dead there". Hard disagree. I arrived early since the line can stretch to New Jersey on matinee days, which today is. I spent all of yesterday ensuring my Ryder Day itinerary was actually possible, including scoring tickets to his all-time favorite Broadway musical.

Just before leaving my apartment, I finally heard from Sally. Her response to my email was gloriously succinct, all caps: YOU ARE A GENIUS. And then: More Soon. I have no idea what that means precisely, but it sent a tiny thrill through my chest, nonetheless.

It's five to eleven, and still no sign of Ryder, but punctuality has never been his superpower. Finally, I spot him crossing Broadway with something—someone—cradled in his arms. As he gets closer, I realize he's brought Satine. I'm about to ask if he completely misunderstood my instructions when he places her by my feet. She's wearing a tiny red vest emblazoned with SERVICE DOG.

"What the heck?" I ask, eyebrows reaching for the sky.

"Good morning to you, too," he says, smiling too innocently.

"Oh, good morning." I lean in for a hug. "I'm really glad you're here."

"Me too… I guess."

"Is she a service dog now?" I ask, keeping my voice low enough that the Broadway-loving tourists around us can't hear.

"Yes, of course she is," he says loudly. Then, under his breath, "For two hundred dollars on the Internet."

"I don't know if they'll let her—"

"Believe me," he interrupts, "nobody is going to say a word."

"But I have a lot of things planned," I say, suddenly worried that my Broadway extravaganza will be derailed by an unauthorized canine.

"You do? Why? It isn't my birthday."

"It doesn't have to be your birthday to plan a special day for you," I say, suddenly terrified he won't even like it. Did I think big enough? What I do know is that I had an embarrassingly good time planning it, so I can only hope that enthusiasm will transfer to reality.

Ryder looks around and finally registers where we're standing.

"Are we going here?" he asks.

"Yes," I say, bracing for protest.

Instead, he threads his fingers together and moves them back and forth excitedly like a rocking boat. "Oh, goodie!" he says with unexpected glee. I smile as we move to the front of the line. Ryder picks up Satine and holds her against his chest, making sure her vest is front and center. The host gives us a once-over.

"Two?" he asks.

"Yes," I say, holding my breath.

"This way, please."

We follow him inside to a world of bright lights, Broadway belters, and sensory overload. It's a happy chaos filled mainly with grandmas and little girls in princess dresses. We're directed to a small booth where I finally exhale. Even if Satine starts an impromptu howl-along, nobody will hear her over this glorious cacophony. It's our next stop that has me truly worried. We settle in, and Satine curls up next to Ryder with the practiced ease of a tiny impostor. I give him a look that reluctantly concedes his point.

A server approaches, dressed in all black with colorful pins and pens tucked into a small apron.

"What can I get you?" she asks with suspicious normalcy.

"I'll have water and coffee, please," I say. "And the waffles."

"I will have a chocolate milkshake—is it too early for that?" Ryder asks, and the server shakes her head. "And the Holy Moly French Toast, please."

"I'll get that started," the server says as she turns. I lean across the table.

"Are you feeling better?" I ask.

Just as the word "better" leaves my mouth, the energy in the room shifts, and our server whirls back around to face our side of the room.

"Be our guest! Be our guest! Put our service to the test," she belts out with such performative intensity that I'm convinced she's singing directly to me. My face burns, but then I realize she somehow makes everyone feel that way. I glance at Ryder, who's half beaming, half smirking. Satine lifts her head at the first few notes, judges the performance, then promptly returns to her nap.

"Tie your napkin round your neck…" Another server picks up the verse, armed with an actual napkin, descending upon some poor soul at a nearby table. I send a silent prayer of gratitude that I've been spared the napkin treatment.

We watch as the performance unfolds with such Broadway precision I feel like I should be paying for orchestra seats. All the while, servers somehow manage to deliver drinks and food without missing a beat. Every time a song ends, and I lean forward to speak to Ryder, another one begins. Eventually, I surrender to musical theater purgatory, and we eat in companionable silence. Ryder demolishes his Holy Moly French toast and drinks every drop of his milkshake with childlike enthusiasm. Each song seems to outshine the one before: 'Food, Glorious Food' from *Oliver*, 'Popular' from *Wicked*, and then—without my even requesting it—'A Whole New World' from *Aladdin*.

Ryder has been into it the whole time, but when the first few notes of this song float through the diner, I swear he nearly levitates. This is our go-to karaoke song; it's his absolute favorite. He closes his eyes and listens, mouthing every word with reverent precision. When it ends, he looks at me with a smile that could power Manhattan.

"That's next," I call across the table, struggling to be heard in Broadway Bedlam.

"What's next?" he calls back.

"*Aladdin*. We're going to see *Aladdin*."

"I know that's from *Aladdin*!" he yells back.

"No." I shake my head. "We're going to the show. After this. To the matinee."

"What? Why?"

It feels impossible to explain my motivations in this noise factory. So I just say, "I don't know. I wanted to."

He reaches across the table and squeezes my hand. Then he pulls out his phone, and at first, I think he's checking something urgent, but then my phone buzzes, and I realize he's texting me from across the table like we're middle schoolers passing notes.

What's up?

I look at him and shrug, but he juts his chin toward my phone, insisting I answer.

I just wanted to do something nice for you.

He reads it and types furiously.

What is this? Make a wish or something? I'm not dying.

He sends it, and as I read it, I watch his face tighten when he realizes what he said. He types again, backpedaling.

I mean, I didn't mean that.

It's okay, I type back. But in that moment, a thought hits me— Luna! I should do something like this for Luna. I mentally bookmark that idea and refocus on Ryder. I text back: *I can show you the world, shining, shimmering, splendid.*

He reads it and scowls in that way that's meant to look irritated but actually means he's touched. I expect him to push back again, but he surprises me and doesn't. He smiles and blows me a kiss that feels more genuine than any words. I ask for the check as our server delivers a song from *Phantom of the Opera* with enough emotion to make Andrew Lloyd Webber weep. I pay, Ryder gathers Satine, and we emerge onto the street that somehow feels both chaotic and blissfully quiet after the diner.

"That was awesome," Ryder declares. "Every single New Yorker should do that."

"I agree," I say, laughing.

"So we're going to *Aladdin*?" he asks with poorly disguised excitement.

"We are!"

"I assume the show is at two? Can we walk her around a little?"

I bite back the question about finding someone else to take care of her. I can't imagine smuggling a dog into a Broadway show, but this day is for Ryder, so I swallow my anxiety.

"Come on, puppy," Ryder coos. "Let's take a short walky."

I watch as Satine prances down the street to a small dirt patch around a tree where she performs her business with surprising dignity.

"We could start heading south," I suggest. "It's on Forty-second Street."

"Oh, I know," Ryder says with exaggerated emphasis. "Sometimes I stand outside the theater while the show is running and try to hear the music coming from inside. This is a dream come true."

"Really?" I laugh. "Why didn't you just get a ticket?"

"I don't know," Ryder says, and we both laugh at the ridiculousness.

I thought I knew everything about Ryder, but somehow missed that he'd never seen the show. If I had known, I would have bought him a ticket ages ago. But even as I think that, I recognize the lie. I was too wrapped up in myself and work to notice what mattered to him.

"I wanted to talk more," I say, shifting gears. "About the other night."

"Do we have to?" he asks, his smile dimming. "I don't want to ruin this."

I don't push, but I want to. We barely talked yesterday, though he did assure me he was okay, and I shouldn't worry about his overall existence. But letting it all go now feels wrong, especially since it's finally out there. I decide I'll try again after the show.

We head to the New Amsterdam Theater with the same anxiety tightening my chest, but once again, Ryder holds Satine with her SERVICE DOG badge prominently displayed, and nobody challenges our canine companion. Luckily, our seats are on the aisle, so I slide in first while Ryder takes the outer seat. Satine performs two perfect circles before settling onto his lap with a sigh that suggests Broadway might not be her scene.

The show is breathtaking. I love every moment, and judging from Ryder's sparkling eyes and constant lip-syncing, I'm pretty sure he's having an out-of-body experience. We don't even leave at intermission. Satine sleeps through the entire spectacle, apparently unmoved by magical lamps and flying carpets.

Afterward, we head to an early dinner at Joe Allen. We're led to our table, Satine settling underneath with another dramatic sigh.

"She's a good dog," I observe.

"The best," he says, reaching down to pet her. "So what is this? An all-Broadway day? And why am I the lucky recipient? Dinner's on me, by the way."

"No, it isn't," I say firmly. "This is my plan and my gift. And I don't know, I think it's because I've been planning this trip for Gerald and his wife, and it's been surprisingly fun. His assistant asked me to help with his retirement gift, and I had the idea for a vacation. Then you were so down that night, and I wanted to do something for you. I guess I was in planning mode."

"Lucky me," Ryder says.

In another life, I would have heard sarcasm in those words, but now I know he means it sincerely. I feel a strange sense of accomplishment wash over me. I always thought my actions needed to impact thousands to matter. Like, if we didn't reach fifty thousand customers, it was all meaningless. Have I been catastrophically wrong this entire time?

"What was going on the other night?" I ask after we order. "Come on, it's me. You can tell me anything. You rarely talk about any of that. Honestly, I thought you were okay with your life now. Have you been pretending? You're such an undeniably brilliant interior designer. I always felt you were meant for this, but I didn't know you when you were dancing. I feel like a failure as a friend—as your best friend. I didn't realize how much you still think about it."

Ryder takes a thoughtful sip of his red wine, eyes meeting mine over the rim.

"Here's my deep, dark secret," he begins. "I have never, ever, until two days ago, truly believed it was over. I always thought I would heal, that I would find my way back, and that I was meant to dance. I told myself there were plenty of dancers who were much older than I am, plenty who came back after injuries, plenty this, and plenty that. But when I went to the studio on Monday, I knew. I just knew. And so, I had to accept it and mourn it. And now, well, now I'm having the best day of my life with my best friend."

I'm mortified when tears spring to my eyes unbidden. Thank god the server chooses that moment to deliver our steak frites. I lift my knife and fork, grateful for the distraction. Still, I wonder if there's more to Ryder's feelings. I don't really believe it's that simple. But I also don't want to ruin the day. Plus, if I'm not eager to cry publicly, why should I push him to emotional vulnerability? I decide to let it rest for now, and we relax into dinner, laughing at the posters on the wall commemorating legendary Broadway flops. For once, I don't dwell on my own losses; I focus entirely on Ryder.

"One more stop," I announce as we begin heading east. "Do you think Satine is up for it?"

"She's up for anything," he says loyally. "What could possibly be next?"

"Frozen hot chocolate at Serendipity."

Now it's Ryder's turn to look suspiciously misty-eyed. He once told me that when he moved here from Singapore alone as a teenager, Serendipity was his first stop. He literally got off the plane and took a cab there because he'd seen it in movies and read about it in magazines. It was the most New York thing he could imagine doing. He also confessed he hadn't been back since, though he'd always meant to return.

We walk east and north to East Sixtieth Street. Satine seems to love the leisurely pace, so we take our time. There's no reservation or curtain time pressing down on us. Everything feels calm, suspended in a perfect moment. We step inside, execute our now-practiced routine, and nobody questions our four-legged plus-one. We order, and soon enormous, frosty goblets of frozen hot chocolate arrive at our table. The server places one in front of Ryder, and I watch as he takes a long sip and closes his eyes. When he opens them, he's wearing an expression that's half smile, half barely contained emotion.

"I can't remember a more perfect day," he says quietly. "You were my own personal genie today. You made all my wishes come true."

A feeling of complete satisfaction washes over me. It's shockingly easy to make someone happy when you know what matters to them. Just embarrassingly, stupidly easy.

I reach across the table and squeeze his hand, then give Satine a gentle pat. After that, there really isn't anything more that needs saying.

Chapter Eleven

I wake up the next morning with that particular brand of restlessness that comes from having a purpose but no outlet. Gerald's trip to Denmark and Finland is planned—complete with a detour to see the Northern Lights (which look like God spilled a cosmic lava lamp across the sky), a visit to a reindeer farm (where I'm 99% sure Santa vacations in the off-season), and an afternoon at Tivoli Gardens (the theme park that Walt Disney himself channeled when creating his own magic kingdom). I gave Ryder the day of his dreams. What more is there to do?

And then I remember Luna and the thought I'd tucked away while Ryder and I were at the Stardust, staring up at the popcorn ceiling of possibility. I realize I am not totally finished; there is more to do. Maybe, now that I think about it, the most important plan of all.

I reach over to grab my phone, which is charging on the nightstand like a patient waiting for its morning coffee, and I text her quickly. I talked to her two days ago, and she sounded like a tired version of herself—Luna on 0.5x speed—but I haven't seen her since the day of the brunch. I need to lay eyes on her.

Coming over, I text. *I'll bring pastries.*

I get up, put my Grace & Company Lucie shower cap on (a purchase Luna once said made me look like a "suburban Betty

Boop"), and take a quick shower. I keep glancing at my phone through the fogged-up glass to see if my screen will light up with her response, like waiting for a shooting star you're not sure will come. I jump out of the shower to double-check, but nothing.

Under normal circumstances, she responds so fast that I have often teased her that her phone is practically superglued to her hand. But today, not so much.

Then I remember a possible reason for her silence: chemo. When we talked, Luna mentioned something about that starting this week, but was fuzzy on the details—a watercolor where I needed a photograph. When I asked her to tell me more about it, specifically the when and the where, she changed the subject with the smoothness of a politician dodging a tax question.

I think about putting a schedule together of people who can go to chemo with her. I know that's a thing—a thing I hoped we would never have to deal with—but I am also fairly sure it is a thing Luna would hate. I think small talk might be one of her least favorite activities in the world, right up there with unsolicited advice and people who say 'irregardless'.

But I wonder if having company and support is more important than all that. Of course, in that scenario, I should be the first one to go with her, which she might have anticipated, and might be why she wouldn't share any details. So, in the absence of a real plan, I'll just go to her apartment and wait. How long can it take anyway, assuming I'm right and that's even where she is right now? The answer is, I have no idea—a shrug fashioned into words.

I check and see that Dominique Ansel Bakery on Spring Street is open, and I know I have to go. It's twenty minutes in the wrong direction, but worth it for the cronuts—a combination of a croissant and a donut, Luna's favorite, and proof that sometimes the best things in life come from refusing to choose. I don't even let the question of whether or not she'll be hungry cross my mind. I jump in an Uber to go north and then walk the last few blocks to clear my head.

I am two blocks from Luna's apartment when I get a text. I jump like I've been shocked. But it's from Ryder. It says in all caps, BEST DAY EVER. BEST FRIEND EVER. LOVE YOU! I heart the message and write back, also in all caps: SO GLAD. WISH WE COULD DO IT ALL OVER AGAIN. BEST FRIEND EVER. LOVE YOU!

He hearts that message, and I'm just about to call him to see if he has heard anything from Luna when another text comes through. This one is from Luna, and I breathe a sigh of relief that feels like my first full breath in hours.

Sorry! Was napping. Today isn't great. Can we try for later this week?

I stop and think about just turning around and heading home. I don't want to bother her if she's feeling that bad. I feel the weight of the pastry bag in my hand, full of buttery promises, and I decide I'll go and drop it off, and then I'll leave her alone for the day. I get to her apartment and buzz. I see Luna's mother peeking through the door behind the main glass door. I wave furiously, like I'm guiding a plane to its gate. She is acting like she's trying to figure out who I am, squinting at me like I'm a math problem she can't quite solve.

"Hannah!" I call. "Hannah, it's me!"

We have done the whole please-call-me-Hannah routine after I called her Mrs. Cumberland well into my thirties. I don't have time for that silliness anymore. If she says to call her Hannah, I am going to call her Hannah, even if it feels like calling your elementary school teacher by their first name.

Slowly, Hannah opens the door, leaving it slightly ajar, but she doesn't move to let me inside. We stand in the entryway, just looking at each other, like two people who picked up the same item at a store.

"I just want to drop off some pastries. I wanted to see Luna, but she just texted to say she isn't feeling well, and I don't want to bother her."

"She's not doing well," Hannah says, shaking her head. "She can barely lift her head."

I can't believe what I'm hearing. The words hit me like a physical blow. "Is there anything I can do? Can I help? Is there anything she needs? Anything you need?"

Hannah hesitates, then nods. She opens the door, lets me step inside, and then, out of nowhere, collapses onto me. It is so shocking that I have to take a step back to steady myself, like someone just pushed a grand piano into my arms. I drop the bag I'm holding so I can reach out and steady her. We stand like that for a few seconds, with her hugging me really hard. When she finally pulls away, I expect to see her crying, but she is totally dry-eyed, like someone who has moved beyond tears into a new state of being.

"I don't think I can do this," she whispers. "I know I don't have a choice, and I know a mom doesn't ever have a choice, but I don't believe that bullshit about not being given more than you can handle. That is total and complete crap."

I smile weakly because I hear Luna in her words—the apple didn't fall far from the tree; it just rolled a few feet and grew thorns.

"You're right, it is pure bullshit and total crap," I agree.

"I'm so glad you're here," she says, taking me by surprise.

"It's been, I don't know what the word is, impossible, I guess, watching your only daughter wither away."

"Can we go inside?" I ask, leaning down to pick up the bag, now slightly squashed like my hopes for a normal visit.

"Yes, of course," Hannah says, looking like she is coming out of a daze. We climb the stairs into the apartment. I am desperate to get inside, but I am also afraid of what I am going to find in there, like opening the door to a room where Schrödinger's cat lives.

We walk into Luna's bedroom, where she is lying on her bed, on her back, propped up against a bunch of colorful pillows like a queen on an uncomfortable throne. Her face is as white as a sheet. Her hair looks greasy. When she sees me, she smiles, and for a moment, she's just Luna—my Luna.

"Took you two long enough," she says.

Hannah excuses herself, presumably to let us catch up. Luna and I look at each other.

"She's driving me fucking crazy," Luna says. "And also, thank God she's here."

"What's going on?" I ask, perching myself on the side of her bed, trying to take up as little space as possible, like I might disturb some delicate balance in the universe.

"I had chemo early yesterday morning." She looks at her watch. "The sickness kicked in about an hour later. For some reason, I thought I would be the exception, that it wouldn't affect me that way, even though I was warned. I have been throwing up nonstop since then."

I nod and take her hand. It feels small and cold, like a bird that fell from its nest.

"I'm so sorry, Luna."

She gently pulls her hand away from me like she's taking

back something precious. "No, please, no pity."

"That isn't pity," I say, trying very hard to define what I'm feeling. Is it pity? What even is pity? I know I am truly sorry she's going through this, and I wish she weren't more than anything—more than I wish for money or success or even happiness.

"Just be your normal self," Luna instructs.

My normal self? That's a hard one. Everything I think to tell her about seems boring or so irrelevant next to what she is dealing with, like complaining about a paper cut to someone in the ER with a gunshot wound.

"Any chance you could eat something?" Hannah says from the doorway, startling us.

"I brought pastries," I offer, holding up the bag like it's a peace offering.

"Why don't we start with some dry toast?" Hannah suggests gently.

"Mother, what are we fucking toasting to? My demise?" She laughs, which is then followed by a series of heavy coughs that rattle her small frame. "Sure, Mom," Luna says once she can talk again. "Toast sounds strangely good."

We're quiet while we listen to her mother half-jogging to the kitchen, the sound receding like a tide.

"I'm so glad to see you," I say.

"Me too," Luna says uncharacteristically sweetly.

"I came here to share a big idea I had," I say slowly. "But I'm going to save it. I don't think it's the right time."

"Well, I wouldn't wait too long," Luna says, sounding like herself again. "Who knows how much time we have? Come on, spill it."

I take a deep breath, like I'm about to jump off a high dive.

"I want to take you somewhere," I blurt out. "I want to take you on a vacation—somewhere incredible, the trip of a lifetime, whatever you want to do. Where have you always wanted to go? I want to plan your dream vacation."

Luna looks at me like I just said I brought a magic wand, and I am going to try to cast a spell that will get rid of her cancer. She leans back, closes her eyes, and slowly shakes her head.

"I don't know if you are seeing this," Luna says, her eyes still closed. "But that little walk from the bathroom to my bed? The one where I didn't throw up for twenty going on thirty minutes? That's pretty much my dream vacation now. And the all-you-can-eat toast prepared for you and brought to you in bed? This resort is killing it."

Hannah is back with the toast and a cold drink. I scoot to the side, and then she waits for Luna to open her eyes. When she does, she sits up a little higher. Hannah and I watch as she takes a nibble of the toast and then a slightly bigger bite, like a wary animal approaching food.

"Good," Luna says, like that is all she can muster.

She manages to eat half a slice and take two sips of what I think is ginger ale in a very old, vintage-looking McDonald's glass that says 'The Hamburglar' on it. I remember the day Luna found it, along with two other glasses, one with Ronald McDonald and one with Grimace, at a cool flea market on Amsterdam Avenue.

"My mom had glasses like these when she was a kid," Luna had said, like she'd just come across a gold doubloon or something. "I have to have these."

I think about asking Luna if she remembers that, but I don't. It feels like a day from another life, a memory from a parallel universe where cancer doesn't exist. I have to look away for a second. I lean closer to her once I gather myself, and we're alone again.

"We don't have to go right now, but I really want to do this for you," I press on. "I love the idea of a spa, a wellness retreat. I'm thinking maybe in Arizona, Sedona specifically? They have those energy vortexes there that I think are really good for you. They realign something, I'm not sure what. The air there is good for everyone, and I'm thinking we should go super fancy, as fancy as it gets."

"Em," she says, my name on her lips like a gentle warning.

"Maybe having something to look forward to would be good." I try to sound upbeat, like a cheerleader for a team that's down by fifty points. "Sorry. I should have waited to talk about it."

"No, no." Luna waves me off. She looks so tired. I feel a pang of panic that I'm going to have to leave soon. Hannah is surely going to usher me out, like a museum closing for the night.

"Lu, I just… I don't know, I'm in planning mode, I guess," I say when she doesn't say anything.

"I love planning mode," she says, perking up a little. "What gave you this idea?"

So I tell her about Gerald and about yesterday with Ryder, and she listens like I'm telling her the secret to eternal life. I tell her that it's the first time I've felt like I lost myself in something in a good way since those early days of StyleShop. I tell her that I love her, and if I am going to give to anyone, it should be her.

"How many wishes are you granting?" Luna asks.

"Huh, good question." I pause. "Well, yours, as soon as I can."

"All this talk reminds me of that perfect week you had with your father when you were little," Luna says, sounding the tiniest bit slurry, like she's had half a glass of wine. "Remember? You've told me about that so many times. How he planned a spring break vacation, and you said it felt like he had an invisible checklist of all your wishes, and he somehow knew each one and made it come true?"

"Oh my God, I can't believe you remember that! That was the best. We fished, took a baking class, and went to a county fair. We stopped at every single pizza place we encountered and then did a rating of all of them. I was obsessed with pizza back then."

"Who are you kidding? You still are," Luna says, a hint of the old teasing glint in her eye.

"I guess I am!" I state proudly, like I've just been caught in a minor scandal I'm secretly proud of.

Talking about pizza makes me think of Ryder and how he said I was his genie yesterday, and how I made all his wishes come true.

"Look, I love the idea of a trip, but I literally can't imagine getting from here to the door," she says, bringing me back to the present. "Right now, getting to Arizona feels like getting to the moon or maybe Mars. I do want to go someplace with you, if I can, if I feel better, after the chemo. I mean it when I say I would like nothing more."

"Not if," I say more urgently than I mean to. "When."

"Okay, when?" Luna says, but I get the sense she is appeasing me, like a parent telling a child they'll go to Disneyland "someday".

"Let's plan our trip, but not for now, for down the road," she says.

"Yes, for down the road," I echo. "And would it be crazy to grant a few wishes for other people in the meantime?"

Luna smiles, a sun breaking through clouds. "Aunt Pearl?"

"Yes!" I love the idea. "And Billie."

"You can take them first while I get back my strength after this round of chemo. You should take advantage of this momentum," Luna says seriously.

She's so good at making sense of things, at organizing the chaos in my head into neat little boxes. "I want you to know there is nobody more important than you."

"There certainly isn't," she snaps. "But, since we've established that I can't go right now, who else might be on that list? What about your movie star mom?" she says genuinely without the regular eye rolls that usually accompany any mention of my mother.

"My mom?" I say incredulously. "The queen of dodging responsibilities?"

"Well, yeah, but she's been better lately, and maybe these trips aren't only about fun or giving to people who have given equally to you. Maybe they're about healing," she says more gently than I've ever heard her say anything, like she's whispering a secret to the universe.

"Okay." I nod slowly, not hating the idea, letting it settle into my consciousness like a cat finding the right spot on a windowsill.

"Did you miss anyone?" she asks, looking more animated than she has since I got here. "You already did Ryder. We'll plan ours someday soon after chemo hell is over, your Aunt Pearl, your mom, and Billie! I love it."

I'm nodding more quickly now. I love it, too. "So," I say, talking to myself as much as I'm talking to Luna, "that's five people when all is said and done, five adventures. And this might sound a little pompous or, at the very least, presumptuous, but since you asked, I see it as five wishes coming true, assuming I hit it right."

"Lady, you always hit it right," Luna says with what feels like her last burst of energy for the moment.

"I love this, Luna." I relax for the first time since I got here. I move to the end of the bed and put one of the cast-off pillows up against the wall. I lean against it. I can feel my eyes getting heavy, like they're being pulled down by tiny weights. "You know, you always help me come up with my best ideas."

Something passes across her face, and then it's gone. I might say fear if I had to put my finger on it.

"Em, that's not true. You come up with so many great ideas yourself."

"No, not really. You helped me come up with StyleShop. I mean, you did that. Without you, who knows what I would have done all these years? I mean, you are at the core of anything important I do."

Luna smiles. "Let's agree I'm fabulous, but so are you."

"Five wishes it is," I say, mostly to myself. "So Ryder got his day as a Broadway tourist. I am going to find the best spa for you, for us, one that serves healing food and has the freshest air, one where people go who have claimed to be cured of whatever ails them. I just have to figure out what everyone else doesn't even know they want yet, which will make all their dreams come true."

Luna smiles. I think she wants to say more, but she's too tired, words beyond her reach. I'm surprised Hannah hasn't kicked me out yet. I sit up. Luna doesn't protest.

"Thank you," I say. "I came here to try to help you, and you helped me. I guess that's the story of my life, of our friendship."

"You have no idea how much you helped me and how glad

I am that you ignored my text," she says as I stand up. "Will you come back tomorrow? Who needs Sedona? We can have our own spa here."

My mind starts racing. *Yes! We can have our own spa here! I'll get all the supplies. I'll get candles. I'll get cucumbers. I'll get special tea.* I notice Luna is looking at me. I bet she can read my mind like it's a billboard in Times Square.

"I'm just kidding," she says. "Your company is elixir enough."

I lean in for a hug. She feels even smaller than the last time. How much smaller can she get? I don't let myself answer that.

I say goodbye to Hannah, who is dozing on the couch but jumps when she hears my footsteps, like I've startled her from a dream. No wonder I got to stay so long.

"Thank you," she says. "For the breather. I hadn't closed my eyes for like twenty-seven hours or something."

"I'll come back tomorrow," I promise. "Luna asked me to."

Hannah nods, and I have two distinct thoughts as I walk away. The first is that I am losing a piece of myself. The second is that I have the same feeling I had when Luna helped me create StyleShop—excitement and the sense that I'm on to something great. Five wishes, I repeat to myself. Five wishes. I can't wait to keep going.

Chapter Twelve

"Excuse me," I hear as I walk past a man and a woman standing on the corner of Sixty-eighth and Broadway. I have that moment of New York existential crisis—to engage or not to engage, that is the question whether 'tis nobler in the mind to suffer the slings and arrows of outrageous small talk or to take arms against a sea of strangers.

"Excuse me," the woman calls out again, staring directly at me with the intensity of someone who's spotted a celebrity but isn't quite sure which one. It's a busy sidewalk. There are at least seventeen other people they could've chosen, all of whom look more helpful than I do on my best day.

"Can I help you?" I concede, fully aware that this could range from simple directions to a twelve-minute interpretive dance explaining why I should fund someone's one-way ticket to Albuquerque. But I'm a sucker for human connection in this concrete jungle, even when my better judgment is screaming and waving caution flags.

"This is a really dumb question," the man says with the sheepish smile of someone about to ask if Central Park is man-made. "And I think we probably already know the answer to this, but are there any campgrounds in New York City?"

They're both wearing enormous backpacks that look like

they could house a small family of raccoons—his is red; hers is blue. The packs are stuffed and tattered like they've been dragged through twelve national parks, but they're unmistakably from REI, which means they probably cost more than my monthly rent. The woman is cute, maybe early twenties, with a nice green sweater that somehow looks both expensive and like she found it at a charming roadside thrift store. Her blonde hair is pulled up in the kind of perky ponytail I haven't been able to achieve since I was twelve. The man looks similar in age, maybe slightly older, with short dark hair, glasses, and a gray sweatshirt that says 'Florida' with an alligator next to it— the kind of souvenir you buy ironically and then end up wearing unironically because it's just so damn comfortable.

"Sorry, we'll figure it out," the woman says in a rush. I've been staring at them for what is apparently too long. They probably think I'm mentally calculating how much their kidneys would fetch on the black market. Or that I'm one of those crazy New Yorkers they've included in their travel bingo card.

"I don't know about campgrounds," I say, finally engaging my brain-to-mouth connection. "But I'm pretty sure there are hostels. Also, I'm confident there are campgrounds not too far outside the city, in New Jersey or Westchester. You should Google it. It would be a fairly easy train ride." I resist adding *assuming the trains are running, which is about as reliable as a weather forecast from a fortune cookie.*

"Told you!" the woman says, gently smacking the man on his shoulder with the casual intimacy of someone who's earned the right to invade his personal space.

"You said you wanted to see New York City," he says. "So here it is." He gestures around like a game show host unveiling a prize that's simultaneously spectacular and disappointing.

"Great," she says. "Thanks." But there's a warmth to her voice that makes me think she genuinely appreciates his terrible planning. It's the kind of warmth that says, I signed up for this circus, and I'm enjoying every ridiculous moment.

"Good luck," I say, silently adding, *You're going to need it if you think you're pitching a tent in Central Park without getting arrested or worse, featured on someone's TikTok.*

I walk away thinking, *Ah, youth, what are they doing? Don't they have phones with access to the entire knowledge of humankind?* I hope they make it through the night without becoming an urban legend. And then, when I am a good block away, I look back at them and have the strangest feeling, one that is extremely rare for me—like spotting a designer bag at a sample sale that isn't damaged. I want to be them. Well, not them specifically because their shower situation is about to get dire. But I have the urge to be younger and totally free, when every single thing in the world was possible. Unlike now, when it feels like so many doors have been firmly closed or are closing right in front of my eyes with the dramatic finality of a Broadway curtain.

And then I have this image of me and Jasper, wearing backpacks, not quite as large as the ones the couple had on but still heavy enough to make my future chiropractor wealthy. We had been together for less than a year, still in that magical phase when you want to share everything you care about with the other person, and before you know them so well that you stop trying on too many fronts because you've already seen them floss and there's nowhere to go but down.

Jasper had been a big camper before I met him. He had done a lot of hiking and backcountry trips in Australia and then in the western states like California, Wyoming, and Montana when he moved here. He'd climbed a bunch of mountains and hiked a few well-known trails—the names of which all blended together for me in a geographical smoothie. Is Point Lobos a mountain or a trail? I could never remember, and frankly, it sounded like a brand of upscale salsa.

I wouldn't say I pretended to be interested, but there was that element of falling in love that makes everything about the other person intriguing, even if under normal circumstances you'd rather watch paint dry. With that in mind, I pretended to remember which was a mountain and which was a trail with the dedication of someone playing the memory game at a party. I asked a lot of questions. What's it like to wake up in the morning miles from civilization? How do you cook? How do you go to the toilet? I had never camped, so I felt like I was taking a class called 'Surviving in Nature 101: For People Who Consider Room Service a Human Right'. Sometimes, I would see cool articles about a trail or a trip someone took, and I would cut it out and save it for him like a deranged scrapbooker. Other times, I would see a sale advertised at Orvis or Patagonia for a camping mug or funny dried food, and I would buy it for him, convinced these were the breadcrumbs that would lead to his heart. Let's just say all of that led Jasper to believe it might be something I would like to do one day, which is what happens when you build an entire personality trait out of politeness.

On the eve of our first anniversary, he told me he had a surprise for me. I was beyond excited. In my mind, I had made it completely clear that I was desperate to go to Bermuda, the way people make things clear in romantic comedies—through a series of meaningful glances and casual references that somehow everyone understands except the actual person you're trying to communicate with. I had never been there, and that pink sand called to me with the siren song of Instagram possibilities. I had even done some research about resorts and dropped subtle hints about them, like leaving browser tabs open on my laptop or sighing dramatically whenever someone mentioned turquoise water. Clearly, those hints were too subtle, possibly microscopic.

He told me to be ready on a Friday afternoon and to clear the whole weekend plus Monday, but his one caveat was that he would pack my bag. At that point, we were basically living together anyway, so he asked me to give him space so he could get my things together without giving away the secret. I carefully put my best summer clothes toward the front of my closet, along with a new bikini I had just bought with all the strategic planning of a chess grandmaster, and then I left and went to a coffee shop, where I continued to do research on where to eat in Bermuda with the confidence of someone who's already booked the trip.

Of course, I glanced at my closet as soon as I got back. Many of the things I had left in the front were not there anymore, so I assumed he had packed them, adding to my Bermuda certainty. When Friday afternoon rolled around, I kept waiting for him to say we should take a cab to the airport. Instead, he told me to meet him in front of my building at 3 p.m. He pulled up in a rental car—some sort of small SUV that looked like it was designed for people who want to pretend they go off-roading but actually just need extra space for Costco runs—and he waited while I processed the fact that it was unlikely we were driving to Bermuda unless physics had changed dramatically while I wasn't paying attention.

I got in, and he was so happy, so excited. He played Van Morrison all the way as we drove north, far north, to Vermont. He knew exactly where we were going. I still held out hope that we were going to a resort, the way people cling to hope that their delayed flight will somehow take off earlier than scheduled. I noticed that instead of using my usual bag to pack, he'd packed a brand-new backpack. There were two in the back—his well-used one and one I had never seen before that looked suspiciously wilderness-ready.

He pulled into a campground, and I was thinking—no way, no way, no way. But I didn't say it, because sometimes keeping your thoughts to yourself is the greatest gift of love there is. He drove around the winding road, finally pulling up to a beautiful spot by a running river. It was late June, so it was just getting dark. He got out, took the tent out of his backpack, and set it up with the efficiency of someone who's done this a thousand times. It was tiny, roughly the size of my bathroom in New York, which is already the size of a generous postage stamp.

We had stopped for a bite on the way, so there wasn't much to do. He made it cozy—he had thought to bring pillows and a lantern we could use inside the tent, and plenty of blankets in addition to our sleeping bags. He was trying so hard, like a golden retriever bringing you its favorite toy. But I was miserable. I spent the whole night watching a huge slug crawl from one side of the tent roof to the other, like the world's slowest and most disgusting NASCAR race. I was afraid to close my eyes. Every time I tried to, I imagined the slug inside our tent, working its way into my sleeping bag to whisper slug secrets into my ear. Meanwhile, Jasper slept soundly, which might have been the greatest betrayal of all.

"Coffee?" he said so innocently when he woke up, as if we were in a Folgers commercial and not what felt like a biodegradable prison cell. I was in a total state. I literally hadn't slept, and I thought, *Does he know me at all? Has he met me? I'm* the person who once called the front desk because the air conditioning in our hotel room was 'too breezy'. Of course, the slug never got inside. I could have slept, and it would have been okay. But I didn't feel that way. I felt like I was one tent zipper away from reenacting a horror movie.

"I figured car camping would be your best introduction," he said, reaching for me with hopeful eyes. "We can progress to more serious camping down the road."

"I'm never going to do this again," I said, sounding way angrier than I meant to, like I was auditioning for the role of Unreasonable Girlfriend in a sitcom. "I want to leave. Or go to a hotel." Preferably one with room service and a spa, and walls made of something more substantial than nylon.

Jasper looked shocked, like I'd just told him I was secretly a werewolf.

"Come on," he urged. "You haven't seen this place in the sunlight."

He unzipped the tent and got out. I followed, because what choice did I have? It's not like I could call an Uber from the middle of nowhere. It was so beautiful—the river and the trees and wildflowers everywhere, like someone had hired Mother Nature as an interior decorator with an unlimited budget. There was a small place for a fire, and I couldn't see any other campers. The words *What is wrong with you* ran through my mind. Jasper had gone to so much trouble, and I was happy to be with him. I loved how he smiled when he saw a bird and how his hair looked like it was on fire when it caught the sun in the right way, like he had his own personal lighting designer. I loved how he knew exactly what to do, how he had the right soap to wash up in the lake and a small camp stove, which he used expertly to cook our breakfast. I tried to relax. I let him make coffee and blueberry pancakes, and then we took a stroll, which is what outdoorsy people call a walk when they want it to sound more charming.

"Starting out easy," he had said, like we were embarking on a gentle introduction rather than what felt to me like Bear Grylls' boot camp.

I laugh to myself a little now as I remember that stroll. We had barely gone a quarter of a mile when I slipped on rocks on the hill leading down to the riverbed, because, of course, I did. The universe has a sense of irony that Shakespeare would envy. Sure enough, I twisted my ankle—or as I like to call it, my body's way of saying *I told you so*. Jasper didn't laugh at me. He didn't say I should be more rugged or remind me that I'm the person who once complained that flip-flops were "structurally unsound footwear." Instead, he felt terrible, helped me back to camp, took down the tent, and drove us to a hotel. It turns out he had a reservation at a very nice inn nearby all along, just in case his idea backfired, which is the kind of thoughtfulness that makes me wish I could go back in time and hug him instead of pouting.

There, I spent the day in a luxurious room with my foot up. Jasper brought me delicious food and even booked me a manicure in the hotel spa. He took such good care of me, though he had the night before, too, I realize now. But he got it exactly right on the second and third nights. I think of what Luna said about the spring break with my dad, and it felt like that with Jasper at the inn, like he had an invisible checklist of all the things I loved and managed to make them all happen for me, despite my swollen ankle and injured pride.

The hotel actually had a 'pillow menu', and he had the concierge bring up a few choices like we were sampling fine wines instead of things to rest my head on. I still remember it as one of the top hotels I have ever been to, and that's saying a lot from someone who judges hotels primarily on the quality of their complimentary toiletries. By the following day, I thought I felt better enough to get into the lovely indoor/outdoor pool and get dressed to go to dinner.

After we checked out and were in the car, about to drive back to New York, he turned to me.

"It wasn't Bermuda, I know," he had said. "Next time."

He was so kind, so thoughtful. So many times during our years together, I had just bulldozed right through that with the determination of someone who knows exactly what they want, even when what they want isn't necessarily what they need.

When we got back, I went to the doctor because the swelling really hadn't gone down, and my ankle looked like it was trying to become its own separate entity. It turned out I had actually broken a tiny bone in my ankle. I had to wear a boot for eight weeks, looking like a cyborg from the calf down. By then, Jasper really felt awful. Did I reassure him enough? Did I reassure him at all? Or did I just use the boot as an excuse to make him carry my groceries and fetch me ice cream at 11 p.m.?

I have the urge to call Jasper. To tell him I'm sorry. To laugh a little at how silly I was, how predictable, like a character in a rom-com who doesn't realize what she has until it's walking out the door with perfectly tousled hair. I pull my phone out. Could I call him? Would he even answer? I think of his voice, how he always said "Hey, love" when I called, like I was the most important interruption in his day.

Here's the thing about regrets—I will never be able to go back to that moment, to that weekend, to that year, and redo it, no matter how much I might want to, no matter how many times I replay it in my head like a movie with alternate endings. Maybe it's my recent birthday, I don't know, but I am starting to see things in a different way, with the clarity that only comes from distance and too many late-night glasses of wine. I can't go back, but I can go forward. I wonder, though, is that enough? Or am I just telling myself the kind of comforting lie we all need to keep putting one foot in front of the other, even when one of those feet is metaphorically (or literally, in my case) broken?

Chapter Thirteen

There is something about that early trip with Jasper that I just can't shake. I keep thinking about that moment in my closet when he packed so hopefully for me—the careful way his hands smoothed each folded item, like he was sending pieces of his heart along with me. In the end, he had included the bikini I'd deliberately left in plain sight. I know he thought we'd swim in the river near the campsite, but of course that never happened. I had used it, though, in the hotel pool—chlorine-scented evidence of plans gone sideways.

The idea of gathering things for a trip, anticipating what you'll need but not really having any idea where it will take you, sparks something in me I can't extinguish. I have wondered how I'm going to tell Billie, Aunt Pearl, and my mother about my trip ideas. Yes, I am really going to do this. And I know, without question, that they are going to think I'm joking. I would bet my entire severance package on it.

Well, no time like the present to prove myself spectacularly wrong or right. Without letting myself think about it too much—because overthinking is my superpower and my kryptonite—I call Billie. It rings and rings until I'm mentally composing a voicemail that doesn't sound desperate. I am just about to give up when she answers.

"My partner in crime!" she practically yells, her voice bright enough to power a small city.

"You have no idea," I say back, already feeling the smile stretch across my face.

"It's a hell of a day over here," Billie says, moving right by my comment with the momentum of a freight train. "Both boys are sick, and it's like a vomit volcano. Make that two vomit volcanoes. With perfect timing and surprisingly excellent aim."

"Oh, God, Billie, that sounds horrible," I say, my nose crinkling involuntarily.

"I have two trash bags full of things I liked or loved in varying stages, as recently as this morning, that can never be used again. They are unsalvageable," she says, sounding surprisingly cheery given her current circumstances, like someone who's found Zen in the apocalypse. "I'm not even going to try. As they say, they are garbawwwge now." She emphasizes the long a with theatrical flair.

"I'm so sorry. Is there anything I can do to help?"

As soon as I say it, I regret it with the force of a thousand suns. The last thing I want to do is go over there and risk getting sick. I am a terrible friend, and I should feel terrible.

"No, but thank you," she replies, and I breathe a silent sigh of relief that makes me feel even worse. "I think we just may have turned a corner."

"I hope."

"Oh, no, spoke too soon," she says, cutting me off. "Gotta run, or we are going to have to throw this whole house away. Plus"—she lowers her voice to a whisper that somehow contains more emotion than a scream—"I can barely stand to see them so miserable. It breaks my heart. Please, pray for us."

I'm left holding the phone to my ear, thinking, once again,

that that could but never will be me. I don't let the sense of loss creep in this time, that familiar hollow ache I've gotten good at ignoring. Instead, I think of Billie and how I can't wait to do something for her; she's always looking after everyone around her with the dedication of a guardian angel in yoga pants. I wish I could wave a magic wand, make her boys better, and pluck her out of there. I'm really sorry she's dealing with that, but I'm sort of glad I didn't have a chance to mention the trip because suddenly I have a much better idea about how to tell her.

I sit down and write a list of every single idea I have about her trip. I run out of room on the paper, so I go to my closet and get an old pink poster board, something left over from an impromptu StyleShop presentation I never used—a relic from my former life. At the top, I write each name in my best attempt at calligraphy: Billie, Aunt Pearl, Mom, and, of course, Luna. I make columns with military precision. I have a million thoughts swirling in my mind about destinations and ways to get there, and dreams and wishes. I go back and forth with concepts—cold or hot, city or country, ocean or land, mountain or lake—until I think I possibly have it. I put the poster board against the wall and take a step back. It is beautiful, if I do say so myself, like a conspiracy theorist's vision board but with less foil and more color-coding.

I take a photo of it in case I have to remember any details, grab my bag and keys, and head out. My first destination is Target, a few blocks away—the mothership calling me home. I also plan to go to the container store, one of the local gourmet food stores, the bathing suit store, and the liquor store, and there is one white cover-up I have admired in a shop window that I plan to buy, like I'm preparing for a heist but with credit cards. I could be doing marketing research for Gerald, but that can also wait. He has me working on their social media, which is so much fun, I wonder why I removed myself from that sort of thing at work. I can't get enough of it, and I think I might have an idea they will like, but I'm not meeting with him again until next week, so I have plenty of time. I lose myself in shopping until I am so tired and so weighed down with heavy bags and unwieldy boxes that I just want to sit and rest, preferably for the next decade.

There's a bar on the corner. I realize it is only four in the afternoon, but would it be so bad if I went in for a glass of wine? The universe has yet to punish anyone for day drinking in moderation. I walk in. It's early, so it isn't crowded. I take a seat at the end of the bar and stack my things on an empty stool like I'm building a retail monument.

"Chardonnay, please," I say to the bartender. She nods, pulls out a glass, and gives me a generous pour that suggests she understands the weight of existing as a human in the world today.

"Thanks." I take a long sip, thinking I made the right choice. I thought I might try to get Billie's mystery box to her today— she clearly needs a pick-me-up—so I shouldn't drink too much. I sit back and look around. I'll send the box first, full of scintillating hints, then once her curiosity is piqued, I will email an official packing list.

Perfect, I think to myself, just as the door swings open, letting the sunshine into the dark bar with all the subtlety of a spotlight. I can't see who it is since the light is bright behind them, creating a silhouette that could be anyone or no one. I take a sip as the figure walks into the shadows, and I see his face. I try to swallow fast, but the wine gets caught in my throat. It sputters there, and then I feel the burn as I try to keep it inside my body, but the reflex to get it out is too strong. I cough loudly as it escapes from my mouth in what can only be described as a fine chardonnay mist. The bartender and the one other person at the bar turn to look at me, as does the man who just walked in, and basically, I wish I could go back to twenty minutes ago and make entirely different decisions. Or perhaps never have been born.

"Emerson!"

Unbelievably, it is Jasper. Hearing the notes of his lyrical accent makes my already watering eyes sting like I've been hit with emotional tear gas.

I gather myself, clear my throat, and sit up straighter, as if good posture can erase the fact that I just choked on wine at the mere sight of him.

"Are you okay?" he asks, coming toward me with that familiar look of concern.

"Yes," I say, surprised to find myself laughing. "I guess I was shocked to see you."

"As I am to see you." There is a pause that contains multitudes. "Mind if I take a seat?"

I glance next to me. I have so much stuff piled up here. There is literally no place for him unless he wants to perch atop my purchases like a retail mountain goat. He sees it and moves to the other side of me, taking the empty seat to my left.

"What can I get you?" the bartender asks.

Jasper looks at me, and for a moment, it's like no time has passed at all.

"I was actually coming in for a quick burger and a Coke, but a glass of wine sounds pretty good right now. I'll have whatever she's having."

"Gotcha," the bartender says, backing away, clearly sensing the crackling atmosphere between us.

We smile nervously at each other for a few seconds, like two people who once knew the contours of each other's souls but now can't figure out appropriate small talk.

"What are you doing here?" he asks.

"I'm surprised we haven't run into each other before this," I say at the same time.

We laugh, and it's both familiar and strange—like hearing a favorite song played in a different key.

"You first," I offer.

He tilts his head the way he always used to, meaning he really wants me to go first, but then he nods once and clears his throat.

"I just wondered what you're doing here," he admits. "Not that you need a reason to have a glass of wine. What I mean is, what are you doing on this block in this neighborhood right now?" His hands make little circles in the air as if trying to draw the right words from it.

"Oh, um, I'm working on a big project," I say, not sure how much I want to share with him about my wish indulging. For one very brief moment, I let myself picture us right here, together, with our daughter in a highchair, the three of us, and then I shake that image away. It is as real as a unicorn, a Sasquatch, or a pot of gold at the end of a rainbow; it does not exist in our world. That thought sits in my chest like a stone.

"What sort of project?" he asks, like he's truly interested. He was always truly interested in a way that made you feel like the most fascinating person alive. "You are completely out of StyleShop, right?"

"Yes, that's all done. For better or worse, but mostly better." I try to sound confident, like someone who has their life together and didn't just spend four hours buying random items for trips that might never happen.

"Cool," he says, and I have the oddest sense that he is so familiar and also such a stranger—like running into your childhood home after it's been redecorated by new owners.

"Thanks, yes, it's been a journey, but this whole last year has been," I say. Then I add, "As you know," which instantly feels like poking a bruise.

Jasper nods, his eyes crinkling at the corners in that way that always made me feel seen.

"So, the project," I say after the slightly awkward silence. "It's, um, it's really at the beginning stages. But I think it is going to be great." I sound like someone pitching a half-baked idea on Shark Tank.

"Well, with you at the helm, I have no doubt. It's nice to see you excited about it."

"What about you? What are you doing here?" I gesture vaguely at the bar like it's a surprising destination, not, you know, a public establishment where adults frequently go.

"I'm rehearsing around the corner. I'm collaborating on a new album. We started so early this morning that it feels like dinnertime, thus the craving for the burger." He pats his stomach lightly, and I force myself not to track the movement.

The bartender puts a glass of wine in front of Jasper.

"Thanks." He lifts it up and bends it slightly toward me. "Cheers."

"Cheers," I say, not lifting my glass to meet his. That just feels like way too much, like crossing a boundary that shouldn't be crossed. We both look away. I would bet my life savings that we are both thinking about our toast at Bad Roman.

"I heard your song!" I say, a little too loudly. "On *Hello America*. It was really good!" I sound like someone's enthusiastic aunt who doesn't understand the music industry.

Jasper takes a long sip of his wine, and I watch his throat work.

"Thanks," he says.

"You are really just so talented," I add, mentally kicking myself for gushing.

"Thanks," he says again, shrugging his shoulders like he isn't sure, like someone complimented his shirt rather than his life's work.

"You are," I say, hating how earnest I sound.

Jasper takes another long sip of his wine.

"So, everything's been good with you?" he asks once he's swallowed.

I almost don't tell him. But he knows Luna, too. He's known her for as long as he and I have been together. Luna was there from day one.

"I'm not sure if you've heard," I begin. He immediately recognizes my tone and leans in a little, his eyes right on me like twin searchlights. "But Luna is sick."

He shakes his head vigorously like he didn't know.

"Sick? With what?"

"It's serious," I say because it is serious, and it is also completely shocking, and I want to warn him. I pause for a second. "She has stage four lung cancer."

Jasper gasps and puts his hand to his mouth like he's trying to physically hold back his reaction. "Oh no," he says, his voice hollowed out.

"It's so awful." I let down my guard with him for the first time since he walked in the door. "The prognosis isn't good. She just started chemo. I... I..."

"I know," he says before I have a chance to finish.

I nod, thinking he might actually know what I was going to say, that I can't believe I am going to lose someone else I love to cancer. That some days it feels like the universe is playing a particularly cruel joke, like I'm collecting grief the way other people collect vinyl records or vintage teacups.

"So, are you going to get the burger?" I ask, feeling like I've dropped the worst sort of bomb. I have probably ruined his day, which, of course, was not my intention.

"Oh, I don't think so," he says, pulling back a little, realizing that's my way of saying I don't want to talk about Luna anymore. "I have to get back. And I guess I'm not as hungry as I thought I was." His glass is still more than half full, but he doesn't seem to care, like he's suddenly lost his appetite for both food and conversation.

"It was really nice to see you," I say, which feels like the most ridiculous understatement.

"Yeah." His eyes radiate a combination of warmth and sadness that makes my chest ache. "It's really nice to see you."

"Are you doing okay?" I ask in a rush. I realize I hadn't asked him.

"Yeah, I'm doing alright." He says it like someone who has rehearsed being alright until they've convinced themselves it's true.

He hops off the barstool and walks carefully around all my stuff. I think he might hug me, then I worry he is going to shake my hand, which seems like the worst thing for some reason, like we're closing a business deal on our shared history. But he surprises me by leaning his forehead in to touch mine for the briefest instant, so brief I could've almost missed it, except I don't. The contact sends electricity through my whole body.

"Please give Luna my best. And please know I'll be thinking

about her."

"I will and thanks," I say, as if these words are adequate when they clearly aren't.

He bows slightly and then turns and walks toward the door.

"Jasper?"

He turns.

"Did you pay for my birthday dinner?" I had considered writing to him to ask, but I worried he would interpret that as an excuse to talk, maybe a hope to reconnect. So I didn't. I haven't.

He stands there quietly for a few seconds, but I already know the answer. My instinct was right.

"I did. I hope it was a great night." His voice is soft, almost wistful.

He turns again before I have a chance to say anything and moves toward the door.

"Thank you," I call out. "It really was..." I let my voice trail off.

By the time I said thank you, he was already pushing the door open, and there was a swoosh of loud air, so I don't think he heard me. And really, what was it anyway? Great? Lonely? A reminder of everything I'd lost? I sit back on my stool and take deep breaths, touching the place on my forehead where his met mine for that fraction of a second. The bartender is there with another glass of wine.

"On the house," she says, picking up Jasper's glass and taking it with her.

She must see different versions of this all day long—the walking wounded trying to navigate the wreckage of their hearts in public spaces.

"Thanks," I say, draining my first glass and then picking up my second. It feels nicely heavy and cool in my hand. *Okay, we'll never have to run into each other after our breakup for the first time again. At least that's done.* I drain my second glass, pay, and leave a big tip, and then I lug all my stuff home like a sherpa ascending Everest.

I lose myself in filling boxes for Billie, my Aunt Pearl, and my mother, which will give hints about the trips I'm planning for them. My idea for Billie is the most well-formed, and I put amazing things in it—olives, the lacy beach cover-up, and a small toy donkey, along with a note saying, *I am taking you away!* with the dates followed by a question mark. Then, *All you have to do is say yes!* I add blue and white tissue paper to the box, colors of Mediterranean seas and whitewashed buildings. There will be another piece to it, but I plan to send that later after the box arrives.

I decide to hold on to the other two boxes and add to them, since those trips will come later. I spend some time writing a note to Aunt Pearl. I know her. She has to see it in writing, or she won't believe it. She probably won't believe it anyway. She'll think it's an elaborate scam or a practical joke. I put the box and the letter in a bag with long handles that I put over my shoulder, and I head out again. I feel about as busy as I was at the height of my working days, and for that, I am glad. I am about to call my mother when a text comes through. It's from Jasper.

Good to see you today, Em. I'm so sorry to hear about Luna. I'm here if you need anything or even if you just want to talk.

I read it three times. Then I text back, *Thanks, Jasper, that means a lot* and I add a smiley face emoji. I think for one second about all the things our texts are missing—the I love yous and heart emojis, emojis with heart eyes, and Xs and Os. And then I think something else—how there is much more here than I ever would have expected. Could we actually be becoming friends? Or is this just what happens when the sharp edges of heartbreak finally begin to smooth?

I smile as I pull up my mother's contact and call her.

"Darling," she says, her voice carrying its usual combination of warmth and distance.

"Hi, Mom, I don't have much time, but I want to tell you something."

"Oh no, what is it?" Her voice immediately shifts to alarm mode.

"No, nothing like that," I say, for the first time in so long—maybe ever—feeling sorry for her that her mind immediately goes to something bad. "I didn't mean to startle you. I'm taking you on a surprise trip. I'll give you the dates as soon as I have them, but it will be this summer. I really want to, so please don't push back or say no. I have the money to do it, so you don't have to worry about that. It will be nice for us to have time, just the two of us."

I realize I am talking and talking because I don't want to hear her answer, which, I am sure, will be negative in some way. But I force myself to stop. There are only so many ways I can say it and so many reasons I can give. There is a long pause.

"Mom?"

"Emerson, that's lovely. That's the best news I've gotten all year."

All year? I tell myself that's just an expression. She doesn't really mean it. There must be some other good news she's gotten in the last twelve months. A role, a callback, a compliment—something.

"Okay, good," I reply. "It's settled then."

"Where will we go?" my mother asks, sounding totally

unlike herself. She is always so hard-edged, so sure of herself. If I had to put a label on it, I'd say she sounds like a little kid on Christmas morning.

"It's a surprise."

"Well, that's lovely," she says again.

"'Bye, Mom. Have a good day."

"I will now," she says, and I wonder how much of a façade she puts on most days to make all of us think she is doing just what she wants to do. I mean, I know her career hasn't ended up the way she hoped. But she always acts like she is the best one in the room, like we are all so lucky to be in her presence.

"I'll be in touch," I say.

"Emerson?"

"Yes?"

"Just don't schedule it when I have an audition, okay?" she says, and there's the mother I know.

"I would never do that, Mom." I'm glad she can't see my face as I say it. What's that quote? If you are going to do something nice for someone, be all in? I'm trying. I'm really trying.

I walk into the shipping store a few blocks away. I send the box by courier to Billie's apartment and have them fax the letter to Aunt Pearl. She never checks her email, and a text with a photo of a document will likely confuse her—technology and Aunt Pearl have an antagonistic relationship at best.

"Thanks," I say when I'm handed the receipt for both.

I walk out with the sinking feeling that now I'm done. I think I've become addicted to having tasks to do. I decide to go home and work on Billie's packing list. I want it to be a big surprise, with some hints so she can get excited.

I am just finishing when Aunt Pearl calls.

"I got a strange fax today. I think it's a scam." Her voice has the wary tone of someone who watches too many consumer alert segments on the local news.

"About a trip?" I ask.

"Well," she says, clearly confused. "Yes."

"It is not a scam," I assure her. "I'm taking you on your dream vacation."

"What? Why?" Her suspicion is almost endearing.

"Well, because you're the best aunt in the world."

"Then shouldn't I be taking you?"

I laugh. "Not this time, Aunt Pearl. This is my gift to you."

Another call comes through. I glance at the screen and see it's Luna.

"Oh, Aunt Pearl, I have to go. I'll call you tomorrow. I love you."

"I love you, too. And for the record, you are the best niece."

I smile as I switch over to Luna.

"Lu, hi! Are you okay?" I say in a rush.

"Just because I have cancer doesn't mean there always has to be something wrong," she says, deadpan.

"Ha ha."

"I wanted to tell you that Jasper sent over dinner. My favorite burger and those fries we love, the place we used to go, remember? Did you tell him? Have you talked to him?"

"Actually, I just ran into him today. For the first time since, well, you know." Since he shattered my heart like fine China dropped from a great height.

"I'm going to thank him now, so I should go before I lose all my energy, but I just wanted to talk to you first."

I nod, then realize she can't see me.

"Thanks for that," I say.

"How was it?" she asks. "Seeing him?"

Unbelievably, another call comes through. It's Billie. I don't want to waste a second of talking to Luna, so I let it go. I'll call her right back.

"It was, I don't know, sad and good. I was reminded of how kind he is."

"Yeah, he was always so fucking kind." There's an edge to her voice, like she's not sure if that's a compliment or a criticism.

"I was thinking, I don't know, that maybe we could be friends," I say.

There's a pause.

"Yeah, maybe." Luna sounds tired, the kind of tired that sleep doesn't fix. "Well, good night. I'll talk to you tomorrow."

"Okay, I'll come see you."

She doesn't say yes or no. She just ends the call. I sit for a second, and then I call Billie back.

"YOU ARE THE BEST FRIEND IN THE WORLD!" she screams into the phone with enough volume to wake the dead. "IS THIS FOR REAL?"

"It is for real! And I'm thrilled you are on board."

"Are you kidding me? Can we leave tonight?"

"Speaking of which, how are the boys?"

"Better. Finally."

"Oh, I'm so glad. I hope you can rest a little now."

"I am going to dream about our trip. Where exactly are we going? I know there were a few hints in the box, but please tell me! I have to know!" She sounds like she might explode from excitement.

"Do the dates I proposed work?"

"Yes, yes!" she exclaims. "But you are not answering my question."

"You'll know soon enough," I tease. "But wait, there. I'm

going to hang up and text you something important. It might give you a few more hints."

"I can't wait!"

I hang up and find the paper I was working on. I take a photo and text it to Billie. Then I turn off my phone. If she asks me again, I will tell her.

BILLIE'S PACKING LIST:
- Flip Flops
- Bikini
- Passport
- Power adaptor for Europe
- Quick dry towel
- Dramamine
- Shawl
- Sundresses
- Sandals
- Beach books
- I'll leave the rest up to you…

When I wake up the next morning and turn on my phone, there is a message from Billie. *You had me at flip flops.* I smile, make coffee, and get to work booking the trip. For the first time in a long time, I feel like I'm exactly where I'm supposed to be.

Chapter Fourteen

"Did you feel that?" I ask Billie, my fingers itching for something—anything—to grip onto as the world beneath us shifts like a moody teenager.

"Feel what?" she asks back, her attention fixed across the pool toward the bar, completely oblivious to how the deck just performed its best impression of a carnival ride.

"That, I don't know what to call it, that movement," I say, just as it happens again. The ship rocks beneath us like it's trying to shake us off, as if we're unwelcome fleas on its massive back.

Billie is looking across the pool toward the bar, her lips curved into a smile directed at an extremely attractive man, who returns it with interest. She offers him a small flirty wave, the kind that if you blinked, you'd miss it. Except I don't. It still catches me off guard when I remember Billie is proudly in an open marriage—that she could actually be with that attractive man at the bar if she wanted, and it wouldn't be a bad thing. It wouldn't be cheating on her husband. It would just be Billie, living her life on her own terms.

Once again, the deck sways, but this time it feels like we went over a huge wave, the kind that should come with a warning label and a height requirement. Maybe I should have done more research about the ship before choosing it. Did I mention this is my first cruise? Without thinking, I grab Billie's arm to steady myself like she's my personal life preserver. That gets her attention.

"Oh, sweetie, you just need to get your sea legs," she says, reaching out to make sure I have my balance before leaning in for a hug that smells like coconut sunscreen and confidence. "Be right back."

She walks toward the man, nestling into the small space between him and the handsome couple next to him with the ease of someone who's never questioned whether she belongs somewhere. I smile, because this is what I want—for Billie to have the best week ever, the kind of week that becomes a story she tells at dinner parties for years to come.

We flew into Athens two days ago. Every single detail was perfect—our flight in business class, where we reclined like queens, and the last two nights at the extremely luxurious Hotel Grande Bretagne, where we mostly rested and ate grilled fish and caught up on our sleep like it was a competitive sport. We left the hotel once, to take an amazing and memorable excursion to the Acropolis, where Billie insisted on doing dramatic poses next to every column. This morning, we boarded the ship for a seven-day cruise—the centerpiece of Billie's dream vacation.

I could have chosen a quiet and elegant option, the kind where people whisper and wear linen, but instead went with the loud, family-friendly choice. It is much more Billie's speed, and the way I see it, there's nothing better than being around a bunch of rowdy kids when you don't have to tend to them. Plus, Billie hates places where you have to watch yourself and lower your voice. She wants to be free and loud and, well, just basically herself. And that's what I want, too.

Also, the itinerary is great, including many of the Greek

islands that Billie has mentioned were on her bucket list. I splurged for the highest tier of accommodations, one of the suites, so we have a huge cabin on the ninth deck with two small bedrooms, a big living room, an amazing balcony that makes you feel like you're floating over the ocean, and our own personal butler. The first thing Billie did when we walked in and he was there to welcome us was hand him a fistful of hundred-dollar bills and tell him he had the week off, like we were in some kind of comedy about rich people who don't understand how the world works.

"It does not work that way, ma'am," he said politely. He couldn't have been older than twenty, maybe twenty-two, with the earnest face of someone who still believes in following all the rules.

"Can't it, though?" Billie had said, as if the rules of employment were merely suggestions that could be negotiated with enough cash.

"I don't have anywhere to go," he said seriously. "Plus, I must work."

"Then come in and sit down," Billie had said. I laughed. The butler, who we would learn is named Theo and was from a place called Skiathos, just shook his head and looked nervous, like we might be the strangest assignment he'd ever been given.

Now I ease over to a column in case I have to grab something should the ship move again, and I glance at Billie. We planned on exploring the ship for a little while, but she is in a deep conversation with the mystery man, leaning in slightly, her laugh carrying across the deck. We have a welcome dinner at 5:30, which seems early, but my sense of time is so messed up anyway, it doesn't matter. I think about going over to say I'll see her later, but I don't want to mess with her groove. I wave, but she doesn't see it, so I walk back to our cabin slowly, almost losing my balance every few steps like I'm playing a solo game of Twister.

Theo is there, standing at the door like a sentinel guarding a treasure.

"Do you need anything, ma'am?" he asks. "A hand, maybe?"

"Oh, thank you, but no."

Butler service always sounded intriguing to me, but now I can see I am just going to worry about him the whole time, like having an audience for my every move.

"Do you just wait here for us all week?" I ask, but I ask it nicely, like I'm genuinely curious rather than horrified. "I've never had this sort of service before."

"Yes, ma'am," he says politely. "Anything you need."

"What if I don't need anything today?"

"But you might," he says just as the deck rocks forward and then back like we're on the world's most expensive see-saw. I frantically try to grab the wall, but I'm too far, and Theo reaches out and grabs my wrist gently, saving me from an embarrassing fall. "That's nothing, ma'am," he says. "Just a little wave."

"Thank you," I say, beginning to feel the slightest bit nauseated, like my insides are trying to rearrange themselves.

I head inside and look through my bag. I had put Dramamine on Billie's packing list, but I'd forgotten to get it myself—just one more example of how I'm better at taking care of others than myself. I go into Billie's room, but it isn't in plain sight, and neither is her cosmetic bag. I don't feel right going through her things without asking, even though I know she wouldn't mind, so I go back out to find Theo. He is standing there politely. I wish I could get him a chair or at least a magazine.

"Any chance you have some motion sickness medicine on you?" I ask.

"No, ma'am, but the ship store has some. I'll be right back."

For a second, I think about saying I'll go, but the deck shifts again, and the nausea gets worse, like a wave of its own gathering force.

"Thank you. And please call me Emerson."

He nods and practically jogs down the hall. Even though I want to tell him he doesn't have to do that, I'm grateful. There is little I hate more than feeling nauseated. I go inside and sit on the couch, willing the feeling away through sheer force of will. I am still totally jet-lagged, and I haven't eaten much today. I look through the basket on the small but well-stocked bar and find some crackers. I tear them open and eat a few. It helps a little. And then Theo is back with a box that has only Greek writing on it. It could literally be anything from motion sickness pills to breath mints to a pregnancy test.

"Are you sure this is for motion sickness?" I ask.

"Yes, ma'am, I mean Emerson," he says, his correction endearing him to me even more.

"Thank you."

He goes back out into the hall, pulling the door closed behind him. For the first time since I met him, I am so glad he's here. I want to take the medicine and feel better. I can't read the directions, so I ease two pills out of the package, thinking two is the normal amount to take in most cases. I pull a blue glass bottle of expensive water out of the small fridge and take them. I go into my room and lie down, thinking I'll let them sink in, and then I'll head out again in a few minutes to see what Billie is up to.

"Em, Emerson." I hear my name being called, and the damn

ship is swaying again. Or maybe it never stopped, I'm not sure which. I just want to escape back into the nothingness of sleep, but Billie is being relentless, like a human alarm clock you can't snooze.

"Em," she says. I open my eyes and sit up. It is totally dark outside and in my room. There's a light on in the living room. The ship isn't swaying. Billie must have been shaking me.

"Oh, thank goodness," she says. "I was starting to wonder if I needed to get help."

"What time is it?" I ask. "Should we go to dinner?"

"Oh, sweetie, that ship has sailed," she says with a grin at her own pun. "I did bring something back for you, though. Are you hungry?"

"Ugh, I'm a terrible friend," I say, standing up. I feel woozy but okay, like I'm walking through a dream. "I took something. I think it was motion sickness medicine, and I must have taken too much. Whatever it was, it knocked me out. I want every minute of this trip to be perfect. I'm so sorry you had to go to dinner alone."

"Oh, I didn't go alone," she says. For the first time, I notice she is wearing a fairly formal dress, her long hair is up in an elegant bun, and she is fully made up like she's auditioning for a role in a movie about beautiful people on vacation. "I went with Mark."

"Is Mark…?"

"Yes, he's the guy from the pool bar," she says, smiling big, her eyes sparkling with mischief.

"Oh, I'm glad." I sit on the edge of the bed. "Did you?"

"We did! And he was delicious," she says with a wink. "I'm so glad I met him, but I've moved on."

"You have? Already?"

"I'm not going to spend this fabulous week with one man." She tosses her hair like the main character in a romantic comedy. "Hey, do you want to go do karaoke in the lounge? We have a day at sea tomorrow, so we can stay up late and sleep as long as we want in the morning."

"Sure, let me just get myself together," I say. I don't want to go; I just want to get back into bed, but I also don't want to let Billie down. I decide to skip the food she brought for now, and I brush my teeth and hair. I consider changing, but decide not to bother, and I follow her out the door.

"Hey, where's Theo?" I ask.

"Oh," she says. She had gotten a few steps ahead of me, and now she comes back and lowers her voice like she's about to share a state secret. "I told him we really wanted him to relax a little. He pushed back, as he had earlier, but I finally convinced him. We exchanged cell numbers, and I just said if anyone questions him, it was one hundred percent our decision and that they should call us."

"Oh, okay, great. Can I have his cell? Just in case?"

Strange how dependent you can get on something you never had before.

She shares his contact. "Theo, the nicest butler on the ship."

I smile, save the contact, and follow Billie to the lounge on the fifth floor. I expected something small and intimate, maybe five or ten people singing, but it is less a lounge and more a huge ballroom. There could be two hundred people in here. When we walk in, a man is singing 'Islands in the Stream' with his whole heart, like he's been waiting his entire life for this moment. Everyone is listening and cheering. Billie claps with glee—she is so joyful, and I take a step back and just look at her. I want to savor the moment. This is exactly what I hoped for. That is until

Billie grabs my arm and says, "We need to get on that list."

"Oh, Billie, you know I don't sing," I plead, panic rising in my throat like bile.

"You do now! Plus, you are never going to see these people again. And, let me add, you do sing. I've seen you do 'A Whole New World' with Ryder many times. What, do you like him better than me?"

"I do not. I love you both equally."

"Okay then." She drags me toward the stage like I'm a reluctant child and she's a determined parent.

"And every single time I did that, we were at a bar with three other people."

There's a sign-up sheet on a table, and Billie leans in and scribbles our names. From what I can tell, we are fifth on the list. We settle in, get a drink, and a couple sings 'Shallow', their voices blending together like they've rehearsed for weeks. And then, just my luck, the next three people on the list don't respond when their names are called. *Please,* I think to myself. *I'm not ready.*

"Emerson and Bill?" a woman in a ball gown calls. She looks a little like Cinderella after the fairy godmother but before midnight.

"Billie," Billie corrects her nicely and grabs my arm.

I don't move. I am a statue, a mountain, an immovable object.

"Come on, please," she begs.

"I can't do it, Billie. Too many people. Please, I'll watch you."

She hesitates for a second, and I think she is going to push me or, at the very least, say something that makes me feel guilty, but she just smiles and kisses me on the cheek.

"No problem," she says. "I didn't really think you would."

She takes the stage confidently. She bows, and everyone cheers. I have no idea what she's going to sing. The music begins, and it's 'Rainbow Connection'. The cheers get even louder. She begins to sing, and she sounds just like… Kermit the Frog. Everyone laughs and claps. I scream, "Go, Billie!" She manages to pull it off and gets a standing ovation. She milks it, bowing and bowing until she finally waves and gets off the stage like a conquering hero.

"I don't want to follow her," I hear someone say. "She was way too good."

"That was so great," I tell her. "Everyone loved it."

"There's nothing like getting out of your own life and just doing what you want—though I will say my boys would have liked that," she adds. "Thank you for this. Thank you so much. I wish there were a word stronger than thank you."

The days begin to flow. One day at sea, the next somewhere great—Mykonos and Crete and Thessaloniki and finally Santorini, which was really the inspiration for the trip.

We are giddy as we get off the ship. There are so many stairs leading up and up and up to the top of the island, like a stairway to heaven made of stone. The ocean is all around us, blue as far as the eye can see. We wait in line for a donkey. I can smell them and cover my nose with my hand, but Billie doesn't seem to be bothered. If anything, she seems to love it. A man motions for her to come over and get on as he holds the donkey steady. Before she does, though, she leans in and pats the donkey's head. He closes his eyes as if he is in heaven. The man laughs. Billie whispers something in the donkey's ear, and then she is on the donkey's back, moving up toward the top of the island.

My donkey seems grumpier, like it woke up on the wrong side of the stable. I pat its head, and it snarls a little. The man just shrugs. I assume they wouldn't let a tourist ride a bad donkey, so I get on, and we follow Billie. My donkey sighs deeply with every step, and I wonder if he hates me. I hold on so tightly and just wait to get to the top. Billie, meanwhile, is waving her hands around and singing; she might possibly look the happiest I have ever seen her. I ease my phone out of my pocket and snap a picture, capturing her joy forever.

That night, our second to last on the ship, Billie asks if she can take me out to dinner.

"I mean, I guess you can. But it's all included, so…"

"Just say yes," she says, her tone making it clear this isn't a request.

We take our time getting ready. When it's time to leave, I head toward the elevator as we always do, but Billie stops me.

"Out here," she says.

I furrow my brows, but I follow her out the door onto the quiet deck. There is Theo, standing formally next to a table set up with a white tablecloth and candles. There is a bottle of red wine. The scene looks like it belongs in a movie about people much more glamorous than us.

"If I didn't know better, I would think you were trying to seduce me," I tell her.

"You are so much more important to me than any man I would seduce," Billie says seriously. "You are. I don't think these words are enough, but you are the best friend a girl could ever ask for, and not just because you gave me the trip of a lifetime. Of course, that is part of it. I will never, ever forget any of this. Please, sit. You told me the other day you missed pizza—well, my dear, Theo can work magic."

We sit down, and Theo bows and smiles. He seems so happy to have something to do. He places a basket full of bread on the table and then two plates with silver domes. He lifts the domes, and there are delicious-looking margherita pizzas, the edges blistered and bubbly. I take a deep breath and savor the familiar smell.

"Wow," I say. "This is, I mean, this week is about your dreams, not mine."

"Well, right now, my wish is to make your wish come true," Billie says, choosing a piece of pizza and taking a bite. "I put together all of your greatest hits."

I laugh. I don't want to spend the evening arguing about whose dreams are more important. As I have that thought, I also think this has been the trip of a lifetime for me, too.

We eat in comfortable silence, with Theo standing by. Eventually, he brings a beautiful salad with tomatoes, feta, and olives, and then finally a small chocolate cake with pink roses made of frosting that says 'Thank You, Emerson!' Theo carries it carefully to the table with a lit pink candle. "Make a wish," Theo says in his thick Greek accent.

I close my eyes and think, *I hope the other three trips are as good as this one. I hope I can make Aunt Pearl and my mother, and especially Luna, as happy as I've made Billie.* I open my eyes and blow out the candle.

"What did you wish for?" Billie asks.

"You know I can't tell you. That's like Wishing 101."

She leans in for a hug.

"By the way," I add. "I've been meaning to ask, what did you whisper in the donkey's ear?"

"You know I can't tell you," she says, and we both laugh.

After the cake and insisting that Theo join us for a slice, we offer to help clean up.

"No, no, I've got this," he says, waving us away. "This has

been my easiest week yet."

We are both very glad to hear that.

The next morning, Billie comes into my room and sits on my bed. I am just waking up, but I try to look alert, like I've been up for hours contemplating the meaning of life.

"Last sea day," she says.

"What should we do?"

"Karaoke?" she asks, her eyes lighting up.

"Sure," I agree, knowing there's no use fighting the inevitable.

Thirty minutes later, we are back in the lounge. It's crowded, but not like the other night. Apparently, karaoke is a twenty-four-hour activity on this ship. There is only one person on the list ahead of us. Billie looks at me with her eyebrows raised.

I nod.

"Yay!" she says, clapping her hands like a kid who just got told we're going to Disney World.

"What should we sing?" I ask. "I am open to anything."

"Anything?"

I nod again.

She doesn't tell me what she picks. The person ahead of us is singing 'Tomorrow' from *Annie*. Not the best choice, but that just gives me the confidence I need. When Billie steps onto the stage, I follow her. My heart is beating really fast, and I can't stop swallowing. Funny how I could speak to a full conference room or even a packed auditorium, about business or fashion, but this, this is hard for me.

When I hear the first few notes of 'A Whole New World', I smile at Billie, and then we are doing it, singing loud, not missing a word. I think of Ryder and our day. I think of my mother, how happy she was about the trip, and about Aunt

Pearl, how she thought it was a scam at first. I think of Luna. We finish the song, and, to my absolute shock, we get a standing ovation, albeit a small one. I hug Billie. She hugs back even harder.

"That was the best," she says as we walk off the stage and over to the bar. "Is it too early for a martini?"

"Definitely not." We take a seat and order. "So after Mark, you never found another guy you wanted to spend time with?"

"Nah. The night with Mark was great. It satisfied my curiosity and reminded me I am free to do that if I want to, but it was enough. I wanted to spend the rest of the time with you."

"Well, I'm honored," I say, feeling a warmth that has nothing to do with the alcohol.

"That karaoke was the bomb," Billie says. "Look at you coming out of your shell."

"Well, yeah, but it took all week."

"You never give yourself enough credit." Billie takes a sip of her martini. "You've worked so hard. You've just come out of a very long relationship. Why aren't you allowing yourself to feel more joy?"

"I don't know." I stare into my drink like it might contain the answer.

"This beating yourself up has to stop. You deserve so much happiness and delight and merriment and pleasure. I would love to see you stop looking backward and really look forward now. Do you know what I mean? Let this right now—this moment, this week together—be the start of your new chapter. Are you in?"

Maybe it's the martini so early in the day. Maybe it's the singing. Maybe it's the swaying of the ship, which I now barely notice. Maybe it's the wish I made on the pink candle last night.

Whatever it is, I want to shout yes. I would love that, to let this be the start of my new chapter; I am so tired of my old one.

"I'm in," I say to Billie. "I am so in."

***

Two days later, after saying goodbye to Theo, disembarking the ship with tears streaming down our faces, and then spending one last night in Athens, we fly back to JFK in our lovely business class seats.

"Best week of my life," Billie says as we get close and the captain announces our descent into New York.

"Me too," I agree. "Thank you."

"Thank me?" Billie says. "I think you have that twisted up. Thank you."

We both look out the window as the lights of the city come into view.

"I miss my little monsters," Billie says, almost to herself. "Great to go away, great to come home."

"I'm so happy for you, Billie," I say quietly. She grabs my hand and squeezes it.

Once we land and we're allowed to take our phones out of airplane mode, Billie calls home.

"We're here," she says to whoever answers. "I can't wait to hug you!"

I text Luna. *Hey Lu, just landed. Good trip, but I missed you. I hope your week wasn't too tough. Coming by tomorrow. I have some souvenirs for you. Miss you! Love you!* I send it, but I don't expect to hear anything. I know she's been less connected to her phone of late. But a minute later, a text comes through. It is a heart emoji from Luna. I send one back to her. Suddenly, I am so happy to be home.

Chapter Fifteen

I wake up the next morning thinking I'm still on the ship. The phantom swaying makes me feel like I'm floating in a bathtub that someone just climbed out of. I grab my phone to Google whether that's normal or if my inner ear has officially gone rogue. That's when I see seven unread texts, and my heart performs an Olympic-level gymnastics routine in my chest.

Tough night, today might not be the best for a visit.

From Luna at 5:30 a.m. Who texts at 5:30 a.m. unless they're either a) still awake from the night before or b) experiencing an emergency? Before I can spiral further, I read the next one:

Sorry, all good, ignore that.

Then,

Nope, but a visit might be nice after all, heading to the hospital.

That one was at 6:15. She sent another at 7:05.

Em, I'm scared.

I stand up so fast the room tilts, my eyes darting around frantically like the answers to the universe might be hiding in the dust bunnies under my dresser. What happened? Why the hospital, and if I want to get to her—which I do with the desperate intensity of someone who's just realized they left their passport in a taxi—which hospital?

Lu, I text with shaking fingers. *Where are you?*

Then I read the rest.

Fuck it, I'm not going to resist anymore, I am so tired of fighting, I am the river.

Resist what? What does 'the river' mean? Is this some metaphysical breakthrough or painkiller-induced poetry?

Call my mother. I might not be able to check my phone.

And finally,

Love you, Em.

Those three words hit me like a meteorite. Luna doesn't say 'love you' casually. She says it like she's bestowing a rare gift, something precious and finite.

I scroll through my contacts for Hannah's number and call her, trying to ignore the scenarios playing out in my head like the world's worst choose-your-own-adventure novel. What if she doesn't answer? What if I can't find Luna today? What if…

"Emerson." Hannah's voice comes through heavy with the sound of someone who hasn't slept. "She is asking for you. We're at Sloan Kettering. Third floor. I told them you're her sister. Immediate family only right now."

"What—" I begin to ask, but she cuts me off.

"Just come, quickly," Hannah says, and the line goes dead.

Somehow, I dress myself and head to the hospital on York Avenue. I have no memory of brushing my hair or hailing the cab, but suddenly I'm pushing through the revolving door, trying desperately not to look at the words Cancer Center looming above me like they're written in the sky.

It's impossible not to wonder what everyone around me is going through. In some cases, it's hard to tell who the patient in a group is, like trying to identify the birthday person at a restaurant. But other times it's brutally clear, written in the hollow shadows beneath eyes and the way bodies lean like saplings in a storm.

On the third floor, I tell the nurse at the desk that I'm Luna's sister. She looks at me with a kindness so genuine I feel myself cracking like old paint.

"Honey," she says. "Why don't you have a seat over there? I'll be back in a moment."

She points to a row of chairs that look like they were designed by people who hate the human spine. I'm about to choose the least offensive one when Hannah appears behind me. If I thought she looked harried and stressed when I saw her at Luna's apartment a few weeks ago, that version of Hannah was on a spa retreat compared to this one.

"You're here," she says, relief washing over her face like sunrise.

"Of course," I say, confused. In what universe would I not come?

"She's… I know she wasn't thinking clearly when she texted you this morning."

"What happened?" The question comes out small, a child's voice.

"I thought for a minute, for a few minutes really, that we were nearing the end." The anguish in her voice makes me think of glass breaking. "Maybe that we were even at the end."

The end? No. Luna had said four months, and we still have some of those four months left, I think to myself with the desperate logic of someone trying to argue with gravity. I want to tell Hannah she's wrong, that she's miscalculated, but I remember that chart I saw about grieving and how you should never push back or claim to grieve more than the people closest to the sick or dying person. I could argue that I'm on equal footing in the who-has-more-to-lose department, but I know in my heart that isn't true, so I don't dispute her. I wait for her to be able to talk again, which feels like waiting for the continental drift.

"But they got her back," Hannah says, looking past me at something I can't see. "She's a little better."

The relief I feel is like nothing I've ever experienced before—like suddenly remembering how to breathe after being underwater too long. "Can I see her?" I ask.

"Of course. If you don't mind, I might go get a cup of coffee once you're in there with her. And maybe some crackers. I haven't eaten anything in a while and now, finally, I feel like maybe I could."

I curse myself for not thinking to ask if she needed anything, but, again, I am losing track of what I am supposed to be doing, what is right in this situation, which keeps changing like a game where someone rewrites the rules every five minutes. I simply follow her in a daze to a closed door marked 323. For some reason, I know I will never forget that number, like it's been tattooed on the inside of my eyelids.

As I walk behind her, I feel the boat swaying again, up then down, up then down. Maybe it isn't the boat at all, but the Earth moving off its axis. How close did we come to losing Luna? Even as I think the words, they feel impossible—losing Luna—like maybe we left her in a taxi or forgot about her at a rest stop. I imagine dialing her number, letting it ring and ring, but she is nowhere to be found. She isn't anywhere.

Hannah pushes open the door, and there she is, lying against a mountain of white pillows like a queen holding court, sitting up a bit, not looking half as bad as I expected. Her color is okay, and her eyes are open. She smiles when she sees me, and it's the smile that undoes me—that quintessential Luna smile that says, *Yes, everything is terrible, but also, isn't it kind of hilarious?*

"Luna." I rush toward her. I stop myself before I crush her with a hug, suddenly aware that she might be more fragile than she appears, like expensive crystal disguised as everyday glass. I choose the chair next to her bed.

"I'm fucking dying," she says, but she sounds much stronger than I expected. Everyone must be wrong around here. Everyone must be crazy. Maybe she needs a second opinion. Maybe all the doctors are secretly veterinarians.

"Are you sure?" I ask dumbly, and she laughs. I listen to the twinkly notes like they're a song I'm trying to memorize.

"Pretty sure," she tells me. "My blood count dropped to dangerous levels." When she says the words 'dangerous levels', she raises her hands to indicate air quotes, like she's mocking a B-movie villain.

"Your mother said they…" I stop. I don't want to say the words *got you back*. "…helped you." It's the best I can come up with, which feels like describing the Grand Canyon as 'a big hole'.

"Yep." Luna points to her IV. "You should have seen me two hours ago. I sounded like a windbag. I could not catch my breath. There was no air, anywhere, that I could find. Steroids do wonders."

"Thank God," I say, with the fervor of someone who just found their lost child in a department store.

"Don't get too excited," Luna cautions me. "There is only so much boosting one can do to a body on its last legs."

"Luna," I say quietly, putting my hand on hers. Her skin feels paper-thin, like I could accidentally tear it just by thinking too aggressively.

"The good news is that they are letting me go home. The bad news is that there is talk of moving me to comfort care, referred to around here stupidly as the 'angel kiss'. I don't know about you, but I don't want to be kissed by an angel. That hot resident who keeps doing rounds? That's a different story."

She stops talking, and I can only imagine she's thinking that not only will she never kiss that hot resident, she'll likely never kiss another man again. I look away, studying a spot on the wall like it contains the secret to time travel. She takes a deep breath and keeps talking.

"I guess the dirty little word nobody wants to say to me is 'hospice'. But I will not be hoodwinked. I know what's going on."

"Luna," I say again. What I don't say is everything else — that she can't die, that she has so much more to do, that I can't imagine my life without her, that she has to hang on at least until I can take her on a trip. Maybe we can find a cure there, among the vortexes and arid desert air, like searching for buried treasure with a map drawn in crayon.

"Here's the thing that sucks the most," Luna continues. I lean in. "I can't go on that fucking woo-woo healing trip in the middle of nowhere with you." Her tone is sarcastic, but her glistening eyes tell a different story — the one neither of us wants to read aloud.

I feel like she heard my thoughts. I squeeze her hand and feel the emotion swell between us, a tide with nowhere to go. Obviously, the trip pales compared to everything else she is facing, but it feels just as significant. It feels like somehow, by not going, the timeline of the inevitable has raced forward. It's in our face. A future where there will be no adventures and further planning. It makes this all feel so final. I get up and nestle onto the bed beside her, careful as a cat finding its spot.

"It's okay," I say, trying to hold it together like a paper bag in the rain. "It's not about the trip."

"I was hoping you would say that," Luna says with a mischievous smile that makes me think she just palmed the Ace of Spades.

"What do you mean?" I sit up, alarmed, and nearly fall out of bed, wondering what will come out of her mouth next. With Luna, it could be literally anything from 'I've decided to become a monk' to 'Let's steal a penguin from the zoo'.

"Let me ask you…" She sits up a little straighter. "If it isn't about the trip, what is it about?"

"It's about doing something for you. Absolutely anything."

"All righty then," Luna says, still smiling like she just pulled off the world's greatest con.

"What? Do you have a wish for me to grant?" I'm smiling back at her, half excited, half terrified, like someone about to ride a roller coaster they're not entirely sure is up to code.

"I do," she says.

"Okay, tell me, I'm ready."

"You can throw my fucking funeral!" Luna exclaims with a surprising abundance of energy, like she just announced we're going to Disneyland. She pauses momentarily, but before I have a chance to say anything, she adds, "While I'm still here to enjoy it." She's studying my face intently for my reaction, eyes alight with the kind of mischief that has defined our friendship.

If anyone else said that, I would scoff or refuse or assume they were making a very bad joke. But this is Luna we're talking about. I sit up straighter.

"Can we rebrand the title of the event from Luna's Fucking Funeral to something a little, I don't know… less morbid?"

"Abso-fucking-lutely not. I'm dying, it's my choice," Luna announces, ending with her best Disney villain laugh, the kind that would make woodland creatures scatter in terror.

I nod slowly, then a little faster, like my brain is booting up. The shock has passed now, and my mind is racing like it's being chased. We'll gather all her friends. I'll even ask her college roommate to fly in from San Francisco. We'll cater it. I'll get all her favorite foods. Maybe it could be themed. Hawaiian? No, too cheerful. Gothic Victorian? Too on the nose.

"Earth to Emerson," Luna says, and I realize she has been talking and I have not been listening, too busy mentally arranging funeral flowers while the not-yet-deceased is speaking.

"Sorry, I was planning in my head."

"Of course you were," she says with that famous Luna eye roll that should be immortalized in an art gallery. "Here's the thing. There isn't much time to plan. It has to be tonight."

"What? No, I need a few days at least, preferably a week," I say, now jumping off the bed to make my objection more impactful, as if physical altitude will strengthen my argument. "I need to arrange the invitations, the venue, the food—getting everyone's dietary restrictions will take at least a week. Plus, there are people that live outside of the city, outside of the state, that I want to get here."

Luna grabs my hand, anchoring me before I can float off into a spiral of party planning anxiety.

"Em, none of that matters." Her energy drops all the way down to calmness, like a feather finally touching ground. "Truth bomb… I am never again going to feel as good as I do today. The doctor said the steroids would give me a kick, which I already feel, but the effect will diminish over time. Their effectiveness will continue to be less and less, you know, effective. This is it, baby. It's you against the clock. My funeral will be tonight."

Chapter Sixteen

Eight hours later, I take one last look around Billie's rooftop before heading down to meet Luna and her mom. Hannah texted that they're ten minutes away, and I want to greet them in the lobby with a welcome basket—a little sneak peek of what's waiting upstairs. I want Luna to be able to absorb every moment, every inch of love, and every word we share. I'm not sure if this will be our last chance to pour into her deeply, but it feels like it could be.

As soon as Luna was released from the hospital, I called Ryder, who dropped everything to come meet me. While waiting for him, I called Billie.

"Luna's dying—" escaped my mouth before I could stop it.

"I know, sweetie," she said with the gentle tone reserved for those moments when the universe has decided to be especially cruel.

"She's been in the hospital overnight. It was scary and… well, our healing desert trip has been replaced by her funeral… while she's still alive. And it's happening tonight."

"Wait… what…?" The gentle tone morphed into confusion.

"No time to explain, but this is my opportunity to grant her last wish." It was the first time I'd framed it that way—her last wish. Was someone's last wish more powerful than all the other wishes that came before? Like some cosmic rule where the universe finally decides to play fair, just once, when it matters most? I wasn't sure.

"Okay, got it. Event planning assistant incoming. I'll help you," Billie said. "Actually, I can do even better than that. Let's do it here, at my place."

"Are you sure? Won't the boys be, I don't know, freaked out by a funeral?"

"No, I think they can handle it. But I was thinking we could do it on the roof of my building. It's beautiful up there and perfect for a celebration of life. It's got those fairy lights and adorable paper lanterns. There are tables and a pergola. You've been up there, you know."

"I don't think I've been there at night, but it sounds perfect. That would be great."

"It's settled then," Billie said, with the conviction of someone who has just decided to move mountains.

Now I feel my phone buzz and look down. It's a text from Hannah. *Five minutes away.*

"They're five minutes away!" I call out like we're preparing for a surprise birthday entrance. If only. Billie is here with her husband, and Ryder, of course, a few of Luna's former coworkers, and all the friends I could think of who live in New York City. One friend, Ellen, had plans to see Billy Joel at Madison Square Garden, and she didn't even take a full second to say she would rather be here. I managed to get Luna's cousins to come in from Greenwich, and her two uncles rushed in from Westchester.

As promised, the lights are twinkling overhead, and the paper lanterns are glowing like tiny moons caught in a net of stars. Ryder spent the day making posters with all the photos I had of Luna, and Hannah sent all the baby photos she had on her phone, which we printed out. They're carefully taped to the white walls by the elevator. There's Luna riding a pink, sparkly bike—one of the few times I've ever seen her near something pink and sparkly. There's Luna in college with a bunch of friends, a cigarette dangling from her fingers like she was born to hold it. There's Luna hugging me at the party celebrating the start of StyleShop, both of us grinning like we'd just pulled off the greatest heist in history. I can't look too long or too closely at any of them without the reality of this moment sinking in like a stone in water.

We placed flowers everywhere, and Ryder insisted on bringing a small Halloween coffin, near which he's put paper and pens so everyone can write a private note to Luna that she can take with her and read when she's alone. I had pushed back, but Ryder said, "Come on, Luna will love it," and I gave in. I think he might be right. Luna always did have a thing for the macabre.

"Here," Ryder says now, thrusting Luna's welcome basket toward me.

"Thanks," I say, accepting it and making sure it has everything I want Luna to see before she comes up here: cigarettes (because, really, at this point, why not?), beer, flowers, confetti, and Twizzlers, her favorite. I nestle an envelope in the middle of the treats with Luna's name on it. Who knows where I found time today to write down all the ways that Luna has impacted my life, but I squeezed so much in there. I have more to say, of course, but I wanted to get this out since I'm not sure when or if I'll have a chance to share more.

I snap back into the present moment. "I'll be right back," I call, pushing the elevator button, basket in hand, feeling my heart beating—no, pounding—as I get closer to the lobby. I expected to walk out to the street and wait for their Uber, but when the elevator door opens, there are Luna and Hannah. Luna is wearing a black lacy dress that I have never seen and bright red lipstick that makes her look like she's ready to conquer the world, or at least what's left of it.

"Hot," I say, because sometimes the simplest truths are all we have.

Luna curtsies, a gesture so delicate it nearly breaks me. I look at Hannah. She smiles at me. How she is even standing, I have no idea, but I turn back to Luna and hold up the basket.

"Welcome to your funeral, bestie. For you." The words are surreal on my tongue.

She looks surprisingly strong, and once again I think this situation, this cancer prognosis, must all be a mistake—some cosmic clerical error that will be corrected any minute now. Luna smiles as she looks through the basket. She reaches for the envelope and raises her eyebrows to ask if she should read it. I nod. She clears her throat, and I think she's going to read it out loud, but she doesn't. When she's finished, she puts it back in the envelope, which she places back in the basket. She one-arm hugs me tighter than I can ever remember as she repeats into my ear the last line of my note: "Never before and never again will a better friend live and die."

"I'm ready," Luna says with 110 percent enthusiasm, the kind of enthusiasm that breaks hearts and rebuilds them stronger in the same breath. I follow her and Hannah into the elevator.

When we get out on the roof, everyone claps. Luna smiles and does a twirl. It's totally out of character for her, and out of the corner of my eye, I see Hannah's face begin to crumble, but somehow she gets it under control and musters a smile that could fool anyone who doesn't know her as well as I do.

"The guest of honor," Luna's uncle calls.

"Guest of honor. I'll take it," Luna replies with a playful smirk and a glint of mischief in her eyes. "Let's not forget, this is my fucking funeral." She throws her arms up in the air like the lead singer of a rock band about to stage dive into a sea of adoring fans.

There's an initial awkward silence, followed by cheers that feel like the perfect response to a situation none of us know how to navigate.

"You're damn right it's a funeral," Ryder calls, matching Luna's energy and stepping forward, and I am so grateful for his ability to rise to any occasion. "Let me kick this thing off."

I had been so taken with the lights and the lanterns, always looking up, that I hadn't noticed until now that there are folding chairs set up facing a chaise lounge that is flat. Ryder points toward it, indicating that Luna should lie there. It looks way too much like a real funeral for my taste, like we're practicing for something that's coming too soon.

"I don't know," Hannah begins, echoing my unspoken thoughts.

"This is fucking awesome," Luna says at the same time, moving quickly to the chaise lounge, lying down, closing her eyes and folding her hands over her stomach. She raises her head and says, chuckling, "I didn't think you would have the guts," then lies back down, giving us the thumbs-up like she's about to ride a roller coaster rather than play dead at her own funeral.

"Come on," Ryder says. "Everyone, take a seat!"

I can tell some people are uncomfortable, and I try not to look too long at Luna because she looks way too much like an actual corpse at the moment. But she is smiling, and there is nothing right, regular, or acceptable about this scenario anyway. I take a seat in the front row, trying to ignore the feeling that I'm attending a dress rehearsal for something I'll never be ready for.

Ryder walks to a small table he set up as a podium.

"Thank you all for coming," he says very seriously, and I hold my breath, having no idea how he is going to play this. It occurs to me that letting Ryder take the lead here may not have been the best idea, but there's one thing I know for sure: I couldn't have done this. As usual, Luna is right; I would not have had the guts.

"Life isn't fair, but it can certainly be delicious," Ryder begins gently, and somehow I know immediately it is going to be okay, or at least as okay as this sort of thing can be. "Tonight, we are here for our dear friend Luna. For one moment, close your eyes. Think about how we rarely get to hear what people really think of us or the ways in which we have impacted their lives, and let's give Luna that gift tonight. Let's fill this rooftop with all the feels and bring words to the incredible human that is Luna. At any time during the evening, feel free to make a speech, but I want to get the ball rolling now. Billie? Can you get this on video?"

Billie nods, holding up her phone.

"Now, we don't want to be here for hours so keep it tight, like Uncle Barry's facelift." The crowd and Uncle Barry break into laughter, the kind that feels like a collective sigh of relief. "Think one sentence, a short paragraph, or even a word that sums up our Luna. I'll go first." He turns to look at her on her chaise. "I have always admired your ability to be one hundred percent you. You live in your truth, don't take any bullshit, and the way you show up to life and play full out has inspired me to be more of myself. I'm eternally grateful that I have you in my life. Who's next?"

Luna's former coworker Peggy steps up.

"I've been thinking about this all day," she says, her voice shaking like a leaf in autumn. "While we don't see each other a lot, you're always the first person to check in when I'm going through something, the first person on my doorstep with booze and food, the first person to tell me it's going to be okay. Your loyalty to our friendship doesn't go unnoticed. Love you, Luna. Forever." She bows slightly and steps away, wiping at her eyes.

We go on like this, and I listen to the outpouring of love. I always knew Luna was a special person, but hearing how she's shown up for all these people has me feeling a deeper level of gratitude, recognizing how lucky I am that I've had her as my rock all these years. One person says if they got lost on an endless hike, they would want to do it with Luna, who can always find her way out of a jam, and we all nod. But then there is a moment of awkward silence when I'm fairly sure we're all thinking, *Yeah, but she can't get out of this one.* Every once in a while, Luna opens her eyes and looks at us, smiling, but mostly she lies there, playing her part perfectly. I keep thinking I'll go next, but everyone is so eager, I end up going last. The only other person who hasn't taken a turn yet is Hannah, but I don't expect her to.

I walk slowly to the front. I touch Luna on the shoulder lightly, wanting to feel her warmth, to anchor myself to her while she's still here. I'll keep this quick as everyone is getting antsy, and I already said so much of how I feel in my letter.

"Best friend ever," I manage to say. "And so damn fucking lovable," I add. There is a light wave of giggles in the crowd.

Luna's smile gets even bigger, like the sun breaking through clouds. "There isn't a day that goes by where I don't feel blessed that our paths crossed all those many years ago. You are a trailblazer, a leader, a divine human, and my soul mate. I love you more than my words can express."

Ryder looks at me, knowing I'm about to be a puddle any moment, nods and then screams, "And on that note, let's turn this funeral into a celebration of Luna and let's fucking dance!"

The sound system, which had been quietly playing classical music while we went through our strange pretend funeral, is now at full blast, pumping out pop and rock anthems. I'm sure at least the top three floors of the apartment building must hear it loud and clear. I'll let Billie worry about that. Luna hasn't moved, so I go to her.

"Are you okay?" I ask.

"I'm perfect!" she yells, competing with the speakers. "That was the best. I'll never forget that—though that's fucking easy to say, I mean, how long do I have to remember it for? A week? Two?" Her dark humor has always been her shield, and I love her for never putting it down.

"Come on, let's dance," I tell her. "Only if you feel up to it."

She sits up, takes a deep breath, and then she's in it, dancing, moving, raising her arms. A part of me wants to stop her, to wrap her in bubble wrap and keep her safe, but there is really no point. When someone hands her a cigarette, I have the same feeling, but I don't act on it. And again, when someone brings her a tequila shot. At this point, what's a little lung damage or liver damage in the grand scheme of things?

"There's someone downstairs," Billie whispers in my ear.

"My mother, maybe," I say. "I'll go." I had invited my mother to come, and at first she said she wouldn't miss it for the world, but then she canceled about an hour before, saying the lead in the play she is doing was sick, so it's her time for the spotlight. Story of my life. The show must have ended, and now she's here. I take the elevator down to the lobby, and when the doors open, Jasper is standing there. His bright, shiny hair is a little longer than the last time I saw him. He's wearing a soft cotton shirt that I recognize, and he's holding a bouquet of flowers. I walk right into his arms and break, like a dam that's been holding back an ocean.

"How is it possible that we are having Luna's funeral? How is that possible? She was lying there like she was already dead," I blurt out, the words tumbling over each other.

"I can't even imagine," he says soothingly, his voice a balm on my raw nerves.

He lets me cry for a half a minute into his shoulder, and then he says, "I wanted to see her. And I wanted to make sure you're okay."

"How did you know?" I ask, taking a step back and wiping my eyes.

"Billie called me earlier today."

I think of how he sent Luna the burger. She must have told Billie about that, too.

"Do I look like I've been crying?" I ask him.

He looks me in the face carefully, his eyes scanning mine like he's reading a beloved book.

"Only a little," he admits.

We step into the elevator, and I use one of Maddi's wipes to lessen the evidence of tears. When I look up, I notice we are standing on opposite sides. I smile at him. I'm glad he's here, but I don't know why I felt the need to get so close to him, and I certainly don't want to do it now. Still, I have that sense again that maybe we can be friends, which is so much more than I thought a few months ago.

Back up on the roof, I lose sight of Jasper right away. Luna is sitting on the chaise lounge; the back is up now so she can watch the party. I go over to her and sit on the floor, like a kid at story time.

"Is it too much for you?" I ask.

Luna looks at me, her eyes bright with life even as her body betrays her.

"You did it," she says. "You totally fucking did it. Would it be weird to say this is one of the best nights of my life?"

My instinct is to tell her there will be other best nights, but I know it isn't true. And honestly, I don't want to waste a second of her time with bullshit. Some lies aren't worth telling, even for comfort.

"Em, I don't even know what to say. I have all these thoughts and some seem real, and some seem crazy, but I know I fucking love you. I know I hit the jackpot in the best friend lottery."

"Me, too." Letting myself cry when I saw Jasper was not a good idea. I had been holding it together so well, but now I feel like there is a leak in the dam, and soon the whole thing might collapse.

"You want to grant everyone wishes, right?!" Luna says, taking my hands in hers. "Well, you gave me my wish. When nobody else in the world could, you turned my darkest time into what will be my most treasured memory."

Luna's breathing is more labored now, but she doesn't mention it. I wonder if the steroid is wearing off and if we can get some more.

"I had help," I tell her.

"No," Luna says with some effort. "This is all you. The help you got is because of who you are and how much people love you. Please, Em, don't ever forget that."

"I think you have that wrong, Lu. It's because of how much people love you."

"Well," Luna says. She is so tired now, I can feel it radiating from her like heat. "I have something for you. I sent it to your house because it's not open for discussion."

"You're scaring me," I say, though I'm not sure what exactly I'm scared of.

"Don't be. When it arrives, you have to promise me you'll put it away. Strict instructions: Don't open it until I die."

I don't say anything.

"Promise?" she follows up.

"I promise." And we both turn to watch the party, all the love in her life right in front of her, so tangible and real you could almost reach out and grab it, hold it, and keep it forever.

"I love you," she says, closing her eyes.

"I love you, too, Lu," I whisper, letting her doze a little, pressed against my shoulder, her weight the most precious burden I've ever carried.

***

The envelope arrives on Tuesday. I know it's from Luna because she wrote LUNA all over the back and in the tiniest writing in the return address corner, as if to challenge the post office, she wrote Fucking Luna. She's crazy—what if it had been confiscated? But then I laugh. It wasn't, and she got away with it, as she almost always did. Does, I correct myself.

I keep calling Hannah to ask if I can come see Luna. She never fully recovered after the party, but she's been hanging on. Every day, Hannah says maybe tomorrow, and that she needs her rest. But I know what she's doing, and I bet it comes directly from Luna—she doesn't want me to see this version of her. She wants my last image of her to be at the party, dancing, talking, smoking, and drinking. I think of her getting up off the chaise lounge, standing tall. She went from one person to the next, hugging and joking and thanking them. Then she and Hannah got into the elevator alone, and I watched the doors close, like the final scene of a movie I never wanted to end.

Hannah calls me on Thursday morning.

"Emerson, she's gone," she says in a near whisper.

When I'm quiet for a second, she adds, "What you did for her the other night, it was incredible. She never stopped talking about it. You celebrated her life. You let her hear how much people loved her. You gave her closure. It was the greatest gift."

"Thank you," I utter softly. I am so sad, I don't think I can speak, and here Hannah is being so generous. "Thank you," I say again because I can't think of any other words. I manage to tell her I am here if there is anything I can do. Over the following blurry hours, Ryder and Billie text, saying they love me and that they have cleared their days if I need them. Jasper, who I didn't talk to again at the party/funeral except for a quick wave as he left, also texts. *Thinking of you,* it says. *Here if you need anything. So sorry.*

I pretend it isn't happening. I pretend that Luna is just somewhere else, not with me right now. It takes me all day to pull out the envelope she sent me and open it.

I start to read.

My Dearest Em,

I know more than anything you wanted to take me on a trip. I know you wanted it for me, but I want this for you. And you can't say no to a dead person.

I have booked you a room at Enchantment Ranch in Sedona. I have told all your friends about this, sent them the dates to hold you accountable, and ensure you go. No excuses, okay?

I love you. From your new angel or fallen angel ;-),

Luna xo

Behind the letter is an itinerary entitled 'Emerson's Enchantment Agenda'.

Monday: Morning hike, afternoon spin class, evening massage.

Tuesday: Morning at the pool, afternoon sip and paint.

Wednesday: Morning Pilates, afternoon nature walk.

Thursday: Morning excursion into town (meet at hotel entrance), lazy afternoon.

Friday: Morning choice, afternoon Zumba, evening hike.

I don't want to do any of those things without Luna. I have no intention of going. I notice there is one more piece of paper folded behind the itinerary. I pull it out, and I can barely believe it. It's from twenty years ago, when we were practically just kids. I'll never forget it; we were already best friends, but still in the early phases when it feels like falling in love. We were always talking about our future and what businesses we might start. I was close to creating StyleShop, and we were in the bookshop hunting for business books when she came across the book *The Guide to Being a Best Friend for Life*. We read it together that afternoon, and one of the suggestions was to make a friendship contract. Part of the template had a section called THE ONE VETO. The instructions mentioned that you get one opportunity to veto your bestie's decision during the course of the relationship.

"Who knows when we'll ever use this," she had said at the time. "But I like a way out, or a way through. What if I really want Korean food and you don't? I'll need this!"

We'd laughed and signed it with initials and hearts, and I never thought of it again. But here it is, Luna's veto power over me. It was circled three times. I can't believe she held on to it and remembered to use it! But of course, that was Luna in a nutshell—saving the most important card for when it really counted. And with that, I know I am going to go, because sometimes the only way to honor someone you've lost is to follow the path they've laid out for you, even when every step feels impossible.

Chapter Seventeen

"**I**s this Ms. Bailey?"

"It is," I say, glancing out the window of my beautifully appointed casita at the gorgeous scenery. All that majestic red rock that would normally make my heart swell with something like reverence, but today produces nothing but a hollow echo inside my chest. Luna's actual funeral was a week ago, and the numbness continues to spread through my body like a slow-moving glacier, freezing everything in its path.

"This is Mariah, your enchantment concierge." Even her job title sounds like something from a romantic comedy I'm decidedly not starring in. "I'm sorry to bother you. I've noticed that you haven't been coming to dinner, and while that's totally your choice, I would like to gently urge you to come to our award-winning restaurant tonight called Che Ah Chi, meaning, as you might know, red rocks."

When I don't say anything—because what is there to say when your best friend has orchestrated your entire vacation from beyond the grave?—she keeps talking.

"I've taken the liberty of booking a seat for you at our solo traveler table," she adds.

Also known as the single losers table, I think to myself, with the kind of bitter internal monologue Luna would have smacked me for.

"I know, I know, but it isn't what you're thinking," she quickly adds, like I'm not the first guest to mentally rename their thoughtfully curated seating arrangements. "It is actually quite lovely and a nice place to connect with other fellow travelers who might also be on a solo adventure. Of course, if you would rather, I book a table just for you—"

"That's fine," I say, cutting her off before I can overthink it. "Let's do the singles, I mean solo traveler table." Because what's the difference, really? A sad person sitting alone versus a sad person sitting with other people who don't know they're sad.

"Perfect. I have confirmed your reservation at 7 p.m. at our communal table," she says kindly, and I appreciate her swift linguistic pivot from 'solo traveler'. "I think you will be pleased."

"Thank you," I say, my voice as empty as the desert night sky without stars.

"Ms. Bailey?" Mariah asks with the gentle persistence of someone who genuinely cares or is exceptionally well-trained. Possibly both.

"Yes?"

"Is there anything else I can do for you? Book a massage, maybe, or a mani/pedi? We also have some wonderful excursions available for our guests."

"That's okay." I pull the shades on the big windows and block out the view to immerse myself in complete darkness—a physical manifestation of my emotional state that would make any therapist worth their salt scribble furious notes. A nap sounds better than any of the things Mariah just mentioned. "I'm good for now. But thank you."

"I'm here if you need me," she singsongs, with the bright

optimism of someone who still has their best friend. "We'll see you at Che Ah Chi tonight."

I've been eating all my meals in my room since I got here two days ago. I know Luna wouldn't approve—she'd be horrified, actually—but I can barely get myself into a sitting position. How am I going to eat in a public place? Even so—and despite the fact that in-room dining is one of the features they tout on the website, and it is done very nicely—I feel so alone. Not just physically (which is self-inflicted) but emotionally (even though my friends are reaching out daily), and everything I eat tastes like cardboard. I might as well be eating boiled chicken and rice in my apartment. But even that has more taste than I can decipher right now.

I Google if grief can affect your taste buds. Yes, yes, it can. The internet is a reliable companion to the grieving and anxious everywhere.

I perch myself on the end of my bed and practice box breathing: in, two, three, four; hold, two, three, four; out, two, three, four; hold, two, three, four. A wave of regret crashes over me. I don't want to be here. But Luna wants me to be here. She's probably looking down (or up) at me, rolling around in fits of laughter. *Damn that friends agreement,* I laugh to myself.

The days have been rough. I'm not surprised by this; my best friend just died. Every hour goes by in slow motion. The mornings are the hardest, waking up and remembering that this isn't all a dream. It takes until lunch before I'm able to breathe normally, leave my room, and not cry. By then, I'm so tired from all the effort, all I want to do is get back under the covers. But it wouldn't matter where I was; this is the way I would feel anywhere.

I settle in for a nap, convincing myself that a new attitude for

Emerson will emerge after some rest. At least the bed is among the most comfortable I have ever slept in. Luna went all out, booking me on a first-class flight and then choosing this elegant room. She would be punching my arm if she knew I was moping around and not indulging in all this place has to offer. *Sleep, then get your ass out of bed and go mingle with the singles*, I'm sure I hear her whisper into my ear as I doze off, her voice as real as if she were lying next to me, plotting my social rehabilitation.

I hear a phone ringing that sounds like it's on top of my eardrum. I open my eyes, and for a second, I have to think about where I am. I bolt up in an instant. I grope for the phone and answer.

"Hello?"

"Ms. Bailey?"

Oh God, it's Mariah. I glance at the time on my cell: 7:20 p.m. It's so dark in here, I have no sense of time, like I've entered some grief-stricken temporal vortex.

"Oh no. I'm late. I'm so sorry I didn't wake up as early from my nap as I intended. If there's a penalty, I'll pay it. I don't mind. I'll just order room service again a little later." As if my absence would create some cosmic imbalance at their perfectly orchestrated singles table.

"Of course, you can certainly do that," Mariah says kindly. "But I was actually calling to ask if you could come a little later. A few people are running late, and I don't want you at an empty table. Can you come at eight?"

"Sure," I say quickly before I can give any other answer. Seizing the day—actually the night—just like Luna would want. Perhaps would have demanded, with colorful language and dramatic gestures. "Thank you."

I take a quick shower and choose a pretty hot pink and

orange wrap dress—a riotous sunset palette that Luna picked out for me last year, insisting I needed more color in my life. I look in the mirror and am shocked at how good I actually look. An afternoon nap does wonders, I remind myself, and I grab the hair dryer to assist in making my hair single-and-mingle ready. Luna would be proud. Or at least, she wouldn't be completely embarrassed.

At a quarter to eight, I begin the walk to the restaurant. The air is chilly and dry and smells so clean, like nothing has ever died here. The rocks are red, as advertised, and imposing and undeniably beautiful. The restaurant is all dark wood and open floor-to-ceiling windows. It is full and bustling, but calm and soothing, and I'm surprised to find I'm truly glad to be here.

"Ms. Bailey," the man standing at the host stand says, and I wonder how he knows. Maybe they all look at photos of the guests before we arrive. If I ran a luxury resort, I would implement that. I'm surprisingly happy to be recognized, to be seen, to exist in someone else's consciousness.

"Oh, hi, yes," I say, as if I might be someone else who just happened to respond to that name.

"Please follow me to your table," he says, grabbing a menu.

I follow him through the dining room, making a mental note to thank Mariah for this. Up ahead is a round table with eight seats, two of which are occupied by women, and the rest are empty. The women are talking animatedly; their body language tells me they know each other very well. I stop walking for a second and draw in my breath, seeing for one moment the ghost image of me and Luna sitting there, laughing about something ridiculous, her hand gesturing wildly, a cigarette somehow allowed despite the restaurant's undoubtedly strict policies. The host notices that I stopped walking and comes back to meet me.

He bows slightly, a gentle smile on his face. I nod and begin walking again.

When we get to the table, the two women look up. They are both tan with blonde hair that is down and clearly blown dry. They look fit and pretty, and at first glance, I imagine they are younger than I am, maybe in their early thirties. But as I look closer, I realize they are older than that; one woman has some gray at her part, and I spot wrinkles on their cheeks and necks. I put them closer to my age, maybe even older. Of course, that makes me feel slightly better in that way that makes me hate myself a little.

"Ladies," the host says, "this is Emerson. She'll be joining you tonight. Emerson, this is Destiny and Grace."

"Hello, single lady!" Destiny says, holding her almost empty cocktail glass in the air. "Welcome, my new friend!" Her enthusiasm is both terrifying and somewhat comforting.

"Thanks," I manage to utter, taking a seat and marveling at the staff's people skills, calling me Ms. Bailey but introducing me as Emerson to the table. I store it all away, like I'm gathering intelligence for a spy mission rather than just getting through a dinner where I'd rather not be.

"Where are you from, dear?" Grace asks, sounding like she just walked off the set of *Bridgerton*.

"New York. What about you?"

"London originally, but for the last thirty years, LA," Grace says. We're quiet for a minute while we look at the menus. "Love, these menus are more informational. We don't really have a choice. They just keep bringing out the food until we roll out of here," she leans in and whispers through a quiet laugh, as if sharing state secrets.

I nod and, as though the server heard her, beautiful salads

are placed in front of us.

"Lovely, thank you," I say, staring at a plate of greens artfully arranged in a way Luna would have immediately photographed.

Just as I take a fairly big bite, I hear footsteps behind me. Grace and Destiny look up, their eyes wide like they've spotted a celebrity, or at least someone worth looking at. I turn just as someone takes the seat next to me. I am struggling to chew and swallow the leafy greens so I can say hello without spitting arugula across the table.

"Ladies," the host says. "This is Nicolas. Nicolas, this is Grace, Destiny, and Emerson."

I shift in my seat so I can shake his hand, and that's when I see who it is. My ex-boyfriend, pre-Jasper. The one who ruined my life, at least at the time. The universe, it seems, has a sense of humor that aligns perfectly with Luna's.

"Emerson?" he says incredulously, like I'm an apparition or a long-lost treasure he'd given up searching for.

"Nicolas," I reply, my voice flat as the Arizona desert at noon.

"Oooh, I sense some history here. Do you know each other?" Destiny inquires theatrically, licking her lips after downing a tequila shot, her eyes bright with the promise of drama.

My heart is racing, and my body is tingling. Is this what a stroke feels like? Or is it just what it feels like to confront a past you thought you had carefully filed away in a box labeled 'Never Open Again'?

"As luck would have it, we do," Nicolas says, sounding confident and familiar. I want to get a better look at him, but I don't want to stare. He looks generally the same--tall with a thick head of still very dark hair, no gray in sight. He is wearing tortoiseshell glasses and looks like he just stepped out of *GQ* magazine. At first glance, he looks slimmer; the creases around his eyes have smoothed, and his face is calmer in appearance. The last time I saw him, he was so anxious and upset and had pronounced dark circles under his eyes. But of course, that had been after weeks of fighting and his eventual resignation from StyleShop. When your career and relationship implode simultaneously, it tends to leave a mark.

"I'm not sure luck is the right word," I mutter, wondering if Luna is somehow orchestrating this from whatever afterlife she's inhabiting.

"Where are you from?" Grace asks him, her eyes still wide, and she is practically drooling. She seems much more interested in where Nicolas is from than when she asked me, but I suppose that's the power of a well-fitted blazer and cheekbones that could cut glass.

"Living in London now," he says, which I knew because, of course, I've stalked him online over the years, a fact I will take to my grave. "But I'm from New York."

"Oh, a handsome London boy. I'm originally a London girl," Grace says flirtatiously, making what appears to be an immediate connection to him, as if having once lived on the same island of 66 million people constitutes a profound bond.

"I'm sorry I'm late," he says. "I just arrived. My flight was delayed."

"Oh, don't worry. We haven't been here long. Take a seat. Welcome to the singles table!" Destiny says, and I try not to roll my eyes so hard they detach from their sockets.

"What brings you to Arizona?" Grace asks.

"Work," he says kindly, but he doesn't offer any more information, and I remember how he could be both charming and cryptic in the same breath.

All I can think is that I just have to get through dinner, and then I can go back to my room. I let the three of them make small talk while I finish my salad and then enjoy my delicious salmon with lentils. At one point, Grace and Destiny think they know someone at the bar, so they run off together to investigate, leaving Nicolas and me alone like we're in some cosmic screenplay written by a sadistic rom-com writer. Nicolas turns to me.

"I can't believe you're here, that we're here together at the exact same time," he says with a pleasant smile that once made my knees weak. "I honestly didn't know if I would ever see you again. What brings you here?"

"Well, my best friend died last week. She had stage four lung cancer by the time I found out about it. She was supposed to have four months, but she didn't make it that far. She'd still be here if she did. Actually, she'd be sitting right where you are."

The look on Nicolas's face is of such pure shock that I almost feel sorry for him. He reaches for my hand, and I don't pull away, which surprises me more than his touch.

"Emerson, I'm so sorry," he says, and he actually sounds like he means it. But with Nicolas, you never know, or at least, I never knew.

The last time I saw him, we were at the StyleShop office after hours. It was about fifteen years ago, so it was still all so new. I brought Nicolas on as CFO, and he was good, smart, and never missed a thing. He was attractive and strong and slightly older than me, which, I realize now, gave me some twisted sense of comfort. At first, we worked together well. Then, slowly, we began to flirt with each other. I looked forward to seeing him. I made up excuses why we had to have private meetings, and he was always open to them, eager even.

One night, after we had been working really late, we decided to go get a drink after we were done. One thing led to another, and basically, I made the famous rookie mistake of dating my colleague. It was so much fun at first. We didn't want anyone to know, so we pretended to be professional during the day and snuck a kiss or two when we knew we were alone. We played footsie under the table during important meetings when we knew we could get away with it.

For almost six months, we spent almost every night together until I found out I was not the only woman in his life. Those off nights when he made excuses about being too tired or needing to get organized? He was with a woman he met around the same time we started dating. Now it feels silly, but then it felt like the end of the world. I thought we would get married. I imagined we would spend our lives together, running the company and having a family. I was completely crushed. He left the company—basically, I forced him out—and he moved to London. I haven't seen him or talked to him since.

I've imagined this moment—seeing him after StyleShop became hugely successful, preferably when I was still with Jasper—but you can't have everything. I was going to tell him I was so much better off without him, that he had done me a favor. But now that I'm sitting here with him, I'm shocked to find I don't want to. I sit back and take a small spoonful of my palate cleanser, elderberry sorbet, letting the tart sweetness melt on my tongue—the first thing I've truly tasted in days.

"Tell me more about your friend," Nicolas says, and so, instead of unleashing the fury I've imagined all this time, I tell him about Luna. And it feels so good, like pulling the stopper on a bottle where I've kept all her stories contained.

"She is my best friend. You definitely met her a few times, although she was out of the country on assignment for most of the time we were together." I hear the present tense in my words, and I stop talking for a second, the reality settling over me again. "Do you remember her? Feisty, funny, always pushing the limits."

A smile comes over Nicolas's face. "She cursed a lot, right?" he asks, and just the memory makes me smile.

"That's her," I say, like I'm introducing someone who's just stepped away to the bathroom.

"And she smoked, like a chimney," he adds.

"Yep." I smile at the thought of Luna with her cigarette, the way she'd lean back in her chair, blow smoke rings, and deliver devastating one-liners.

We talk about Luna for a while, and when I get quiet he begins to walk me through his past decade. He got married, has two kids, and now he and his wife have agreed to a trial separation.

"It isn't a surprise," he says. "There has always been some disconnect between us."

I don't ask if he was unfaithful to her, if that is what he always does to people he is supposed to love. I'm surprised that I can't conjure up the anger I've felt for him all these years. It's like grief has rewired my emotional circuits, leaving only room for the largest feelings—the Luna-sized ones—and everything else seems distant and small.

Grace and Destiny return to the table, and somehow now it feels like they are crashing our party.

"False alarm," Destiny says with a shrug.

"Well, maybe not quite," Grace says with a mischievous smile. "I'm meeting that fine fellow later."

"You foxy minx," Destiny says while hitting Grace on the arm, and they laugh, the sound bright and incongruous against my mood.

Nicolas turns to me. "Do you want to take a walk?" he asks, his eyes searching mine.

"We haven't gotten dessert yet," I say, like someone who cares about the proper order of things.

He raises his eyebrows, a question mark.

I think about how I despised him for so many years. There was a time I believed he had ruined my life. But I just don't seem to have the energy to care about any of that anymore. I feel relieved to be with someone familiar who doesn't know every detail about my life for the last few years, who doesn't know I lost a baby and had a failed relationship in addition to a dead best friend. Sometimes it's easier to be with someone who knows only part of your story.

I smile at him and stand.

"Nice to meet you both," I say across the table to Grace and Destiny.

"You, too," they mumble, but Destiny is trying to find the guy on Instagram to show Grace, so they don't look up.

Nicolas puts his hand on the small of my back, and we walk out through the beautiful restaurant. I see a woman with a name tag that says Mariah standing off to the side. When she sees us go by, she smiles, and I wonder if perhaps this was her plan all along—Luna's final gift, delivered by a stranger.

Chapter Eighteen

"Have you seen the red rocks?" Nicolas asks as we walk toward the lobby. The darkness has settled in, but there's still a pink hue to everything. The moon hangs impossibly large and full in the sky, like it's trying to one-up the sun's earlier performance.

"Briefly, on my walk over," I say with all the enthusiasm of someone reading terms and conditions.

"Did you arrive today, too?" he asks.

"Nope, I've been here for a few days. I just haven't really explored much beyond my room's four spectacular walls." The bed and I have become quite well acquainted.

Nicolas gives me a look that's equal parts understanding and pity, and I hate that I don't hate it.

"Well, would you like to see them now?" he asks.

I shrug. Do I? I don't really want to do anything. But surprisingly, I don't want to return to my room either. Moving beyond my self-imposed prison has been a welcome distraction, like finding a window in what I thought was a sealed box.

"It's getting late," I say, which is neither a yes nor a no.

"I would say, trust me, but I have a feeling that's the last thing you're going to agree to do," he says, and we both laugh. It's startling, the sound of my own laughter. "I'm not proposing a hike or anything at this hour, but I saw a small path around the pool on my way to dinner. Come on, I'll show you."

We walk outside, and the temperature has dropped dramatically, a desert chill that wraps itself around us. I don't react to it, though. The last thing I want is for Nicolas to play the leading man, asking if I'm cold and offering me his jacket like we're in some rom-com where I've forgotten I hate him.

We walk toward the pool, which is big and serene, chaise lounges lined up like obedient soldiers, umbrellas down and tied for the night. I follow Nicolas past the pool and onto a tiny path that takes us to a view of the red rocks, which, in this light, look like varying shades of pink and red, as if they're blushing at our attention. I expect him to stop, but he keeps going, and we end up back at the pool. I'd almost forgotten the joy of being out in the fresh air. If I'd known all of this was here, the feeling I would get, I would have come out sooner. Well, probably not.

"Do you want to sit?" he asks, pointing to the chairs around the pool. There is nobody else here. It feels like a monumental decision, and I stand there thinking, as if he's asked me to choose between parallel universes.

"We don't have to," he says when I still say nothing. "I can walk you back to your room, or we can just say good night now."

I continue to stand there like I've completely lost my ability to make even the simplest decisions. Nicolas sighs and gently takes my hand. I let him. He leads me to a chair, places his hands gently on my shoulders, and pushes lightly until I sit down. Then he moves my feet around so that I sit with my back against the seat and my legs straight out. Nicolas sits next to me and arranges himself the same way. He reaches into his pocket.

"This might seem totally crazy, but I have these edibles," he begins.

"Great," I say immediately, suddenly capable of making a lightning-fast decision. "I'll take one."

"Oh, I expected I would have to sell it harder." He laughs.

"Nope, anything to increase relaxation." At this point, I'd probably accept a tranquilizer dart meant for a rhinoceros.

"They are fast acting," he explains. "Ten, fifteen minutes tops. At least, that's my experience. Everyone's different, of course."

I reach out my hand, and he places a sugary orange triangle gummy in it. I raise my eyebrows.

"Pomegranate," he says. "It's the kind that makes you sleepy."

"Even better." I sit up and turn toward him. I put the gummy in my mouth and chew it, enjoying the sweet and slightly bitter taste, thinking he's a genius since I had not thought to pack gummies. I wasn't sure if or where you could get them in Arizona, plus the whole never-leaving-my-room situation made it challenging.

"Thanks," I say, still sitting up and facing him. He smiles and puts one in his mouth, chews, and swallows. I feel an undeniable pull toward him, but I remind myself it's just the grief clouding my judgment. Grief: the ultimate beer goggles.

"Are you doing okay?" Nicolas asks, sitting up to mirror my position. We are inches apart.

"I think so," I say thoughtfully, feeling the first waves of the gummy, which may or may not be my imagination. "Do you want to come back to my room?" slips out before I can stop it, like a secret that's tired of being kept.

Nicolas jerks back slightly, and for a second, I think I made a huge mistake, which I don't even really care about. I can go back to my room alone; it'd be no different than the last two evenings. But before I know it, he's standing up and grabbing my hands. He pulls me back in the direction of the lobby and stops.

"I have no idea where I'm going." His grin spreads widely. "Which way?"

Again, we laugh, and I think to myself, *Wow, a few days ago I wondered if I would ever laugh again.*

"This way." I lead him toward my casita. "I have to warn you. I have no idea what I'm doing right now," I say, which could be my life motto at this point.

"I probably didn't help that with the gummy."

We are moving fast, as if at any moment, one of us might change our mind, and we don't want to give ourselves a chance to reconsider. Our bodies seem to understand something our brains don't quite yet.

"It's absolutely your fault," I say, stifling a giggle.

He stops and pulls me back so I'm facing him. "You're not married, are you?" he asks. "Because…"

"I'm not married," I say quickly, cutting him off.

He looks truly relieved. We pick up our walk toward my room.

"Because what?" I ask, curious.

"Because," he says slowly, "I have no idea what your life has been like these last few years, not really anyway. I mean, I know you sold the company—that news was hard to miss—and, well, because the last thing I would want to do when you are already dealing with so much is further complicate your life."

I nod. I'm torn between being impressed by this and thinking he is probably still the same jerk he always was. But the funny thing is, I don't care. I am suddenly desperate to get close to him, to feel his skin and warmth. To not be totally alone, even if it is just for a few fleeting moments. Sometimes loneliness is a hunger you didn't know you had until someone offers you food.

We reach my door, and I open it. We walk in. I'm shocked that the blinds have been adjusted to halfway up instead of the sloppy way I left them pulled all the way down. Now, they reveal a beautiful tree with fairy lights all over it just beyond the glass, like the universe decided to throw some beauty my way after all. I take it all in, then I pull them back down.

My bed has been made, and there are not one but two chocolate squares, one for each pillow. Mariah was paying close attention, which feels a little weird, but I guess that's her job? And, just to add to that, right in front of us, on the main table, is a bottle of champagne on ice and a small circle of champagne glasses. I count four glasses—and I think that Mariah is smart, ready in case, but not too obvious. Well, maybe a little, but I'm grateful.

"We can have champagne after a gummy, right?" I ask.

"Dr. Google tells me yes. I've done it many times," he says, and then, "Sorry, I did not mean that the way it sounded at all. Yes, I have mixed pot and alcohol and had no problems."

"Good." I reach for the bottle. The cork comes out quickly, making a huge popping sound that feels like it should mark something momentous. I pour two glasses and hand him one.

"Cheers," I say.

"Cheers."

"To… would you say you're an old friend?" I ask; the gummy is definitely kicking in. I take a sip of the champagne, and it is sweet and bubbly and good.

"No," Nicolas says thoughtfully. "Not an old friend. Probably just the opposite. But I'm glad to be here with you right now, Emerson. When I woke up this morning, this was the last thing I ever expected."

"You and me both. The universe has a weird sense of humor."

"Right," he agrees.

We're quiet for the first time since we got to my room, and I notice music is playing quietly in the background. I glance around and realize it's coming from the TV—another thing Mariah probably set up for me. It's Van Morrison, which I love but have no real emotional connection to, so it's fine. It doesn't jolt me back to reality or anything.

Nicolas leans in and stops just about an inch from my face. "Is this... okay?" he asks.

And then we are all in, mushing our bodies together and pulling at each other's clothes. He smells just the same, not whatever soap he might have used or his deodorant, but the base scent, his scent. It has been so long since I was with someone, fully with someone. Jasper and I had stopped being together before we broke up. We went through the motions on occasion because it seemed like we should, but I hadn't felt anything.

As Nicolas eases my underwear off, I wonder for a brief moment if he'll be able to tell I've been pregnant, but I don't think so. And it's part of my story now, anyway. If he doesn't like it... But he really seems to like it. He is totally focused on me, and I let him be. We find our way to the bed, and for the next forty minutes, I am swept away. I don't think about anything but the feeling of Nicolas on my body, his tongue and his hands, and then his penis. It is blissful. And then it's over, and I wait for the weight of life to bring me back to reality, like waiting for the comedown after a high.

"That was... I don't even know what to say," he says, sweaty and slightly out of breath. "That was amazing."

I don't say anything.

"Do you regret it?" he asks gently.

"I don't know," I say honestly. "I'm waiting to see."

He laughs as if to say that's fair.

I keep thinking I'll get up to pour more champagne or to go to the bathroom. In one minute, I'll get up. Maybe I'll ask Nicolas to return to his room so I can be alone. But I don't want to. Being with him feels surprisingly therapeutic in a way that being with a stranger would not. Plus, he lives in London! I never have to see him again. I settle deeper into the mattress, my head on his shoulder, and I fall into a gummy-and-champagne-induced sleep.

***

"I booked a massage," Nicolas says as he gently shakes me awake.

"Now? Who books a massage at this hour?" In my mind, it's still sometime in the middle of the night.

"It's nine a.m.," Nicolas tells me.

"What?" I say, sitting up too fast. I knew I'd been sleeping, but I thought for about an hour. There is brightness peeking through the gaps in the blinds. I wince a little.

"Did you sleep as well as I did?" I ask.

"I think so," Nicolas says, smiling. He leans in for a kiss.

"Wait! I haven't brushed my teeth yet." Morning breath: the great equalizer.

This is another place where Nicolas could say something cheesy like it's nothing he hasn't done before, or I used to kiss him all the time before I brushed my teeth, but he doesn't. He just smiles to himself and says gently, "I don't mind."

I feel myself relaxing a little. I have not slept that deeply in a long time. Since Luna died. Actually, since just before I lost Evie.

"Would you like me to check if they have room for you to get a massage, too?"

I think about it for a second, but then I shake my head. "That's okay," I say. "But will you come back after?"

Nicolas cocks his head and looks at me. "That would be my pleasure." And then he's up and out, and the room feels like all the air has been sucked out of it.

I make myself a cup of coffee and open the blinds. I see the red rocks in the distance, playing back the movie in my mind that was the last twelve hours. I'm still in disbelief. I hadn't even thought about him in years. But if someone had said, what do you think of Nicolas? I would have said, bad news! Not worth my time.

So why did I like being with him so much? Maybe it really is one of the vortexes here. Maybe it turned things upside down. I feel the air slowly come back into the room and realize I am actually looking forward to his return. I find myself humming and looking for my bag. Somehow, while Luna was dying, not only did she manage to plan this trip for me, but she gave me the oddest packing list. When I saw it, all I could think was how much I had wanted to do that for her. I had so loved doing it for Billie. But in classic Luna style, there was nothing very practical on her list, like underwear or a swimsuit. It read:

Please take… Fucking slippers, not wool! (I had to buy those) Your long-lost sketchbook (I had to dig that out of the depths of my closet) Advil, in case you drink too much, you shit (I deserved that) Condoms (which came in handy last night, so maybe there was something practical on the list after all) Cigarettes (she knows I don't smoke, but maybe this was her way of saying, 'Be more like Luna').

How did she know? For the first time in so long, I have an urge to sketch. When I was walking out of the restaurant with Nicolas last night, I saw a woman, probably in her twenties, wearing the most beautiful dress. It was navy blue with subtle lace, and even though I was completely distracted at the time, I thought, *Let me at it. With a few tweaks, I could make that dress perfect.*

Now I grab my book out of my bag, my hand curling around the top, and I feel the familiar yet distant excitement I used to feel when I planned something or fiddled with a sketch I'd been working on. It's like running into an old friend—one you actually like. I walk to the table in front of the big windows, move the almost-empty bottle of champagne out of the way, and lay the book out on the smooth surface. I sit and sketch, first doing a rendition of the exact dress I saw and then, right next to it, drawing one with my improvements. It comes so naturally, I have the sense it is sketching itself.

When I look up, an hour has gone by, and I know Nicolas will be back soon. I close the book, throw it onto the unmade bed, and jump in the shower. I hear the door opening just as I'm getting out. I feel like I have entered an alternate universe—this is what your life could have looked like if you had made different choices!—but it feels like a relief. I wasn't loving the life I'd been living these last few months anyway.

"How was it?" I call from the bathroom.

Nobody answers, and I worry it isn't Nicolas after all.

"Hello?" I call out more urgently, suddenly aware I'm very naked and very vulnerable.

"Hello, hi, sorry," Nicolas answers. "Can I come in?"

"Sure, why not?" I respond casually, as if I'm not still dripping wet.

He enters the bathroom. He looks relaxed, glowing, and so handsome in the light of day. I'm standing at the mirror, wrapped in just a towel, brushing my hair.

"How was the massage?" I ask again.

"Heavenly. But I missed you. They offered an extra half hour at no charge, but I turned them down."

"That might be the highest compliment," I say, turning to face him. I can see us in the various mirrors around the big bathroom. It's not a bad view. "Being chosen over a heavenly massage." I offer a teasing smile.

"Well," he says, giving in to my smile. "I thought we could do some massaging of our own."

He leans in for a kiss. I can smell the oils on him — eucalyptus and something else — and I close my eyes. In an instant, he is tugging the towel off me, and I let it drop to the floor. He leads me toward the bed, and we begin to lie down. I spot my sketchbook on the bed, lying open, and I reach for it; I don't want to crush it. I move it to the side, closing it, feeling that I just did that. But it takes only a few seconds for me to completely forget about it and lose myself once again.

We nap the afternoon away, have food brought in for a late lunch, make love two more times, and then we head to the restaurant for dinner, where we are seated at a table for two. Mariah is there and smiles as she watches the host place menus in front of us. I realize I am starving. I can see Grace and Destiny still sitting at the singles table. They are there alone but are laughing loudly, having a good time. I'm glad.

"Tomorrow is our last day together here," Nicolas says.

I nod, feeling an overwhelming sense of disappointment and possibly relief. Two days being wild and free in paradise after these last twelve months is perfectly acceptable. No harm done.

In fact, nobody will ever know. At that thought, I have to will away the burn of tears because, more than anything in the world, I want to tell Luna. She would get such a kick out of this, I just know it. She'd say something like, "See? I told you that guy had something going for him besides his annoyingly perfect face."

I clear my throat. I am sure Nicolas understands that I'm feeling emotional, but he doesn't call me on it. He sits there patiently, waiting until I'm ready to talk. He is so different now from the man I remember.

"Should we do something?" I ask, once I'm pretty sure my voice won't crack. "Maybe actually leave the resort grounds?"

"If you want to. But I would say today has been near perfect. We could just take the tiny path around the pool again and call it a day."

He smiles and I smile back.

"We could," I say. "Maybe best to spend our last day together inside."

"I want to show you something," Nicolas says.

"Okay." I wait as he reaches into his pocket for his phone and starts scrolling. He finds what he's looking for and holds it up so I can see. It is a photo of Nicolas, me, and Luna in the StyleShop office, the first version of it. We are all in my office with the largest smiles on our faces. I think we had just gotten a huge order, if I remember correctly, and Luna happened to be there when we got the good news. I squint at that photo.

"Had we admitted to our relationship by then?" I ask. We haven't talked about any of the old history. I figured it was best to leave that alone.

"You had just told Luna," he says. "When you talked about her, it had been so long, I couldn't remember her face, but I knew I had this photo. She was… I know you don't need me to say this to you, but she was something. I could tell in only those few times I met her." He pauses. "She always made me feel a little scared."

I laugh out loud, and it feels so good. "That was exactly what she was going for," I tell him. "Most people were a little scared of her. But she was the absolute best."

I stop talking, and I can't look at him. The tears are too close to the surface now.

Again, Nicolas lets me take my time, and I'm grateful.

"She sent me here, you know," I softly say. "I wanted to take her on a trip, but she was too sick, and then, well, you know. We talked about a spa, the clean, dry air, and the energy of the vortexes. But it was too late for her. She insisted, actually demanded, I come. You can't get a better friend than that."

Nicolas is nodding, letting me talk.

"I've been doing this thing," I continue. "Trying to grant people's wishes. I've done it for the special people in my life, and I plan to do it for more—my Aunt Pearl, my mother. But I didn't get the chance to do it for Luna."

"It sounds like you are doing it for her," he says, taking my hand. Our food has come, and I pick at it, but I'm not hungry anymore. And apparently neither is Nicolas. Our steak sits mostly uneaten between us, like a metaphor for something I'm too tired to figure out.

"Let's go back, if that's okay with you, and get some sleep," Nicolas offers.

"I'm so sorry I have brought this mood down to the basement, the subbasement."

"That's okay," Nicolas says gently. "I'm glad you feel you can talk to me."

I realize I don't know any details about his wife at all except that he has two little kids, and he realized, too late, that she might not be the right person for him to make a family with. That piqued my interest, but I don't have the energy to delve into it now. Probably the less I know about that, the better. Plus, we have only one more day together. There is no need to analyze something that won't affect me in more than twenty-four hours.

I look at him as we walk out; he's unbelievably handsome. And so surprisingly kind and patient. If I didn't know better, I would think Luna set this up somehow. But that's impossible. Two days ago, he would have been the last person I wanted to see, or at least one of them. There's no way Luna could have known any different. But still, it feels lucky.

As we leave the restaurant, I think we probably won't have sex tonight, and I hope that's okay with him. But by the time we get to my door, it is all I want to do. He is so hot. He always was, but the calmness that I never saw before adds an entirely new element to his hotness. I reach for his blazer and push it over his shoulders. He raises his eyebrows as if to say now? I nod, and he's all in. We barely make it to the bed, and once we're finished, breathing heavy on top of the sheets, it is only a few minutes before we're going at it again.

We spend the next day in bed, having meals delivered to my room again. I don't get any calls from Mariah asking me to come to dinner.

The next morning, I sit up in bed and look around. I think back to two days before when I could barely get out of bed, for totally different reasons than not getting out of bed now. I feel the slightest twinge of sadness.

"I'm going to miss you," I admit. I hadn't expected to feel it or say it. I imagine telling Ryder all about it.

Good for you, he'll probably say. *You deserved a fuck vacation.*

That's what I'm thinking as Nicolas comes over and sits on the side of the bed. He takes my hand.

"You don't actually have to miss me," he says.

"Why not?"

"Well, maybe I should have told you this before, and I want to preface it by saying there is absolutely no pressure..." He takes a deep breath, and I sit up straighter. I have no idea what he's about to say. "But I'm not actually flying back to London. I'm going to New York for a month to work on a project and, I don't know, give the separation a chance to take."

"What about your kids?"

"They'll come for a few days about halfway through the month."

"Wow."

"Yeah, wow."

We're quiet for a few seconds.

"Are you happy about it?" he asks. "Do you think you might like to see me while I'm there?"

I laugh and fake punch him on the arm. "I'll think about it," I say, smiling.

He nods, kisses me, and we make love one more time before I have to check out of the casita.

Chapter Nineteen

I feel the wheels touch down in New York and immediately think of the last time I arrived home—with Billie from Greece, when my first instinct was to text Luna. The thought of not being able to reach her anywhere sits like a stone in my chest. So I try not to think about it, which is about as effective as trying not to think about a pink elephant while someone's shouting "PINK ELEPHANT" directly into your ear.

I text Nicolas, who happens to be on my plane but is trapped in the second-to-last row by the bathroom. I would have pegged him for a business-class guy; he was always so pretentious during the Nicolas 1.0 era. But he hasn't complained once, at least not that I've heard. It's starting to seem like people really can change, which feels both terrifying and hopeful, like most truths worth discovering.

He texts back immediately.

It's totally your call, he writes. I had asked what the plan was. I look around the cabin at all the people either arriving home or possibly going on vacation, and I know with bone-deep certainty that I don't want to be alone right now.

Nicolas had mentioned his company set him up with a short-term apartment in Turtle Bay near his office.

How about we go to your place? I'm happy to spend a few more days outside my apartment, continuing what Nicolas and I had in Arizona. He sends back a heart emoji, which somehow feels more intimate than anything we've done together.

I'm in the window seat, so I wait while everyone files out, watching the choreographed chaos of deplaning.

"Fancy meeting you here," Nicolas says as he approaches my row. The plane is almost empty now. I am usually in such a rush to get off, like the air I'd been breathing for however long was suddenly lacking in oxygen. But now I am in no rush at all. Nicolas looks at me and slides into the middle seat. He bites his bottom lip. He takes my hand, and I let him.

"Do you feel like I tricked you?" he asks.

"Tricked? Not at all," I reply, though the question makes me wonder if I should feel tricked.

"Is there something else?"

"No." I turn to face him. "Your being in New York doesn't mean I have to see you if I don't want to. It's a big city."

"I've heard that," he says, squeezing my hand.

"We coexisted here for years and never saw each other," I say. "It's more the other stuff, I think. The returning home without Luna here. And other things. I was pregnant a while back. I lost the baby."

I had mentioned Jasper in passing, and Nicolas listened but didn't push in the same way I didn't push to learn more about his wife, but I never mentioned Evie. Now he turns and looks at me directly, his eyes soft with understanding.

"I'm so sorry," he says, his voice filled with genuine sorrow. "Just so sorry."

I nod and rest my head on his shoulder. I wait for more questions, questions that don't have answers, but he doesn't ask them. He leans his head against mine with just the right amount of pressure. I could stay here like this for at least the next few months, or possibly years. As if on cue, a flight attendant approaches us.

"Sir, ma'am, you'll need to deplane, please," he says with practiced politeness. "The cleaning crew is coming on."

We both stand up.

"Sorry," I mutter, suddenly self-conscious.

"Thank you," Nicolas says.

In the Uber, I change my mind approximately seventeen times before saying: "Maybe we should go to my place."

"Sure," Nicolas says without missing a beat. "Should I change our destination in the app?"

"Wait, actually. I'm undecided. I officially have no idea what we should do," I confess, providing irrefutable evidence that my brain has turned to mush.

"How about this?" Nicolas says, taking my hand. "Let's go to my place and see what you think. I'm sort of curious to see it and at least put my bags down. If you don't like it or it doesn't feel right, we'll leave and go to your place."

At that second, his phone rings. He looks at the display, then at me like he doesn't know what to do. I can see it says Reuben. I raise my eyebrows in question.

"My son," he explains.

"Take it, please." I move a few inches away to give him some space, even though I'll still hear everything he says in the confines of the backseat.

"It's really late there," Nicolas says, worry creeping into his voice. "Hey, bud," he says into the phone.

I can immediately hear that Reuben is crying, the sound piercing even through the tiny speaker.

"Whoa, slow down. Are you okay? Is Mom okay?" Nicolas

looks at me with slight panic in his eyes. He quietly says to me, "This happens sometimes." He puts the phone closer to his ear. "Bud, bud, Reub, are you okay?"

I can hear the loud crying slow down, and I catch fragments like "miss" and "love" and "home".

"I know, bud, I know, honey," Nicolas says with such tenderness it makes something in my chest ache. "Is Mom sleeping? Okay, yes, I can talk you through it. Take deep breaths, okay? We can do it together. I'll do it with you. In, out, in, out."

Reuben says something, and they go back and forth like that for a few minutes.

"You can literally call me anytime," Nicolas says. "I love you, bud."

Nicolas hangs up. "He's okay. He misses me. But I hate that moment when he is all-out crying, and I have no idea if it is truly something terrible or not. Every single time that happens, until I get a handle on it and understand he's mostly okay, I think a few hours are shaved off my life. It feels like my heart stops."

"That sounds so hard," I say, meaning it.

He is so kind and unexpectedly patient that, for the first time, I really do wonder what happened between him and his wife. The Nicolas I knew fifteen years ago wouldn't have handled a crisis call with such gentle care.

The driver pulls up to a building on the corner of Forty-seventh Street and Second Avenue. There's a small park across the street. We're near the United Nations, but this isn't a neighborhood I come to very often. We get out. The lobby is bustling and immaculate, but the design feels outdated and lacks any charm. I don't know what I expected—something more elevated? But I don't even know exactly what he's doing now or what kind of company he's working for. We've barely talked these past days, preferring to communicate in other ways.

Nicolas talks to the doorman and is handed a key.

"Nine H," he says.

We take the small elevator up. There are many young people in this building, but they look mostly fresh out of college and graduate school. I do not let the thought form in my head that I am so far beyond that stage. When in the world did that happen? It feels like I blinked and suddenly became the kind of person younger people call 'ma'am'.

The halls have a brown carpet with orange and yellow stripes and that strange smell New York City apartments have when lots of different people are cooking—a combination of curry, garlic, and furniture polish. We find 9-H, open the door, and wander around. It's a nice but small one-bedroom apartment, furnished in that corporate-anonymous way. Nicolas stands just inside the door, looking lost.

"You okay?" I ask.

"Sorry, I'm a bit distracted by the call from Reuben. It made me realize how much I miss my kids."

I lean in and hug him. He hugs me back, and I can feel him relaxing a tiny bit. We both take a deep breath in unison.

"What happened with your wife?" I ask.

He looks at me. "Oh, so you want to have that conversation?" he asks, looking open to it but wary.

"Maybe?" I say, the word tilting up into a question.

He begins to lead me toward the bedroom, where the bed is made and there is a mountain of fluffy pillows, but he thinks better of it and redirects us toward the couch in the tidy living room.

We sit down.

"She had an affair," he says matter-of-factly.

Suddenly, it is fifteen years ago, and I just discovered Nicolas had been unfaithful to me during our relationship. My life was turned upside down, and I so very much wanted him to disappear from my world. I look at him now. Does he remember? I mean, of course, he remembers somewhere in there, but does he connect it? Does he know how ridiculous it sounds? Or ironic? Two days ago, if someone had told me Nicolas's wife had cheated on him, I would have said, without question, that he deserved it. Karma and all that.

"I'm sorry," I say, because I'm surprised that ninety percent of me means it deeply.

"I wanted to stay together," he continues, surprising me. "We have a family, everyone can make a mistake, a marriage is long and complicated, all of that, but she didn't want to. She says she's in love with him."

"Oh," I say. That is not what I expected. "I'm really sorry."

"Thank you. It has not been easy."

"When did you find out? About the affair?"

"A little over six months ago. I actually ran into them together. It was, well, it was truly awful. She didn't even try to deny it or make up a story. She just looked right at me, almost daring me to accuse her of something. I've thought of that moment so many times. I think she wanted to get caught. She had to have, right? She's very smart. She could have probably avoided me or made sure we didn't run into each other. I did run an errand I hadn't told her about—it was a surprise for her birthday, if you can believe it—but still, she knew my schedule for the day. She knew where I was likely to be."

"Wow," I utter. How many times can I say I'm sorry before it starts to sound hollow?

"Well, I didn't mean to bring us down." He pats my thigh

and stands up.

I'm able to pretend we're still at a hotel, though the view is not as majestic—unless you really love New York City high-rises, which I do. He eases into bed next to me, and I think he's just going to peck me on the cheek and say it's been a tough day. But I am so wrong. He inches slowly down toward the bottom of the bed, looking at me and smiling as he goes, and then I forget everything else.

The next morning, Nicolas heads to the office early, and I make my way back to my apartment. Gazing out the window of my Uber, it feels as though I've slipped into an alternate reality, one where things have completely shifted. How is it possible that I'm back with Nicolas again? The universe has a strange sense of humor sometimes.

I unpack, leaving my sketchbook out for the first time in a long time. "Thank you, Luna," I say out loud, acknowledging the gift she gave me in the middle of her own ending. Maybe I'll work on one of the designs later. And then I get to work on Aunt Pearl's packing list. We leave in less than two weeks! I'll be glad to go to a whole different continent and get some quality time with Aunt Pearl. Her wisdom and presence is always so good for my soul, like being wrapped in a warm blanket when you didn't even realize you were cold.

In the way I sent Billie a packing list and a box, I plan to do the same for Aunt Pearl. My idea is to get her a Camilla kaftan—they're gorgeous, and really, you can't go to Australia without one. I know a store downtown where I can buy them. I'm relieved to have something practical to focus on.

I opt for the subway instead of an Uber. When I emerge from the underground, the sky is strikingly blue. As I let my mind wander to the skies of Australia, a flicker of excitement stirs in my stomach. I can already picture Aunt Pearl's face when I reveal our destination. Australia has been on her bucket list since she had an Aussie friend in school. She knows to save the dates, but not much else—she will lose it when she realizes where we're going.

I am turning the corner on Eighth Street when I run right into Jasper. My heart begins to beat extra fast, and it's hard to catch my breath. It hadn't even entered my mind before, but seeing him here in front of me makes me feel like I am totally and completely caught, like I snuck away and cheated on him these last few days. So weird since that is totally not the case. Even so, I'm sure my cheeks are burning red, and I can barely make eye contact.

"Emerson," he says a little breathlessly. "Are you okay?"

I force myself to lift my head and look at him. He is as handsome as ever, his ginger hair so bright in the direct sun, his accent so familiar it twists my insides. *Stop,* I say to myself. He is not mine anymore. And I most certainly didn't cheat on him. Yet here I am, feeling guilty as if I've been caught doing something wrong, when the only thing I'm guilty of is moving on.

I look behind him and see the sign for Electric Lady Studios, and I'm pretty sure that's where he came from. Ryder told me he had mentioned something about working with a new artist at Luna's party, her living funeral, whatever we are supposed to call it. I just remembered that, so much of that night is still a blur.

"Yes, I'm fine," I say, trying to sound nice but uninterested at the same time. I don't think I accomplish either. "It's just, I don't know, still weird to run into you."

"Roger that." He salutes me, and I think, *Was he always so dorky? And why was that endearing once upon a time?*

"Where are you headed?" he asks.

Now I feel like I'm cheating on Nicolas. I am a mess. A total disaster of a human being.

"Oh, I'm, um, taking Aunt Pearl to Australia soon, so I thought the best way to get her excited and prepared is to get her a Camilla kaftan, of course. And maybe get one for myself."

Jasper looks at me; I can't quite put my finger on his expression. He's the one who told me about Camilla kaftans and how his mother can't get enough. He takes a deep breath.

"I can't believe you're going to Australia now." There's a note of sadness to his voice. It sounds more resigned, like this detail is the one that tells him we are really over. "I always thought I would take you there."

It's wild to think that in the ten years we were together, Jasper and I never went. His family visits the U.S. every other year, so he never felt the need to return. He always said he left Australia for a reason. We had planned to go and celebrate the sale of StyleShop, but with the surprise pregnancy—and then not being pregnant—it just never happened.

I'm quiet for a second.

"I guess I did, too," I say finally.

What we don't say is that we talked about taking Evie there. We sometimes argued happily about what age would be the best time—two, five, ten? I have a flash of the day we lost Evie, when we were trying to make sense of it all, thinking of all the things we would never do with her, and Jasper had whispered, "I'll never be able to take her home." I knew at that minute that he didn't mean our apartment; he meant Australia.

The memory is piercing, and I turn away. Jasper reaches out and puts his hand on my arm gently, and it is like he touched me with a live wire. The jolt is so intense. He feels it too, I know, because he pulls his hand away and looks at it like it's betrayed him. I don't want to be dramatic, so I resist the urge to rub the skin where he touched me. We stand there for a second, breathing harder than normal.

"Sorry," Jasper finally says. "I should be going."

I nod like the jolt I felt took away my ability to speak.

I watch as he heads away from the studio. There's a coffee shop nearby, and I duck inside, hoping the bathroom won't be some complicated combination of numbers I have to ask for. I am in luck. I close the door and cry, like all-out cry. Thank goodness I held it together when I was in Jasper's presence, but now I wonder how I will get this under control. *I am not in love with Jasper anymore,* I chant to myself. I am also not alone anymore, or at least not at the moment. I am doing whatever I am doing with Nicolas, and it feels good.

But that touch. We've always had that sort of electricity between us. I close my eyes and remember our first date. It was a freezing cold February day—February 13, to be exact. We both knew the next day was a Saturday and would have been better for a date, but it was Valentine's Day, and that seemed way too serious for a first date. So, we met late on that Friday afternoon and wandered through the Met. After a little while, Jasper said he knew of the best Peruvian hole-in-the-wall nearby. He said I would love it. We went outside, and we were blasted by what felt like an Arctic wind, which picked up icy snowflakes and blew them at us. We laughed at first, and we were almost there by the time I realized I had lost my gloves somewhere; I wasn't sure where. My hands were red, and the tips of my fingers were a little white. I kept rubbing them together.

We hadn't touched yet, but Jasper noticed, and while we were waiting for a light to change so we could cross the street, he grabbed my hands in his and cupped them. Somehow, his hands were warm, but that isn't even what I remember. I felt that same jolt I felt today. It was a jolt that warmed my entire body, and then some. We held hands all the way to the restaurant. And he had been right—I did love it. I don't remember feeling cold again that night or maybe that entire winter when we were together. I also remember that the next day he sent me a bouquet of a dozen red roses.

I stay in the bathroom until someone bangs on the door. Then I wipe my eyes and walk out. There is a line six people deep. Oops. I don't apologize. In fact, I must look pretty awful. But I don't say anything. I don't even look at anybody. I march out and go to the store, where I buy four kaftans and a dress. Retail therapy at its best.

***

AUNT PEARL'S PACKING LIST:
- Sensible sandals
- Your favorite swimsuit
- Passport
- Power adaptor for... Down Under
- Quick dry towel
- Dramamine/sleeping aid for a long flight and water-centric excursions
- Shawl (check the box—it will arrive soon)
- Sundresses
- An underwater camera
- Beach books
- I'll leave the rest up to you...

Chapter Twenty

"Ahhhhhhhhhhhhhhhhhh!"

I smile and hold the phone away from my ear, the kind of smile that feels like it's taking up residence on my face, refusing to budge.

"No way, no way, no way," she squeals. "Is this for real?"

Funny, that's exactly what Billie asked. Like there's some universal language of disbelief that transcends generations.

"It is for real," I say, my smile evolving into something that might qualify as a legitimate facial cramp.

"What did I do to deserve such an incredible surprise?" she asks, and I swear I can feel her heart racing through the phone, like some bizarre cardiac Bluetooth connection.

"Well, being the best aunt in the world for starters," I say, suddenly grateful that some relationships just exist without the complicated tangle of conditions.

"Sweetheart, this is too much. I'm so appreciative, but it's too much money." Her voice drops to that place adults go when they talk about finances—a hushed reverence, as if money might hear us and run away.

"Gratefully, I can afford it," I reply, waving my hand dismissively even though she can't see me. "Don't worry about that at all."

"Well, I do. You should save your money," she says, the classic refrain of someone who grew up counting pennies.

"This year has shown me that life is unpredictable and can be shorter than we expect. We should make the most of our time, being together and doing meaningful things while we still can." I'm surprised by the earnestness in my own voice. Nothing like loss to make you sound like a motivational calendar.

"This is my dream trip, you know," she says, her voice softening. "I have always wanted to go to Australia."

"I know. That's why I picked it. I do listen to you, you know," I say, smiling so big I imagine she can hear it in my voice, like emotional echolocation.

"Ahhhhhhhhhhhhhhhhhhhhhhhhhhhhhh!!" she yells again into the phone, and now we are both laughing so hard we're crying, that strange alchemy where joy becomes so overwhelming it leaks out of your eyes.

"When you told me to save the date, I thought, I don't know, something local to me, maybe a little staycation?"

"I'm trying to think bigger these days," I say, still crying and laughing, wiping my eyes with the heel of my hand. "Not that there is anything wrong with a staycation." Though lately small spaces have felt too much like the inside of my own head—cramped and well-worn.

"I'll be ready in thirty minutes," she says, joking. Her laugh bubbles up again, effervescent as champagne. "I'm just bursting with excitement."

I realize I'm not quite ready to go down under just yet. That recent moment with Jasper continues to linger like a phantom limb. I keep replaying it with the obsessive precision of someone checking to make sure they locked the front door. I can still feel the spot on my arm where he touched me, the epicenter of an emotional earthquake. I even wondered this morning if it looked red in the shower, like I had some actual physical reaction to his touch, a sunburn from a star that burned out months ago.

"Me too," I say to Aunt Pearl now, dragging myself back to the present conversation.

"Counting the days!" she exclaims, then adds, "The minutes!"

"We're going to have the best time."

When we hang up, I call Nicolas. "I leave in a week," I tell him. "So, when I get back, you'll be here only for a few more days." My voice does that thing where it tries to sound casual while secretly begging for reassurance.

He waits for me to say more, but I don't. Some silences are like empty frames, waiting for someone to fill them with meaning.

"I know," he says quietly. "Do you want to come over now?"

"Sounds great." My mind is in overdrive, thoughts spinning like a hamster wheel going nowhere. How will I feel being away from him? How will he feel? What will happen when he goes back to London? I commit to not worrying about any of it, to just do my best to enjoy our time together and not race ahead of myself. I laugh to myself as I walk out the door. I've never been good at that before, so could I possibly be good at it now? Probably not, but I guess time will tell. Spoiler alert: Time is notoriously bad at keeping secrets.

***

Aunt Pearl grabs my hand so tightly, squeezing what feels like all the life force from my limb as we feel the plane descending and finally touch down in Sydney. The look on her face is something I will never forget—pure, unfiltered wonder, the kind adults usually train themselves out of showing. I do my best to squeeze back. The flight has been long enough to watch approximately seventeen rom-coms and question all my life choices, but it allowed me to catch up on the movies I've been meaning to watch. Aunt Pearl took the inclusion of a sleep aid on her packing list very seriously. I'm not exactly sure what it was, but she was knocked out for hours, mouth slightly open in the universal expression of deep sleep.

"I can't wait to stand on Australian soil," she says. She is so gleeful, her delight bringing me so much joy that it almost feels stolen. I smile and nod. I'm slowly coming out of my groggy phase after my first Australian coffee, which should probably be considered a controlled substance given its potency.

I stretch and listen to the captain welcoming us to Sydney. I try to pay attention, but my mind wanders to the last seven days with Nicolas. It was like we were at the retreat in Arizona all over again, except with more talking, more getting reintroduced to these newer versions of ourselves, like meeting someone at a high school reunion—familiar yet completely different. We became closer, and I stuck to my commitment to not overthink the whole situation and just enjoy each moment we have together. A personal miracle on par with water transforming into wine.

"I've felt more like myself these past three weeks than I have in the previous three years," he said to me as I left his apartment the morning of our flight. "This has been such a welcome surprise. I've really enjoyed getting to know you, all over again." His eyes held mine, sincere in a way that made my chest tight.

"I feel the same way," I said, because what good would it do to play it cool? But sometimes, I did find myself trying to find the old Nicolas in the new Nicolas. Was he in there? A psychological archaeology dig. And then I would remind myself to just take it one day at a time and trust that who he is showing me is the real him. Trust—the ultimate extreme sport.

"Unless you get swept off your feet by Hugh Jackman, can I see you when you get back?" he asked, letting out a small chuckle while leaning in and gently kissing the top of my head. He breathed deeply, like he was trying to memorize my scent.

"I would like that," I said, deciding not to remind him that it would only be for a few days before he returns to London, back to his regularly scheduled life. Because nothing says 'I'm emotionally available' like pointing out the inevitable end.

I'm now eager to get to the gate and off this plane, which has started to feel like a time capsule I've been sealed in for decades.

"Is that a koala?" Aunt Pearl asks, startling me and grabbing my arm with the urgency of someone who's spotted a celebrity. She is looking out the window to the far edges of the runway.

I giggle to myself before I lean over her and peer out the window. Jasper always thought it was hilarious that every American assumed there were kangaroos and koalas roaming the streets, like we imagined Australia as one giant wildlife preserve with a few buildings sprinkled in for good measure. He often joked that he had them both as pets growing up, which, of course, everyone believed with an earnestness that never failed to delight him.

Aunt Pearl's eyesight must be incredible—or very bad, I'm not sure which. I can vaguely see a bunch of trees about twenty feet to the side of the plane. There is something gray, but it looks tiny. It looks more like a parrot, but I don't want to burst her bubble. I turn to Aunt Pearl.

"Yes," I tell her. "I think it might be." The white lie feels like a gift, small and perfectly wrapped.

Aunt Pearl sits back, still beaming, her face a roadmap of joy.

"I promise we'll see more koalas and wildlife," I say, hoping I'm right, knowing I had a surprise waiting for her at our first hotel.

I did a ton of research about where to stay and what to do, stopping short of calling Jasper to ask his advice, a restraint that deserves some kind of medal. I was torn between a very nice-looking Park Hyatt right in the city that had views of the Opera House and the Harbour Bridge, and a wildlife retreat just out of town. I was tempted to choose the Hyatt, but then I thought, we could stay at a Hyatt anytime. The retreat looks awesome, and it is a nonprofit, so we're supporting the wildlife while there. It's connected to an actual zoo, and we can walk to it from the hotel. The rooms look amazing, and we have a reservation at the restaurant tonight. We'll spend two nights there, and then begin our journey to the Great Barrier Reef, which, after seeing the Australian animals, Aunt Pearl told me has been on her bucket list since she can remember.

We slog through the airport, and all I want to do is lie down in the nearest corner like a discarded sweater, but Aunt Pearl is riveted by everything—the way the air smells, the people, their accents, and the colorful signs lining the terminal. Her enthusiasm is contagious, and my fog is clearing quickly. I still haven't told her much about our trip, so once we're settled in the cab, I turn to her. She has been so game, just completely ready to follow me anywhere, like we're on some grand scavenger hunt and she trusts I have all the clues.

"So, we're staying at a wildlife hotel for the next two nights," I say, and her eyes light up like I've just handed her the moon. "We can rest a little when we get there, and then we have a sanctuary tour and dinner. It is fancy but also rustic."

"Wowza," Aunt Pearl says, and I laugh, loving how her vocabulary sometimes seems to belong to a 1950s comic book character.

As we pull up, we're greeted by a woman who is so warm she could melt chocolate from across the room, and she leads us into the lobby. It is perfect and elegant, with amazing chandeliers and sleek furniture, but it gives the illusion that we are also outside, like the trees and the flowers were invited in for coffee and decided to stay. We have a view here, too, of the city and the Opera House. It is farther away than the Hyatt would have been, but we can get there pretty quickly. I think it is about a ten- or fifteen-minute drive. Tomorrow, I have a driver reserved to take us all around the city.

We are shown to our room. I chose the tree-top suite versus the 'roar and snore' tent since neither of us are campers, and I'm so happy to see, it looks even better in real life than in the pictures, like a Pinterest board that somehow learned to exist in three dimensions. I can almost see the cloud Aunt Pearl is walking on as she races to the full-length windows overlooking the zoo. In this moment, there is no place I would rather be.

The sanctuary tour is everything I could have asked for. We see koalas (which Aunt Pearl coos at like they're newborn babies), emus, wombats, the laughing kookaburra, and a plethora of Australia's greatest hits of animals. Aunt Pearl loves them all and asks our guide where she can make a donation.

"Let me do that," I say gently.

"You're doing too much," she says, her eyes soft. "Emerson, I can't explain how much joy I'm feeling right now."

"Me, too," I say, and it's true. There's something healing about watching someone else's dreams come true.

We had talked about not taking a nap and just pushing

through, but when we get back to the cool room, the beds call to us with a siren song impossible to resist. The day-one jet lag Reddit warned me about is becoming our reality, a sleep debt collector banging on our door.

"Let's just rest for ten minutes," Aunt Pearl says, and I'm relieved because I feel like I could sleep for three or four days, possibly emerging with a new personality.

The next thing we know, something rings somewhere, and Aunt Pearl stumbles to answer the phone next to the bed. I have a quick flashback to Sedona and Mariah, and I sit up fast, my heart skipping like it's being chased. We've clearly missed something, but what and how much is unclear.

"Oh yes," Aunt Pearl says, not sounding flustered at all. "We are on our way."

I look at her with raised eyebrows.

"We are twenty minutes late for dinner, but they are holding our table. Quick, get dressed!"

"This place is supposed to be delicious," I say as I slip into my favorite silk blouse, the one that drapes beautifully across my shoulders, and pair it with my tailored wide-leg pants. I check my reflection one more time, smoothing the fabric and adjusting how it falls. The outfit makes me feel put-together and confident. I run a brush through my hair and swipe on my bold red lipstick. "The best seafood in all of Sydney, or so the website told me."

"Can't wait!" Aunt Pearl says. Somehow, she looks perfect and not like she just woke up from a two-hour 'nap'. I smile, and we are out the door. I have definitely learned my lesson. Our first-night dinner should always be at the hotel for this very reason. But this place—called Me-Gal—is supposed to be otherworldly. Aunt Pearl hooks her arm through mine, and we walk the path to the restaurant. It is similar to the rest of the hotel—elegant but also rustic in a luxurious sort of way, like someone built a five-star restaurant in a very expensive treehouse. We are led to a table that offers a distant but perfect view of the harbor and the Opera House. We both sigh as we take our seats and then we laugh, not believing that this is our life right now. We decide to do the feast, which is like a tasting menu, and we sit back and look around, taking it all in.

There's someone at the table next to us who looks awfully familiar from behind, the way her hair rests on her shoulders, the way her neck and hands move as she's dramatically laughing at what the person at her table just said. I tell myself I'm being crazy. We aren't in New York. We're in Sydney, Australia! I don't know anyone here. The statistical probability is roughly the same as winning the lottery while being struck by lightning while spotting a four-leaf clover.

But I am so wrong because the person stands up and turns, possibly looking for the bathroom or the bar, and my heart sinks like a stone thrown into still water. I look around, wondering if I can somehow disappear. Maybe I can crawl under the table. Or simply evaporate.

"Sweetheart, what is it?" Aunt Pearl asks, concerned.

"I'll explain in a minute," I whisper.

Just as I say that, she sees me, and her eyes go wide. It is Jasper's mother, Stella. I know she lives in Sydney—of course I do—but never in a million years did I even think about the chance that we would run into each other. And here? It is very nice, but it also feels a little touristy. I mean, what are the chances? The universe has a sick sense of humor sometimes.

"Emerson?" she asks, coming closer. "Emerson Bailey?"

I stand and hope she can't tell that I'm shaking. It's a

Pavlovian response, I think, the way I used to feel the few times I met her. She is so put together, so formal, that it always feels like I am a messy American when I am with her, which is not a usual feeling for me, so it always surprises me. Maybe I just thought she didn't think I was good enough for her son. She must be happy now, vindicated in her silent judgment.

"Stella," I say, accepting her rather warm hug and a kiss on each cheek. She is smiling, and it looks like a genuine smile, not the kind adults give children when they've made an ugly drawing.

"I can't believe it," Stella says. "What in the world are you doing all the way over here?"

"Oh," I say, gesturing toward my aunt. "This is my Aunt Pearl. We're on a trip together."

"How lovely," Stella says. "When did you arrive?"

"Just today," Aunt Pearl replies. "And Emerson is being modest. She is treating me to this trip. The trip of a lifetime! She is granting my wish." She says this with such pride that I feel myself blush.

"Well," I say, and then I realize I have been very rude, the social misstep making me flush hotter. "Oh, Aunt Pearl," I add in a rush. "This is Stella. Jasper's mother."

I can see the flash of surprise in her eyes, but she quickly adjusts and holds out her hand, smooth as silk. "How nice to meet you," she says.

We talk a bit about the magnificent venue, and I keep expecting Stella to say she has to get to the bathroom or back to her table, but she seems in no hurry to do either, like this bizarre reunion is the highlight of her evening. Finally, Aunt Pearl says she is going to run to the ladies' room. To my great surprise, Stella moves to take her seat when she leaves.

"Can I sit for a moment?" she asks when she's practically already seated. What am I going to say? No? That would require a level of confrontation I'm not capable of after a 20-hour flight.

"Sure," I say. "Please." I straighten my posture like I'm suddenly being graded on it.

"It is so nice to see you, Emerson." She reaches across the table and pats me on the hand.

Had I been wrong about her? She seems completely different from the image I remember in my mind. She was always vaguely cold and seemingly uninterested, like I was a boring documentary she was forced to watch.

Now, she gazes at me eagerly across the table. "You've been on my mind so much lately," Stella says.

"I have?" The idea of Jasper's mother thinking about me is as bizarre as discovering your goldfish has been keeping a diary about you.

She cocks her head slightly and clears her throat. "Jasper told me everything," she says gently. "I know you've broken up, and I also know about the baby. What a terrible loss. I am just so sorry for all of us."

I feel the burn of tears, and I will them away, like I'm mentally pushing back the tide. I worry it's my turn to talk now, that I should say something back to her, but I can't think of any words. Also, I can't find my voice, like it's gone on vacation without me. I'm grateful when it's clear that Stella has more to say.

"I might not have been able to admit it then, but you were incredibly good for Jasper. He truly became more of himself when he was with you. I had never seen him that happy."

I am so taken aback that I almost don't know what to do. What in the world is she talking about? This feels like being told

I've won an award for a contest I don't remember entering.

"It's true," she says when I still don't say anything.

"What?" I manage to croak out. "No, I mean, I don't know if that's true. With some space and perspective, I can see I wasn't really that good for him, or maybe I wasn't good enough to him. I fear I was closed off and often emotionally unavailable. Always putting the company before him."

Did I just say that? To Jasper's mother? I've had these thoughts, of course, but I have never said them out loud before. It's like watching yourself sleepwalk off a cliff.

Stella smiles, pats me again on the hand. "Honey, nobody is perfect."

For a brief moment, I feel like a huge weight has been lifted, like Stella finally sees me and has given me permission to be myself. But what does it even matter anymore? Anything I did or didn't do for Jasper is in the past, a museum exhibit I can't edit. I can see Aunt Pearl making her way back to the table. I wait for Stella to notice, and as soon as she does, she jumps up and apologizes for taking her seat.

"No need to apologize," Aunt Pearl says kindly.

Stella bows slightly toward her and then comes around and gives me another hug. She then goes back to her table, leaving me sitting there with the emotional equivalent of whiplash.

"What was that about?" Aunt Pearl asks just as a beautiful plate of oysters arrives at our table. We ooh and aah for a second as the server tells us in the most beautiful accent where each one is from.

"I'm so sorry. That was odd. She seemed to actually, I don't know, to like me, which was not how she made me feel the handful of times I met her before. Anyway, let's move on. We have food to devour, and nothing is going to interrupt our evening. This trip is all about you," I say, mentally shoving Stella's words into the deepest, darkest corner of my mind.

Aunt Pearl leans in for a side hug. "That's the thing about wishes," she says. "They don't always go the way you expect. Sometimes, they show up for the person who was least expecting it."

"Oh no," I respond, shaking my head. "I think you're reading too much into it. It was unexpected and slightly strange, sure, but there's no hidden meaning to this encounter. There is nothing left between me and Jasper."

My voice trails off as I absentmindedly touch the spot on my arm where he touched me, a gesture as revealing as a poker tell. I shake it off and reach for an oyster, determined to focus on the present moment even as the past lingers like a ghost at our table.

Chapter Twenty-One

Aunt Pearl grabs my arm and squeals for the fiftieth time since we arrived. I smile, throw my head back, and laugh because, honestly, she might be the best travel companion in recorded history. She appreciates every single detail of this trip with the unbridled enthusiasm of someone who's spent decades dreaming of paradise and suddenly finds herself standing in it.

She points out the window of the plane, and then it's my turn to squeal—a sound I haven't made since approximately third grade. It's our first glimpse of the Great Barrier Reef as we make our descent into Cairns, all swirls of impossible blue and green like God went a little crazy with the watercolors. We don't actually go to the reef until the day after tomorrow—I have an amazing private tour set up that will let us do as much or as little as we want. We're both definitely still dealing with jet lag, but I have a feeling Aunt Pearl will opt for the do-and-see-everything option, possibly while dressed in full scuba gear. Today, we're going to Kuranda, where we'll relax and settle in, and tomorrow, we'll go to the rainforest.

I chose the Reef House because it's adults-only, and while we both love children, I didn't want to be surrounded by them all day, splashing us in the pool or having a meltdown during an otherwise relaxing dinner where I'm trying to pretend I'm the kind of sophisticated woman who knows which fork to use first. There are multiple pools, a spa, restaurants, and the rooms look divine—like something from a magazine spread titled 'Places You Can't Actually Afford But Will Go Into Debt For Anyway'.

As soon as we get there, Aunt Pearl is so taken with the big pool—a shimmering expanse of blue that looks like it was poured directly from the sky—she says she just wants to sit here all day. So we get comfortable, breathe the amazing fresh air that somehow smells like flowers and saltwater at the same time, and I log into the Wi-Fi, which I haven't done in a while.

It takes a second to load, and I immediately regret going online like I've broken some sacred vacation commandment. The first thing I see is an email from Jasper. I glance around to see if Aunt Pearl happens to be looking over my shoulder, but her eyes are closed, and she looks about as relaxed and content as I have ever seen her—like someone photoshopped all her worries away. I, on the other hand, immediately feel my pulse quicken and my shoulders tense like they're preparing for impact. Why did I have to look? Honestly, it could be about anything. And I certainly don't need to deal with it while I'm in paradise, trying my best to be a woman who has her life together. I snooze the email, decide I don't have to look at anything else, and close my laptop. But I can't shake it. I spend the next two hours wondering what Jasper could have possibly wanted, the question lodged in my brain like a splinter. The subject line only said *Hey!* with an exclamation point that feels both aggressive and insufficient.

"Do you want to explore?" Aunt Pearl asks me with a twinkle in her eyes that suggests she's already mentally mapped out the entire resort.

"Sure!" I say, happy to have the distraction from the Jaspershaped cloud hanging over my otherwise perfect day.

The grounds are beautiful and have the feel of a tropical garden designed by someone who really, really loves plants. Every tree, every flower, every path seems deliberately placed to make you gasp at regular intervals. Everyone we encounter is smiling like they're all in on some wonderful secret. We walk by the mineral pool, where an aqua aerobics class is in full swing — a dozen or so retirees moving their arms in perfect synchronization like a school of particularly cheerful fish. Some people are riding bikes on paths we cross, their hair blowing in the wind, looking like they're filming a commercial for living your best life.

"Miss! Missus!" someone calls our way.

We both turn, and there is a woman, smiling big, with a tray in her hand. She runs toward us, careful not to spill what is in front of her, her movements so graceful she might as well be dancing. As she gets closer, I see there are two beautiful pink drinks with fruit on the side — the kind of drinks that show up in Instagram photos hash tagged #blessed.

"We have been looking for you," the woman says breathlessly. She is wearing a cotton dress with a name tag that reads Aria. "You got away from us when you checked in earlier, and we never got to give you your welcome drinks."

She smiles as she first hands one to Aunt Pearl and then one to me. It feels cool in my hand, beads of condensation sliding down the side like tiny diamonds.

"What is it?" I ask.

"Well, it is our little secret," she says with a wink that makes me wonder if I'm about to drink something that will make me see through time. "But the alcohol in it is gin."

I'm not so sure. Their little secret? But before I have a chance to say anything to Aunt Pearl, she has finished the drink and is moving the pink straw through the ice so she can get every last drop, like a prospector panning for liquid gold.

"Delicious!" she says, handing the now-empty glass back to Aria. "Thank you!"

They both look at me expectantly. I hesitate for a second, then I pull the straw out of the glass and drink it down, all of it, feeling the sweet-tart liquid slide down my throat with dangerous ease. I wipe my mouth, put the straw back in, and hand it to Aria. She looks very pleased, like she's just successfully initiated me into a cult I didn't know I was joining.

"That was exquisite," I tell her. "Thank you."

She bows slightly. "If there is anything else you need, please find me," she says. She backs away, and when she is about four feet from us, she turns and disappears behind a wall of foliage like some kind of botanical ninja.

"I could get used to that," Aunt Pearl says, hooking her arm through mine. "Now that we're fortified, let's continue on our mission."

"Our mission?" I ask, wondering if the drink has already gone to my head.

She stops and looks at me, mischief in her eyes that makes her look twenty years younger. "Did you see that man when we checked in?" she asks. "He had that gorgeous head of white hair and was wearing a red Speedo?"

"Um, no," I say, mentally thanking the universe for that small mercy.

"He smiled at me," she says, her voice dropping to a conspiratorial whisper. "I know lots of people are here with their special someone, but I just have a feeling. I want to find him and see if he's by chance here alone."

That is one part of her dream vacation I had not orchestrated, and if I can help my aunt find vacation romance, I am all in. We continue to wander through the grounds. The flowers look even brighter now that I've had my welcome drink, their colors cranked up to eleven like someone adjusted the saturation on reality.

"Have you ever seen anything that pink?" I ask Aunt Pearl, and she can't remove the smile from her face. We round the corner, and we encounter a pool we haven't seen before. Next to it is a beautiful bar with a thatched roof that looks like it belongs on the cover of a travel magazine. There is a man flipping bottles, and I think of Tom Cruise in the movie *Cocktail*. The bottles catch the light and somehow make kaleidoscope patterns. It is mesmerizing, like watching a magic show where the magic is just really good coordination and upper arm strength. Aunt Pearl is mesmerized, too, and I wonder if this is one of the activities listed on the resort's website or if we've stumbled into someone's very specific fantasy.

"Come on," Aunt Pearl says, tugging at me. "Why are you just standing there?"

She nods toward the bar, and there is the Speedo man. You can't miss him. He has thick white hair and the brightest red bathing suit I have ever seen—the kind of red that makes you wonder if it's visible from space. He is tan and has incredibly defined abs that look like they were carved from mahogany. He is drinking what looks like a piña colada—it is light yellow, icy, and delicious-looking, like summer in a glass.

"Can I have one of those?" I say to the bottle-slinging bartender. He looks up and smiles. Everyone here smiles like they're contractually obligated to.

"You can come closer to the bar," he says gently. I look

around. I stopped about ten feet too soon, standing awkwardly in the open like I'm lost or conducting an invisible orchestra.

"Oh, right, sorry," I say, and I hear an Australian lilt in my voice. I must be picking up the accent. Jasper would get a kick out of that. I shake my head to dislodge the thought and take a seat on one of the barstools. I pat the stool next to me, which just happens to also be next to Speedo guy. Aunt Pearl takes the seat gracefully, like she's been planning this moment since we left home.

"Can I buy you a drink?" Speedo guy says to Aunt Pearl, and I feel a rush of vicarious triumph.

I want to take credit for it, but I can't. Instead, I accept the drink the bartender made, put it on our room tab, and I duck away, back to our original poolside chairs, which are only a little hard to find in my gin-fuzzy state, and my laptop, which thankfully is right where I left it, tucked into my beach bag like a sleeping creature. I sip the drink and pretend I'm not going to read Jasper's email for about three minutes, which is approximately two minutes and fifty seconds longer than I actually resist. Then I open my computer and can't find the email. It takes me a tipsy second to remember I snoozed it for this exact reason, so I wouldn't be tempted, but I find it and click on it like ripping off a Band-Aid.

I talked to my mom, and she said she ran into you. You seemed different, she said. I'm intrigued. I still can't believe you're there without me, but I guess you never know how things are going to turn out. Well, I just wanted to say hello. Cheers, Jasper

I read through the email six times, looking for something, some clue about what he wants or what he means, analyzing it like it's a cryptic message that will reveal the secrets of the universe if I just stare at it hard enough. She said I seem different? Is that true? And if so, how? What does seeming different have to do with it? Was I not good before? But, of course, I know the answer to that. I was not good before. That's a big reason why we broke up. It's true, I think drunkenly to myself, and I decide I better go check on Aunt Pearl before I do something stupid like reply.

I get lost twice trying to find the other pool and the bar and wonder briefly if it doesn't exist, if it was some sort of Australian Brigadoon that appears only once every hundred years, until I come upon it from a different angle. The bartender is still there, flipping the bottles, even though there isn't anyone watching him, like a tree falling in the forest that doesn't need to be heard to make beautiful patterns in the air.

"Hey, did you see a woman here, and a man with thick white hair? They were here not too long ago? Drinking?"

"Ah, yes," he says, setting a bottle down and looking at me. "They went for a walk. They left about ten minutes ago."

Chapter Twenty-Two

It takes about twenty frantic minutes to hear back from Aunt Pearl. *All good,* she finally texts. Then, strangely, *Fantasy Island!*

"Um, okay," I say out loud, because even I know Fantasy Island isn't really what it sounds like, that all those fantasies went terribly wrong. Like a wish monkey's paw, but with more humidity and tropical drinks. I want to drop it and let her have at it, but I can't take the chance.

First, I go to our room—not sure what I'm expecting—but it's empty. Obviously, I don't know where his room is, but I'm prepared to ask the front desk for a wellness check, possibly exaggerate a family emergency, when I come around the corner and see them walking hand in hand down the path. She's laughing, and he is smiling down at her. *Hmmmm.* He could just be drawing her in before he makes his move.

This is ridiculous. And Aunt Pearl is a big girl. I turn, thinking I'll leave them alone and hope for the best, but my foot catches on a vine and I go down hard. There is nothing subtle or discreet about it. Luckily, I do not hit my head. But my knee doesn't feel great. I don't even want to look. They are at my side in an instant.

"Emerson," Aunt Pearl says. "Jack, this is my niece, Emerson;

Emerson, this is Jack. What happened? Oh, you're bleeding."

Jack runs off, and I think, *Well, at least we nipped that one in the bud*, but then he's back with a first-aid kit, and he is gently cleaning my knee and putting ointment on it.

"I was a medic," he explains in a gorgeous lilting accent that makes every word sound like a line of poetry. "It sticks with you. Here, straighten your leg slowly if you can."

He gently feels around and moves my calf up and down, bent and straight, testing my knee like he's tuning an instrument.

"Nothing's broken," he says confidently. "Let's get you up and to a chair."

Once it's determined I will, in fact, live to embarrass myself another day, the three of us spend the rest of the day together. Jack is pretty nice and at least appears to be a very kind man. He keeps asking Aunt Pearl if she wants anything—water, shade, a small tropical island—and we decide, since I am now too foggy and slightly injured to take the lead, we'll have dinner together at one of the hotel restaurants.

Eventually, I trust him enough to leave them alone, and I go back to our lovely room to nap and shower. About thirty minutes before dinner, Aunt Pearl appears to get ready. She comes and sits next to me on my bed. Our perfect room has two queen beds, a view of the lush grounds, and a fruit basket—it is exactly what I hoped for. It feels like heaven, and as I think that, I see Luna's face, and I start to cry.

"Oh, sweetie," Aunt Pearl says. "You've been funny all day, ever since you had that welcome drink—or maybe even before. What's going on?"

"I'm so sorry. This is not about me. It's about you. How's Jack?"

Aunt Pearl smiles. "Jack is intriguing," she says, and I know in that instant they did not go back to his room for an afternoon delight—at least not yet. "But, sweetie, you have to stop saying this is about me. It is about us—being together. Did something happen?"

Now I am crying full out, and honestly, it feels good, like releasing a pressure valve I've been keeping tight for too long. "I really miss Luna," I say quietly. "It's hard to believe I'll never see her again, never be in the same room with her. She's just... gone."

Aunt Pearl folds me into her arms and lets me cry. She rubs my back soothingly. "I know, I know," she says. "Grief is the awful price we pay for love."

We sit there for a while, and I cry and cry. Aunt Pearl keeps soothing me, saying those same things over and over again, her voice a steady anchor in a storm. Finally, I sit up straight, wipe my eyes, and breathe deeply.

"I'll do my best to keep it together." I wipe my nose with a floral-scented tissue that smells like someone's grandmother's powder room. "I hear you, I really do, that this trip is about us, but it is also about you—I want it to be everything you've hoped for."

Aunt Pearl gently grabs my arms and turns me to face her. I look at her. "Your happiness matters to me, too," she says softly. "Is there something else going on? Not that missing Luna isn't enough, but I just feel like something changed for you today."

Aunt Pearl is so smart. You can't fool her. She has emotional radar that could pick up a feeling from space.

"Jasper emailed," I confess. "He spoke to his mother, who told him she saw me, and so he wrote."

"What did he say?" Aunt Pearl asks neutrally, her face a

perfect poker mask.

I pull up the email and read it to her. She nods.

"Nice," she says.

"I guess," I say, like a moody teenager instead of the forty-year-old I technically am.

Aunt Pearl points to my inbox. "There are more."

He has written two more times. This is so weird. Like watching someone perform a dance you've never seen before.

I click on the top one, which also has the subject line of *Hey!* I guess I thought it was the same email as before.

It's funny to think of you in Australia. Does everyone sound like me?

I furrow my brows and look at Aunt Pearl. "Is he flirting? Or maybe he was doing a late-night writing session with a few too many beers?" I ask her.

She also furrows her brows. "Maybe?" She points to another email from Jasper with the same subject line.

What would my wish be?

We both look at that one for a long time, like it's written in hieroglyphics, then I snap my computer shut. We go to the restaurant, where Jack is waiting for us, no longer wearing just his Speedo, which I consider a minor victory.

"How's your knee?" he asks right away.

"Better," I say. I hadn't even thought of it since it happened. "Thanks to you."

***

Over the next few days, Jasper writes more short, pithy emails.

Say hi to the fish for me.

Say hi to the koalas for me.

When people say barbie, they don't mean the movie.

And on and on like that. Little breadcrumbs of communication that I can't quite figure out.

I find myself looking forward to them, but I don't respond. Aunt Pearl and I do everything we planned—the rainforest the next day, the reef the day after that—and Jack comes with us, which I like. He's a great guy, and his charm and thoughtfulness remind me of Jasper—the way he notices small things and anticipates needs before they're spoken. On the last night, Aunt Pearl comes to find me as I'm brushing my teeth in the bathroom.

"Hi, sweetie," she says. "Listen, would you mind if I spend the night at Jack's?"

I finish brushing and walk over to her, trying not to look too stunned. Aunt Pearl, you dark horse.

"I don't mind. But you'll be careful? You feel safe with him?"

"I love you for asking those questions," she replies. "And I do."

Once she's gone, the room is so quiet like being alone in a church. I pull up Jasper's emails and read through them. I have not answered a single one, but I realize his voice has been in my head since he began to write. I did say hi to the fish for him, and all the animals we've seen along the way. But the one I keep coming back to is *What would my wish be?*

Just as I'm wondering what he means exactly, another email pops up. This is really so unlike him. I am beginning to wonder if he's sick like Luna and just acting recklessly and saying anything because he now has nothing to lose. I worry that everyone I love or have ever loved is going to get sick and die. With that revelation, I feel like the air has been sucked out of me, like I'm suddenly in a vacuum. I don't read Jasper's new email, but I click reply on the one about a wish, and I write, *Are you okay? I am really asking.* I wait, but nothing comes. Finally, I click on his most recent email. It says simply, *Where would you send me on my trip of a lifetime?*

I let myself imagine it for a few seconds. I know without question that it, like Luna, does not exist in this world. But still, I let myself picture a trip with me, Jasper, and the baby. We would go to a resort, but an easy resort, maybe one in the Florida Keys. It would be upscale, like a stay at the Four Seasons or Ritz-Carlton, and we'd spend the whole day relaxing by the kiddie pool. We would eat at the hotel restaurant every night, where they would have an elegant highchair and farm-to-table baby food served in tiny porcelain dishes. And we would drive around during naptime so she could sleep. We would stop for ice cream, and Jasper and I would take turns getting out of the car to order.

I'm not crying, even though my longing feels so real I could almost touch it. It's the ghost of a future that never was. Instead, I keep going, imagining nights when the baby is asleep, and Jasper and I order room service and eat it on our balcony: hamburgers, steaks, scallops, and shrimp scampi—all the foods I wasn't supposed to eat when I was pregnant. I see a new email come in out of the corner of my eye. It is Jasper's reply to my reply. I click on it, and my phone rings. I imagine it is going to be Jasper. I read his words before I answer.

I'm okay. Mostly.

"Mostly?" I say into the phone.

"Emerson?"

It's Nicolas, not Jasper, and I quickly snap out of my thoughts, pulled back to reality like a fish on a line. "Nicolas!"

"I was getting worried about you," he says, but he says it nicely. "I haven't heard a word from you."

"Sorry, I know, the Wi-Fi has been really bad," I explain—everyone's excuse everywhere for being out of touch. "I'm surprised you could reach me now. How are you?"

"Is that really it? The Wi-Fi?" he asks, not buying my excuse for a second.

"No," I admit. "I guess I just haven't wanted to deal with what is coming next for us, and I don't know, being this far away has made it easier to put off. I just feel sort of suspended in time and space."

He's quiet for a minute, and I wonder if I've been too honest, if I've ruined something precious by telling the truth.

"Can you hear me?" I ask, more urgently than I mean to.

"Yes, sorry. I need to tell you something. I feel like, by not responding, you somehow knew something was up. I'm back in London, at least for the time being. Reuben's been struggling a lot. He was in the hospital for a few days—nothing too serious—just sick and dehydrated, but we're thinking it was stress-related. My wife asked me to come back because of that, but honestly, I'd already been considering it. I want to be clear—this isn't about you."

I brace myself to feel sad, upset, or frustrated that he didn't tell me before he left. But then I remember he called and texted—he clearly tried to. And surprisingly, I don't feel sad, upset, or frustrated at all. Am I… relieved? Is this what closure feels like?

"I am not saying she and I are going to work things out," he says quickly when I don't say anything. "I'm in a hotel for now, not at the house. But at least I can see Reuben every day, and Hannah. Reub is home and recovering. He's well enough, in fact, that he's coming to spend the night with me."

"It's okay, Nicolas."

"It is? I worried, I don't know, that you would say 'same old

Nicolas'."

"The opposite, actually," I tell him. "You're doing the right thing."

We're both quiet for a few seconds. I can hear people talking outside my room. They sound happy and possibly a little drunk. Celebrating a life I'm not living.

"Are you there?" Nicolas asks.

"Yes, sorry, there was noise outside my hotel room."

"How is it?" he asks as if he just remembered. "How's the trip?"

"It's good," I say, hoping Aunt Pearl is having the time of her life with Jack. "It's really good."

"What you're doing, Em, it's really special," Nicolas says. I hear a knock on his end. "Oh, Reub is here, I better go."

"Nicolas?" I call out to him quickly.

"Yes?"

"We can be friends, right?"

I hear the knock again.

"Definitely," he says, then, "Em?"

"Yes?"

"Thanks for granting my wish. I loved our time together. This might sound corny, but I think it gave me what I needed to come back here. I don't feel as angry at my wife for what she did. I don't know why exactly."

"Have fun with Reuben."

"I will," he says, and he sounds happy.

After we hang up, I briefly consider calling Jasper to ask what he meant by being 'mostly okay'. Is there a part of him that isn't? But I don't. Maybe one day we'll be friends like I hope Nicolas and I will be. I wonder if it'll take as long for me and Jasper. I'm not sad that Nicolas went back to London. He was exactly what I needed, and I'm grateful our paths crossed again. It's also a relief that someone I once thought of as awful seems so good now.

I head toward the balcony, thinking I'll sit out there for a few minutes, away from my computer and phone, when I hear the key card at the door. It's Aunt Pearl, her cheeks flushed and eyes sparkling like a teenager after prom night.

"Hi!" She waves. She looks a little tipsy, happy-drunk in a way I haven't seen her before.

"Hi!" I say back. "Did things not go so well with Jack?"

"Things went wonderfully well with Jack," she admits, and I think I see her cheeks get even pinker. "But I want to be with you on our last night. He completely understood."

I go to her and hug her, and I find I'm crying again.

"Oh, darling," she says. But she doesn't push me, and I'm glad. I don't even know why I'm crying. So many reasons, all of them colliding like atoms in a particle accelerator. I don't apologize this time. I just cry.

"Do you want to drink a bottle of wine out on the balcony?" she asks.

"You literally read my mind," I say, smiling and crying at the same time.

We settle in our seats, the breeze warm and fragrant around us, like we're being wrapped in an expensive perfume.

"This has been the best week of my life," Aunt Pearl says.

"I'm glad," I say, wondering if it has really been her best week. Regardless, it has undeniably been a wonderful week. One that we will always remember.

Aunt Pearl leans back, closing her eyes, her glass of wine resting on the table beside her. I have a lot on my mind, but it feels selfish to bring it up right now. I want this last evening on the balcony to be about her, even though she'd argue otherwise. Before long, her breathing slows, and she starts to quietly snore. She looks so peaceful and serene. I decide to let her rest a bit before gently coaxing her back inside.

"Jasper's been emailing more," I say quietly, knowing she can't hear me. "I started to reply, but I'm going to stop now. I think I need some time alone—to really mourn Evie. It feels like the only way I can ever move forward, to grieve for Luna, for the end of things with Jasper, and now Nicolas being back in London."

I stay quiet for a few minutes to make sure Aunt Pearl is still asleep.

"I came up with this dream trip for Jasper in my head," I continue softly. "It made me a little sad, but I'm done thinking about it now. It's not going to happen, so there's no point dwelling on it. Alright, confession over."

I pull my chair closer to Aunt Pearl and put my head back, close my eyes. Our elbows are touching, and I know I am going to miss her, which, I'm sure, is exactly the opposite of how I'm going to feel when I take the trip with my mother, which is up next.

When we finally go back inside, I see there is another email from Jasper. This time, I don't even look. I ignore it, close my laptop, and go to sleep, Aunt Pearl snoring quietly next to me, her peaceful breathing the only music I need tonight.

Chapter Twenty-Three

I keep having the same conversation in my head; it unfolds like a well-worn argument where neither side ever wins. Why did I think planning a trip for my mother was a good idea? Does she even deserve it? She was basically a ghost throughout my childhood—or if I'm feeling generous, I was simply never her priority. But then I remind myself this isn't about me. It's about the important people in my life, and she is, as my mother, undeniably one of them. Back and forth, back and forth, like a metronome of guilt and obligation.

While I wouldn't say I saved the best for last, there's something almost poetic about this trip being the final one. If there's anything I've learned over these past few months, it's that you can plan until your calendar bleeds ink, and life will still throw curveballs at your head. So, here's to surprises! (And to ducking when necessary.)

Still, the enthusiasm I had for the other trips is nowhere to be found with this one. My mother is clearly one reason, but I'm also brutally aware that this is the last trip. Then what? What will fill the hours that have been consumed by planning these elaborate escapes?

I've never been to the Maldives—a place my mother always spoke about with stars in her eyes—so that will be interesting at least. I pull the packing lists from Billie's and Aunt Pearl's trips and lazily combine them like I'm making a half-hearted playlist. I did check the dates with my mother, so she knows something is brewing, but I decide to send her a sketch of our activities too. While the packing list will come in handy, mysteries only irritate her—a woman who spent her life demanding the spotlight.

Our itinerary reads like a travel brochure fever dream: snorkeling at coral reefs, swimming in crystalline lagoons, waterskiing, Boduberu folk music and dancing, having breakfast on a sandbar, and dinner in exotic places like on a luxury dhoni and—get this—actually underwater. We're staying at spectacular resorts along the way and eating at restaurants that would make food critics weep. I didn't skimp on a single thing, and I feel good about that. You know what they say: if you're doing something for someone, don't do it begrudgingly. Do it with your whole self, or something equally Pinterest-worthy.

Still, it's hard not to remember all the times my mother didn't come through for me: birthday parties where the guest of honor was her absence, school plays where I scanned empty seats, summer days at the pool where I pretended not to notice I was the only kid without a parent.

"Sorry, love," she would call, her voice stretched thin across miles or merely across town. "Love you! Miss you!"

Half the time, she had no idea what she was even missing. She'd be surprised when I told her later about a role I landed or a party we threw. She actually discovered in our local paper that I'd won a poetry award in third grade. Somehow, she'd missed all the conversations about it at home. That about summed it up, and when she mentioned it, despite the fact that I had been working on that poem for weeks, she talked about it almost like she had read some interesting news about a stranger, not her own daughter.

She was always at work or trying to get work. Something about that stops me now. It feels oddly familiar, like looking at my reflection in a funhouse mirror, but I push the thought away. I remind myself that despite everything she did, it never really worked out for her, not the way she'd wanted it to. She's had many, many parts but has never been the star. And I know that realization has finally sunken in for her lately, and she's been having a bit of a hard time. *I can do this*, I chant to myself like the world's least convincing motivational speaker. *I can do this.*

If I could truly grant my mother's wish, it would be to somehow make her a star, finally, or find her that starring role. If I could, I would…maybe. But short of paying someone off to make it happen at this point, which would be the worst possible thing I could do in her eyes, this trip is the second-best gift I can give her.

I scan the packing list and the itinerary with the dates written in bold at the top and email it to my mother with the subject line DREAM VACATION. I wait and wait, and there is nothing—no call, no yelling into the phone, no response at all. I know she checks her email all the time. She still goes to auditions and is always checking in with her manager. When two hours have passed, I call her. She doesn't answer. I call again.

"Hello, sweetheart," she says, her voice deceptively light. "Is everything okay? When you called a second time, I thought it might be important."

She does not say why she didn't answer the first time, and I don't ask because some mysteries are better left unsolved.

"Did you see my email?" I ask.

"Email?"

"Mom," I say, already exasperated. "Remember when I told you to save those dates? Now I'm telling you why."

"Oh gosh, I forgot about that," she says, and I can practically hear her waving her hand dismissively.

I shake my head, but of course, she can't see it, which is probably for the best. "Mom, this is important," I say, thinking Luna would get such a kick out of this. I can hear her saying fucking Ava and shaking her head with a knowing smile that says, some things never change. "I sent an email with the subject line DREAM VACATION. Did you get it?"

"That was you? I deleted it. I thought it was a hoax."

"A hoax?" I ask. "Do you mean a scam?"

"A hoax, a scam, what's the difference?"

"I don't know, Mom," I say, pinching the bridge of my nose. "I'll send it again, okay, while we're on the phone? Let me know when you get it."

I resend it, changing the subject line to THIS IS FROM YOUR DAUGHTER EMERSON because subtlety is clearly getting me nowhere, and I wait.

Finally, a full three minutes later, she says, "Is this for real?"

"Yes. I'm treating you to a fabulous vacation, just the two of us, in the Maldives, just like you always said you wanted to do."

She's so quiet, I wonder if she's still there, and then I realize she's crying. Not the theatrical tears she's perfected for auditions, but something else entirely.

"Mom?"

"Emerson, why? I love you, and I have always wanted the best for you, but to be perfectly honest, I'm not sure I deserve this."

"Why do you say that, Mom?" I push. We never talk about this. It's sacred territory, marked with signs that read DANGER:

DO NOT ENTER.

"Well," she says, and she takes on that tone she has when she's reading a script, "I guess I was bored by many of the childhood milestones."

"I know, Mom." Put on or real, this is not breaking news.

"My point is, you don't have to do this, Emerson," she says.

"I want to do this," I say, wondering as the words leave my mouth if they're true. "I took Billie and Aunt Pearl. You know Luna sent me to that spa in Sedona, which was supposed to be for her. I gave Ryder a perfect day in Manhattan. Now it's your turn!"

"Thank you," she says, sniffling. I think she might be crying a little. Honestly, she's not that good an actress, but I still don't buy it. "I'll start packing."

I don't know what I expected—that she would cancel at the last minute because of an audition or something—but I was wrong. When the day arrives and I tell her to be ready in her lobby so I can come by in the Uber to pick her up, I imagine she will probably still be in her apartment when we get there. I'll have to call her and apologize to the driver, but instead, she is waiting on the sidewalk, a straw hat on her head, a surprisingly small carry-on suitcase by her side.

She kisses me on the cheek and gets in. I want to say, who is this impostor, and what did you do with my mother? But I don't. She has always been good at handling things when she's the focal point and I guess, by design, that's the case here.

Just before I left my apartment, I had a thought. I tried to remember why my mother was so enthralled by the Maldives in the first place, and I finally pinpointed it. When my parents got engaged, they fantasized about going there on their honeymoon. They even met with a travel agent who showed them some amazing resorts. But they didn't have anywhere near the money they needed to go, so they went to the Catskills instead. It was there that my mother got her first call from her manager about an audition, so they cut the trip short by one day. Whenever they made a decision or liked a place, the joke always was, well, it isn't the Maldives, but…

So I found my stack of favorite photos of my father and stuffed them inside the front pocket of my suitcase. I probably won't tell her—that is way too sentimental for her—but I want him with us. As we get out of the Uber and I drag my suitcase from the trunk, I pat the pocket and feel the photos, and they give me comfort. I'm surprised when my mother takes my arm, just as Aunt Pearl had done, and we walk together toward her adventure.

We jumped right in as soon as we landed. We ate dinner at an underwater restaurant, which was like nothing either of us had ever seen before (it was also slightly claustrophobic, like being trapped inside a snow globe), we visited Huvahendhoo Island, and we shopped two days in a row. There was so much to do that it felt like we were running from one thing to the next, and for that, I was grateful. And it was all as wonderful as the guidebooks said it would be, if guidebooks were capable of honesty.

On the last full day of the trip, I planned a snorkeling outing at the Rainbow Reef. It seemed like one of the better excursions, so I decided to save it for the end. I had read about it, and it seemed like a good way to explore the water and get close to the colorful fish. I didn't like most of the organized trips I read about, so instead I booked a private boat with a captain who was also going to be our guide. It was more expensive, but I figured it would be worth it.

As soon as we show up at the dock, I am so glad I did it this way. There are boats overflowing with people; I can't imagine they are adhering to the legal limit. They all look wobbly and overburdened, like floating anxiety attacks. As we get closer, an extremely tan and handsome man walks toward us.

"Emerson Bailey?" he asks in his lilting accent.

"You found us," I say.

"Well, actually, you found me," he says, smiling. "Name's Jim, by the way."

I glance at my mother, who is being unusually quiet. Jim motions for us to follow him to a boat about the size of the others and helps us on, offering each of us his hand. I keep waiting for my mother to make a comment about how good-looking he is; she is not above flirting with someone thirty years younger than she is. Maybe something along the lines of "Who needs to see the fish when there's a hunk right here?" but she doesn't. She stays uncharacteristically quiet. She has been fairly good company, but I don't feel like we've slowed down enough to really talk, which was probably by design on my part. Jim starts the engine.

"So soon?" my mother says, clinging to the side of the boat. Weird. I have never pegged her for not liking boats, and she saw the itinerary and didn't mention anything.

"What's up, Mom?" I ask.

"Nothing, darling." She straightens up and loosens her grip on the rail and I decide I was imagining it. Or maybe she thinks that's how someone is supposed to act at the beginning of a boat ride. You never know with her—her entire life is a performance with no intermission.

I watch as all the other boats go in the same direction, but we go in the other. I walk over to Jim.

"Isn't there just one Rainbow Reef?" I ask.

"Indeed there is. I'm going to show you the best way to approach it. You get the special tour."

I'm not sure what that means, but I try to relax as we move into the ocean. The water is a beautiful shade of blue, and I can already see colorful fish here and there. I can tell the reef is going to be amazing. I can see the other boats stopping and all the people easing themselves into the water. But we keep going, out a bit further and around the other side, and Jim finally cuts the engine. He comes over with a mesh bag full of equipment. It seems like we are in much deeper water than the other boats. Also, the water seems less calm here, choppy with tiny white-capped waves that look like shark's teeth.

"I assume you lovely ladies have both snorkeled before?"

"Um, I haven't," I say, realizing I have no idea about my mother. Not that I know of anyway. I look at her, and she is shaking her head and biting her lower lip like she's trying to hold back words. "That's okay, right?" I ask Jim.

"Absolutely," he says enthusiastically as he looks through the bag and pulls out masks and tubes and flippers and throws them on the floor of the boat. He quickly demonstrates putting the tube through the side of the mask and tells us we can't go down too deep since we don't want to get water in the tube. "It's your air source," he keeps saying, as if we might forget that humans need oxygen. "If it gets foggy, just spit in the mask and rinse it out," he instructs us. "Ready?"

"Um, sure," I say. I'm eager to get into the water. I can see the reef right below us. I can make out some of the colors from up here, like a living kaleidoscope. My mother, meanwhile, has not said a word, which might be a record for her.

"I'll be here watching you," he says. "Go ahead."

I pull off my cover-up and wait for my mother to do the same. I get the equipment set up, ease down the ladder, and throw myself into the water on my back. *Ahhhh. This is good. This is beautiful.* It takes my mother a long time, but she does it slowly, each movement deliberate as if she's being graded. When she reaches me, I can almost hear her breathing; it's like her breaths are shallow and fast, a hummingbird trapped in her chest.

"Are you okay, Mom?"

"Dandy," she says, pulling the mask down and adjusting the tube. She takes one look back at the boat and moves forward, her face in the water. I follow her.

My first glimpse of the reef with my mask on is otherworldly—there are yellow fish and blue fish, and the reef itself is extraordinary, like someone spilled a rainbow underwater. I want to go deeper, but I know I can't; I know I have to keep the tube above the surface. I get lost in it, feeling slight waves take me around a small bend. I think my mother is right behind me so when I see an incredible fish, I turn to wave at her, but she isn't there. I duck my face back into the water and squint my eyes to see if she is somewhere nearby, searching for her legs in the water. Finally, I lift my head, and I see someone waving. That person is pretty far out, and I wonder if they got away from one of the other boats.

"Help!" I hear. I rip off my mask and realize, in that instant, it is my mother. "Please help me!"

I turn and see we have both gotten pulled out by the current. It takes me a few seconds to spot our boat, which now looks tiny in the distance.

"Jim!" I scream. "Jim!"

I try to get to my mother, but it feels like I am moving through molasses, like I am fighting the current. What in the world happened? Could she have gotten bitten by something?

"Please," she's calling. "Help."

Behind us, Jim jumps into the water and moves toward us. I still can't get to my mother, but I'm getting closer. She is bobbing up and down, her mask and snorkel nowhere in sight, and her mouth seems to be taking in water. Every few seconds, she spits and makes a strange gurgling sound. She's never been much of a swimmer, but she was always fine in the water, at least I thought she was. And then from our right side, a tiny motorboat is coming at us fast. It reaches my mother in an instant. I'm pretty sure I saw that boat at the crowded dock when I felt sorry for all of them.

"You're panicking," the driver of the boat calls to her. "Don't try to climb in. You'll tip us. There's a handle on the side, grab on."

What the heck?

The boat reaches her, and she grabs the handle. Her face is completely white, blank as a sheet of paper. She puts her head back.

"Thank God," I hear her say.

"Mom!" I am almost there. Jim is still trying to reach us. I guess I didn't pick the best guide or the best boat, but none of that seems to matter at the moment.

"That's your boat?" the savior asks, pointing.

"Yes," I say.

"You okay?" he asks me.

"I think so."

Now we all make our way back toward our boat. I'm swimming, and the man is slowly guiding the boat that my mother is holding on to with all her might. Jim stopped and is now waiting for us back on the boat. The man pulls his boat right up to our ladder and indicates my mother should climb on, which she does. As soon as she gets on board, she lies on the floor on her back, breathing hard, like a fish out of water (the irony is not lost on me). I have never in all my life seen my mother behave this way—this raw, this unfiltered. I climb up the ladder after her, and Jim gives me a hand, which I take reluctantly.

"Thank you," I say to the man on the boat. I consider asking for his name so I can use his service next time, but I have a feeling I will never do anything like this again.

"Don't mention it," he says, saluting, and he is off, back toward the crowds.

"Mom, what happened? That was so… unexpected."

"I don't know. I was doing okay, and then I was so far out there. And I thought, there is literally no place to put my feet down, and it is so far to anyplace where I could put my feet down. I felt like I was going to die."

"Classic open water phobia," Jim says, as if that's helpful.

I look at him and then back at my mother. I find our bag and get her a towel.

"You're okay now," I tell her. "Why didn't you tell me?"

"I didn't know for sure. That happened only once before."

"It did?" How in the world had I never heard about it? How could I have booked the one thing she was so afraid of, and I didn't know, and she didn't tell me? "I'm so sorry, Mom."

My mother looks at me, pushes herself up from the floor, and throws her arms around me, hugging me in a way that feels like she may never have done before, or at least it seems that way. I am so shocked, and she is so slippery. We both fall back to the floor like a pratfall in a sitcom.

"I'm so sorry, Emerson, I've been a terrible mother," she says in a rush.

"What? No, why are you saying this?"

"Because I almost died! Because my life flashed in front of my eyes."

"You did not almost die, Mom," I say, but did she? If we hadn't been able to reach her, what would have happened? I don't want to think about it.

"I am well aware of my faults," she says quietly, almost to herself. "I was always, always looking outward, never toward you."

I had never thought of it that way, but yes, that is exactly what she was doing. It's like someone has finally handed me the key to a door I've been staring at my whole life.

"Em." She grabs my wrist. "The love you have for a child is terrifying. I knew that going in. It will tear your heart out if you let it. Every single thing—an interaction with a mean kid, an illness, a lost game—can break your heart if you let it. Better to keep busy, to brush by it all. And I was able to do that only because I knew your dad would do what I wasn't doing. He was the best father. He let me, I don't know, escape."

"But you cared about the acting and the parts, right? That was real?"

"Yes, that was real," she admits. "I loved the stage and the attention. I craved it. But it was also a place to hide."

A place to hide. It is like the skies were dark and cloudy, and now they've opened up and there is a torrential rain, a release. It's like I finally understand my own approach, why I was always on my phone when Jasper wanted to share a new song with me or talk to me about his day. What in the world would I have been like with Evie? I sit up and turn away, my heart suddenly too big for my chest.

I feel my mother's hand on my arm.

"Are you okay, Emerson?" she asks, clearly concerned. "This isn't a surprise to you, I know that."

I shake my head. "I'm just like you, Mom. Just like you."

"Maybe," she says, still a little breathless. "But a lot of that is the good part of you, the hardworking, amazing, creative person you have become. You have already had so much more success than I ever will."

"But, I was hiding. Exactly what you said. I was never fully present, or I was so rarely. It, I don't know, it was too bright. I had to protect myself from the glare."

"Exactly," my mother says wistfully. She takes a deep breath like she's preparing to dive underwater again. "There's something else."

"What?" I ask, bracing myself.

"I don't feel I have talked to you properly about Jasper. And the baby."

The loving way she says *and the baby* in that moment, like there was a baby, like for a few minutes or days or months, there was the reality that I was going to be a mother, and she was going to be a grandmother, is almost more than I can take. It's a knife turning slowly between my ribs.

"Properly?" I ask.

"Enough. At all. I just don't feel I've said my piece."

"There's really nothing to say," I tell her. "You know exactly what happened."

"But," she says slowly, "sometimes you lose something very important, the most important, and with it, you lose something you might not have to lose."

The words *it's all lost* roll through my mind like thunder.

"Ready to go?" Jim asks suddenly. He is a very bad guide.

Not only is he interrupting a conversation I never thought I'd have with my mother, one that took her to believe she was almost dying to initiate, but he hasn't even offered us a bottle of water. Customer service: zero stars.

"Yes," my mother says quickly, wiping her face and changing her expression, and, in that instant, I know it is over. I can feel it. That moment, whatever it was, is gone, like sand slipping through fingers.

My mother gets herself up and sits on the bench. I see something change in her eyes. I know we will never talk about this again.

"How old are you?" she says to Jim. "Are you single?"

"You flatter me," he says.

And just like that, I feel so ready to go home. I turn away from them and watch the blue water rush by. I think about how crazy this was, that for about five minutes, my mother felt vulnerable enough to say honest things. And then it hits me, the same way it hit me, how much I'm like her: She is never going to change. Never. I could try and try and try, I could take her on dream vacation after dream vacation, but she is always going to be who she is. And maybe that's okay. Maybe I can finally stop hoping she'll be someone other than who she is. It feels like such a relief.

I sit up and grip the railing tightly. Something else occurs to me. Maybe I can be different. Maybe I don't have to always be the same. I can change. I can do better. In that moment, I vow to be more self-aware, to not spend my life being predictable and selfish. I glance at my mother and silently thank her.

For some reason, that makes me think about Nicolas. He changed. He isn't the same person he was all those years ago. He's doing well back in London, and I am shocked to find myself rooting for him and his wife to make it work. Apparently, she wasn't as in love with the other guy as she had originally thought. He told me in his last text that he's coming back to New York soon to finish up the project he was working on last month. He asked if we could officially be friends. I hearted the message and sent back a smiley face emoji, and I actually meant it, which might be personal growth or just exhaustion.

That leads me to Jasper, who stopped emailing after I stopped responding, and I feel fine about that—or at least, that's what I tell myself. I miss Billie and Ryder, and I have some great ideas for Gerald's company. Even though he is now officially retired, I still plan to stay involved. I look forward to spending some time brainstorming for Gerald's company and maybe getting involved in other businesses, though I have no idea which ones.

I'm worried about getting back and not having something to look forward to, and I'm also eager to get back to some sort of work—I miss it. The longer I put it off, the longer it's going to take to feel any sense of normalcy. I don't know what my schedule will be like or how I'll organize my days, but I guess I'll figure it out. I mean, what other choice do I have?

Once we're back at the resort, we go to our room, drained. I had meant to share the photos of my father with her, but now I decide to keep them for myself. I pat the pocket in my suitcase where they are and silently thank him for being the best father I could ever have. My phone pings, startling me. I haven't gotten a text in days, but now suddenly I have seven unread messages. Three are from Billie saying she misses me, she misses our trip, and she can't wait until I get home. Four are from Ryder with an invitation to some unspecified event. He tells me it's important and that I must save the date.

To Billie, I write, *Miss you, too!*

To Ryder, I write, *What's the event?*

Trust me, Ryder writes back immediately. *And don't be such a busybody.*

Fine, I write back to Ryder. *I'll save the date.*

Whatever it is, I'm happy to have something on my calendar when I get back, an anchor in time.

I am so lucky to have my friends waiting for me at home because it is clearer than ever that my romantic connections are over for now. I try not to think about the spot on my arm where Jasper touched me. That was ridiculous, nothing. Just a ghost of a feeling that refuses to be exorcised.

My phone pings again, and I assume it is Billie or Ryder, but it's Nicolas. I feel like he somehow felt me thinking about him, like some weird cosmic connection that refuses to die.

September 13! he wrote. *Save the date!*

I look at it, go back to Ryder's text to make sure, and then realize it is the date Ryder already asked me to save, strangely. A coincidence that feels too neat to be random.

I write to Nicolas, *Sorry! Already have plans. Another day, maybe?*

I see Nicolas start and stop writing a number of times until he finally writes, *Sure! No prob!* with a smiley face emoji. I heart his message and his emoji, confirm our seats for the plane tomorrow, and turn my phone off for the rest of the night, counting the hours until we can call this trip a wrap.

Chapter Twenty-Four

I've heard of the wedding blues when the wedding is over, and the bride is depressed because all the activity and excitement has evaporated like a puddle in July. But I've never heard of having the wedding blues without having an actual wedding, and I think that's what I have, or at least some mutant version of it.

I didn't expect to be so sad that all the wishes have been granted. No, that's not true. I love that all the wishes have been granted. They were mostly incredible in their own way—even when they appeared to be trainwrecks—but I am sad that the planning and implementation are over. I don't know what to do with myself or how to pass the time. I have work to do for Gerald's company, sure, and I like that, but is that all I'll have to do for the next twenty years? As glad as I am to have that work, somehow I don't think it will be enough to fill the Emerson-shaped holes in my days.

The week stretches out in front of me like an endless beige hallway. I sleep late, partly because I'm tired, mostly because I'm avoiding consciousness. I work on my computer for a few hours, though I have no idea what I actually accomplish most of the time. I eat roasted turkey and broccoli because it's easy and healthy and because, I realize with a start, I am not hungry. Will

I ever be hungry again? Will I ever be busy again? Will I ever not feel like a plastic bag drifting through the wind, wanting to start again? (Great, now I'm quoting Katy Perry lyrics in my internal monologue. This is what rock bottom looks like.)

I wait until 5:00 each evening, and then I pull out my sketchbook and sketch. It is the only time all day the seconds don't drag themselves across the floor like wounded soldiers. I know it is a waste of time, and it isn't going to get me anywhere, but I decide I'll let myself work on my sketches for one hour each day. Before I know it, it is 7:00 or even 8:00, and I look around, thinking, *How did that happen?*

For those few hours while I sketch, I feel hopeful, or at least not desperate, and then I wake up the next morning alone and drifting, and the cycle starts all over again. I keep reaching out to Ryder and Billie to see if they have time to get together, but they are both elusive and full of excuses that sound suspiciously rehearsed. I was so despondent yesterday morning that I even called my mother to see if she wanted to have lunch. Maybe, somehow, we could talk more—like actual humans who share DNA and not just awkward holiday meals.

"Oh, honey, I would love to," she replied. "But I have one audition after another this week. Rain check?"

"Sure, Mom," I'd said, vowing to never look to her for emotional support again and also feeling strangely at peace with that, no longer angry. "Break a leg."

Even though Billie is too busy to see me, she is somehow also in on the plan for Friday and keeps reminding me about it, to not make other plans and to not forget.

"I'm counting the hours," I told her every time she called, once again, to make sure I would be there. "I literally have nothing else on my calendar except 'stare at wall' and 'contemplate existence'."

She laughed, but I was serious. There was no way I was going to forget it, whatever it was. When your social calendar consists of conversations with your houseplants, you don't forget your one actual commitment.

"Where are we going again?" I ask when we're on the phone, and she seems distracted by one or both of her boys making what sounds like a rocket launch in the background.

"No way!" she says every time. "I'm not falling for that. You'll see soon enough."

So now, finally, after one of the longest weeks in the history of human existence, I am getting ready for the mystery event. I don't even care what it is. I'm just glad to have a reason to brush my hair and leave my apartment. Billie told me to meet her in the lobby of her apartment building. I assume we'll go out from there, maybe meet Ryder for dinner. She told me to "look nice", but that was all the direction she gave me. I decided to go all out, and I'm wearing a shimmery gold floor-length gown. I either look really good or like an Oscar statuette with anxiety issues.

I'm here, I text when I get to Billie's lobby. I was given explicit instructions not to just 'come up', like a vampire needing an invitation.

Wait there, Billie texts back with suspicious speed. *Coming down*.

Again, I assume she'll come get me and we'll head out and find Ryder, who has been as hard to pin down as Billie this week. I wander around the lobby, smiling at the doorman, thinking they could use some better art. The current paintings look like something a hotel would buy in bulk.

"Hi!" Billie calls, and I whirl around. "You look beautiful."

She is also dressed up, in a cocktail dress that looks so familiar it almost takes my breath away. Where have I seen that before, and why do I have such a gut reaction to it? I squint at her, trying to figure out where I've seen her dress before. Is it from StyleShop? It is blousy and sits just right at her waist with an open collar that would be good for work or a night out. As I think all these things, I realize with a jolt that it is my design! Or someone else in the world is thinking the exact same way I'm thinking, which seems statistically improbable.

"Where did you get your dress?" I ask, coming closer and feeling the fabric between my fingers. I tug lightly on one of the tips of the collar. Billie just smiles at me, a Mona Lisa smile that says, *I know something you don't know.*

"What is going on?" I ask. She just keeps smiling like the cat that ate the canary, then found another canary for dessert.

"Is that…?" I continue and then stop because she is nodding furiously.

"It's your design," she confirms.

"But how?" I ask. "I never had a sample made. It was just a sketch in my book of impossible dreams."

If it is possible, her smile gets even wider, threatening to split her face in two. "Come with me," she says, walking back toward the elevator.

"I thought we were going out."

"Come with me," she says again, and I feel a little like Charlie being beckoned to follow Willy Wonka into a factory of pure imagination (or possibly doom).

We get into the elevator, and I can't get over the dress. How in the world did she even find it? It's in my sketchbook, which I mostly keep hidden on the high shelf in my closet like a diary or my collection of embarrassing high school photos. For a second,

I'm worried we're going back up to the roof, which I don't want to do. That was Luna's party, Luna's wish, and I don't know that I ever want to go out there again. But before I ask, the elevator stops on Billie's floor, and she gets out. She turns to me and touches my arm.

"It's time for your wish," she says.

My wish?

Without another word, I follow Billie. It is so quiet, I can't figure out what is happening. What sort of wish could be in her apartment? The hall seems longer than ever, like a treadmill that's going backwards, and I feel like we just keep going and going, which I know is overly dramatic but accurate to my emotional state. Finally, Billie stops in front of her door, knocks lightly twice, waits a beat, and then throws it open. She stands back, and I look inside.

I see Ryder first, and he smiles and waves, then I see Aunt Pearl. I spot friends from StyleShop whom I haven't seen in ages. I scan the room for Maddi, and sure enough, there she is. Gerald is also here. I'm shocked when I see Nicolas standing off to the side. He waves when he sees me. Every single person is wearing one of my designs, like I've accidentally stumbled into a parallel universe where I'm actually Vera Wang.

There is a neon sign hanging on the wall that reads STYLE ME SATURDAY, the name of my old fashion blog and what I sometimes, if I've had a little too much tequila, tell my friends I would call a fashion line if I ever had one, always following with some version of "but of course I'm not talented enough for that" or "it's just a crazy dream, like my other dream of marrying Paul Rudd".

There are also mannequins placed around with rough but beautiful renditions of some of my other sketches, some with wineglasses in their fake hands. Two are set up like they are about to kiss. I point to them, and Ryder places his hand over his heart as if to say *that's all him.*

"How?" It is the only word I can get out of my mouth. At my question, Nicolas's smile is the biggest, and then I have a crazy memory of my sketchbook at the retreat in Arizona and how I was so sure I had left it closed, but when I saw it next, it was open. He must have looked through it then. But how in the world did he get the sketches? It wasn't like he could make copies out of thin air. "You did this?" I ask Nicolas.

"Not really," he admits. "I saw the sketchbook, yes, and I had an idea to do something, to make you see how talented you are. So I talked to Billie and Ryder and, well, basically they took it from there."

"How?" I say again. Apparently, it is the only word I know right now, like a toddler who's just learned to talk.

"Well, when you were in the Maldives with your mother, Billie used the key she has to your apartment to go in and get it. She and Ryder made copies and voila."

I shake my head. I literally can't believe it. My friends broke into my apartment to steal my secret fashion designs so they could make them real. This is either the sweetest thing that's ever happened or the beginning of a very niche psychological thriller.

Ryder lets that sit for a second, and then he lifts my hand into the air like I'm a prizefighter who just knocked out the reigning champion. "Presenting the one and only Emerson Bailey, fashion designer extraordinaire and the best darn friend anyone could ever ask for."

Everyone cheers. Ryder leans in to hug me, then he points around the room like there is so much to see, and there is. I notice there are rows of chairs set up in Billie's big living room, and I'm led to the one in the front. Ryder hands me a shot of tequila and stands there until I drink it. And then it begins.

I hear the beats of what I think of as fashion show music—like what plays in my head when I'm trying on outfits in my bedroom—and one by one, beginning with Ryder, everyone walks down a makeshift aisle, doing a flourish turn at the end and coming back. They are wearing my shirts, my dresses, and more casual shirts I've been playing with lately. Some of my friends from work simply carry blown-up sketches, but Maddi is wearing a yellow summer dress that makes her look gorgeous. For a second, I think, *Wow, I'm good*, and then, *Well, a brown paper bag would look good on Maddi, so I shouldn't get too excited*.

I see Ryder waiting in the front of the line and wonder if we've reached the end of the fashion show. I stand, whistling and applauding noisily, but he smiles and waves me down. The music changes. It is still instrumental but slower, slightly less upbeat. I can see him counting in his head, *one, two, three*, and then he is walking again down the runway, holding up a framed photo of Luna wearing a shirt I had made for her years before as a gift.

It is the lightest pink, because she hated pink. But she also loved it and said she wouldn't be caught dead wearing it, but this pink was perfect—not too bright, barely even pink at all. Luna adored it. I try very hard not to think about her comment about being caught dead wearing it, which feels like a cruel joke from the universe now.

I have to look away. I've felt teary since I got here, since Billie said, "It's time for your wish." But now I am a mess. I don't even try to hide it. I just cry openly, not taking my eyes off Ryder and the photo of Luna's face. People start whooping to lift the mood, and I am laughing and crying at the same time, that specific emotional cocktail that makes you feel both completely unhinged and totally alive. Everyone hugs me—my aunt, Ryder, and Billie.

Nicolas comes up to me and smiles. "Happy Wishing Day. Once things settle, let's talk."

"About what?" I ask.

"I want to talk about taking this fashion line to the next level. I have some ideas."

"It isn't exactly a fashion line," I protest. "It's more like a collection of drawings that somehow escaped into the real world."

"It will be if I have anything to say about it."

"Okay," I say slowly, not sure what he has in mind but definitely intrigued. "Thank you."

He leans in close and smiles. "I should thank you. I can't explain it, but I feel like you helped me figure it all out. I just…"

I can see he is struggling to find the right words, so I smile and wave him off. I get it, I really do, and I'm glad. I give him a quick hug. It feels like enough, I think, to both of us.

The evening is all beyond my wildest dreams, my most indulgent wish. In a million years, I never would have thought this could happen. And the funny thing is, I don't think I would have allowed myself to acknowledge that this right here—my favorite people in the world bringing my fashion designs to life and talking about taking it to the next level—is truly my greatest wish.

That's not true—bringing Luna back and giving Evie a chance at life are my greatest wishes. But neither is possible in this world as we know it. Still, I can't help but think that if only Luna could be here, it would be the most perfect night of my life.

If only Evie were somewhere, anywhere, with a babysitter, waiting for me, I would be the happiest person in the world. I'm back to just crying now. I miss them so much. Will it ever not hurt like this? Will grief ever transform from this knife-twisting pain into something softer, like an old bruise that only hurts when you press on it?

Aunt Pearl comes up to me, puts her arms around me. "I'm so proud of you."

I'm crying too hard to talk.

"Your mother wanted to be here, but she had a callback of some sort."

Now suddenly I'm laughing and crying at the same time, then laughing more than crying. A callback? At this hour? But it's okay. It is finally okay. My mother is who she is—a woman who will always choose her career over her daughter—and I don't need to keep hoping she'll transform into someone else, someone who shows up.

Before I have a chance to respond, everyone gets quiet. The slower music is still playing, but suddenly nobody is talking. We all follow Billie's gaze to the door. Jasper is standing there. He is wearing a sweater I designed for him a long time ago, off-white wool with a slightly complicated turtleneck. Everyone moves out of his way as he walks in, moving toward me.

I want to disappear. This is too much. I wanted everything up to this point but not this, not Jasper. They have definitely gone too far. It was perfect, and now it's something else. Friends can't force love to come back to life, no matter how much they think they want to or no matter how much they might believe I want it. But maybe that isn't what they're doing. Maybe they are inviting him into the friend phase of my life.

The upbeat music is back on, louder than before—somehow I know Ryder did that to give us some privacy—and suddenly everyone seems very busy, talking in small groups, trying to give me and Jasper a chance to talk. And I know, despite my thought that we might just be friends, that is not what my best friends want for me. They want more, and I just don't see how that is going to be possible.

Jasper walks over. He leans in for one of our awkward hugs. Again, his touch is electric, like I've stuck my finger in a socket, but in a good way. He's here. He came to my wish. That has to count for something.

"I'm going to go get a drink," he says quietly. "Do you want anything?"

"No thanks," I say, though what I really need is a time machine.

I look around the room at all the people I love, and then I watch Jasper walk toward the bar that Billie set up. He's so thoughtful, giving me the chance to gather myself. He always was so thoughtful. But that's not the problem; that was never the problem. I tell myself to breathe through it. He'll leave soon enough.

And then I notice something surprising. Instead of my heart rate being through the roof, which I would expect after the shock of seeing Jasper, it is slow and steady, calm, like he's having the opposite effect on me than I would have anticipated. Like, instead of bringing chaos, he's bringing peace.

"Huh," I say out loud.

"What?" Ryder says, sidling up next to me. Where did he come from? Probably hiding behind a curtain this whole time, watching his matchmaking unfold.

"Nothing," I say. "But you took it too far. You jumped the shark."

Ryder looks unfazed, smiling like he knows something I don't. "Maybe," he says. "I guess time will tell."

Chapter Twenty-Five

I wander around the room, studying the designs with the intensity of someone trying to memorize a map to buried treasure. Then it hits me all at once—this is what I want to do. It's what I've always wanted to do. I wonder again what Nicolas could have possibly meant by wanting to take it to 'the next level'.

The party is winding down like a music box running out of steam. Aunt Pearl has already bid her goodbyes. Ryder and Billie are doing tequila shots with the determination of college freshmen, and I migrate toward them like a moth to flame. They hand me one, and Ryder counts—one, two, three—and we all drink as if synchronized swimmers.

Jasper materializes behind me, and Ryder hands him a shot without missing a beat. I step back, letting him into our circle, feeling that same unexplainable calm wash over me with him so close. Again, Ryder's silent count, and on three, we all drink. I spill a little and laugh as I wipe the liquid from my chin, feeling it burn all the way down.

"Where's your family?" I ask Billie, suddenly realizing there's been no sign of her boys or husband all night.

"Camping," she says with a decisive nod. "But my kind of camping. They're hanging out at a campsite during the day and retreating to a motel at night. I told them it was too cold to spend the entire night outside."

"Nice," I say. "My kind of camping, too."

The words escape before I can catch them, and I feel my cheeks flush hot enough to cauterize wounds. Camping. The spectacular disaster of our first anniversary trip.

"I'd say not camping is your kind of camping," Jasper says, somehow reading my thoughts like they're subtitles running across my forehead. But he's smiling. There's no snark in his voice, just shared history.

"I'd say you're right," I reply, my lips curving upward against my will.

"Can we talk?" Jasper asks, and the room suddenly feels ten degrees warmer.

I don't know, can we? Should we? But I don't voice any of that. I'm so full—of love and the exhilarating possibility of a new professional direction and the miracle that I was somehow granted my own wish after all the wishes I'd granted—that I just nod, and we retreat to the quiet corner of the living room.

"How did you know?" I ask. "About this?"

"Actually, Nicolas invited me," he says, and I blink like I've just been told gravity is optional.

"How is that even possible?" I ask, feeling like I've missed several crucial chapters in my own story.

"Sometimes things are not as clear-cut as they seem," Jasper says with such philosophical gravitas that I almost want to laugh—it sounds like something from a fortune cookie—but I don't. He's standing close enough that I can feel heat radiating from his skin, making it hard to focus on anything else.

"I was with Nicolas," I blurt out like someone ripping off a bandage. "After we broke up, obviously. It's part of why I was being weird when you were emailing me from Australia."

Jasper nods, his expression unchanging, like I've just told him it might rain tomorrow. "I wondered," he says simply.

I wait for the interrogation, the raised eyebrows, the hurt—but none come. He genuinely doesn't seem bothered, which is more disorienting than if he'd been upset.

"We ran into each other at a retreat. Actually, it was a retreat Luna sent me on," I explain. At Luna's name, Jasper reaches out and touches my arm. The contact sends electricity zinging through me like I've stuck my finger in a socket. I meet his eyes for a fleeting second before continuing. "I was so depressed being there without Luna. It was the most beautiful place, all these red rocks, but I could barely leave my room. I ran into him, and he was having his own… relationship trouble."

Again, Jasper nods with the serenity of a Buddhist monk. I clear my throat. What am I doing? I sound like I'm in a confessional booth.

"It's okay," he says, his voice gentle. "You don't owe me any explanations."

I look away, suddenly fascinated by a painting on the far wall. What exactly am I doing?

Jasper reaches for my hand, and I nearly jump when his fingers close around mine.

"Emerson," he says, my name a slow, deliberate incantation. "I've missed you. I think I made a mistake. The worst mistake of my life."

I have the distinct feeling that I'm standing at a crossroads—I could run, or I could face this head-on. Part of me wants nothing to do with it, still convinced we're not meant to be together, that the breakup should stand like a monument to our mutual failure. What really has changed since then? Nothing tangible. So why are we even having this conversation?

But then I remember how he appeared out of nowhere when I needed him most—even if I didn't realize it—at that bar, on the street, and at Luna's party-slash-funeral. Is this my wish? Having this second chance? Has some cosmic fairy godmother sprinkled magic dust on my path? Wishes can be so damn confusing. I look Jasper directly in the eyes.

"What mistake do you think you made?" I hold my breath without realizing it.

"Walking away from you when things got hard," he says without hesitation, like he's been rehearsing this answer for months. "Not doing every single thing in my power to find a way to have a life together, to preserve and nurture the love we had."

A few minutes ago, I was going to ask if he'd been with other people, when I told him about Nicolas. I thought that was where the conversation was heading, and I wasn't at all sure how I'd feel either way. But looking at him now, I realize I don't care. If he had fallen in love with someone else, he wouldn't be here, looking at me like I'm water in a desert.

Life is long—if you're lucky—and messy, and I guess it doesn't always follow the neat little script you've written for it. Maybe that's okay? All I know is that the days and weeks and years stretched out endlessly before me with no real anchor, and now, finally, I understand why. Jasper is my anchor. He's the one who gives my days form and meaning. I realize we're still holding hands, our fingers interlaced like they've found their way home.

"You aren't the only one who thinks they made a mistake," I admit, surprising myself. "I wasn't the easiest person to live with. Honestly, you could barely get my attention most of the time."

"Do you want to get out of here?" he asks with a sideways smile that makes my stomach flip like an Olympic gymnast.

I look around one more time, at my friends and my fashion designs come to life, then back to Jasper. How can it be that I felt so hollow when I woke up this morning, and now I'm overflowing? Is this real? Can I trust it?

"Sure," I hear myself saying, as if someone else has momentarily hijacked my vocal cords.

We walk hand in hand to the door. Everyone has gone quiet, watching us like we're the finale of a TV show they've been binge-watching for years. I feel almost silly, like I'm in a rom-com and everyone else is in on the script except me. I can imagine Billie and Ryder plotting this, debating how it would play out. I look at Billie, and she has tears in her eyes. I glance at Ryder, and he gives me a thumbs-up worthy of a cheesy '80s movie. My dear, meddling friends. They know me better than I know myself.

"We're gonna head out," I say, and everyone laughs like I've delivered the punchline to a joke they've been waiting for all night. So casual, so normal, and yet so earth-shatteringly extraordinary.

"This was the best night, the best wish," I tell everyone. I have the strangest sensation that we're leaving a wedding as the couple of honor. Everyone came to support us, to shower us with love, and now they're seeing us off. Why do I keep thinking about weddings? I am being ridiculous. Who knows what happens next? I certainly don't, and for once, that doesn't terrify me.

"Thank you all," I say. "I will never, ever forget this."

We walk out, down the long hall to the elevator. It's there

that Jasper kisses me. His lips touch mine, and I realize in that moment it's the missing piece, the answer to my emptiness. Then a panicked thought: *am I completely losing my mind?*

I pull back.

"Wait!" I say, my voice echoing in the empty hallway.

He pulls back but barely. He's smiling like someone who knows a secret I haven't figured out yet. Is it possible that I never stopped loving him? How did I survive these last months? And then I think of Evie, and my heart plummets like a stone in water.

"If we couldn't get through losing Evie, how are we going to get through other things?" I ask. "That was the worst possible thing, but there could be other things, and then what? We'll just break up again?"

Jasper looks at me, his eyes full of something I can't quite name. "Are we back together then?" he asks, his voice hopeful.

The elevator door opens, and we step in. We each face forward, but we're both smiling so wide our cheeks might crack.

"We're going to have to take it slowly," I say, not believing my own words for a second.

"Of course," he agrees, just as unconvincingly.

"Do you want to come over?"

We laugh, the sound filling the small space with something that feels dangerously like joy.

When the elevator door opens in the lobby, we hesitate for a heartbeat. Then he takes my hand and leads me out, through the lobby, into the city, and finally home.

***

The next morning, I wake up and for the briefest second believe I'm alone, with another empty day stretching before me like an endless desert. And then I see Jasper looking at me, and the world rights itself. He reaches out and touches my hair like he's making sure I'm real.

"I want to tell you something," I say, my voice still rough with sleep. "After you sent that email, I kept thinking about your wish and what dream vacation I would give you."

He nods, waiting.

"And it just wasn't possible," I say, the words catching slightly.

He nods again, patient.

"Because your dream trip, our dream trip, would be the three of us—you, me, and Evie—and she isn't here. She's never going to be here."

I thought I would cry when I said that, but I don't. The pain has changed shape, becoming something I can carry without collapsing.

"I've thought about this so much," he admits. "It's like, what do we do? Not be together because we miss her so much? Just be sad and lonely for the rest of our lives because being together makes us miss her more, because it makes us think of what could have been? I mean, is that what Evie would want if she had a say?"

"No," I say, and now I am crying, the truth of it so clear it's blinding. "No, that's not what she would want."

We're both crying, our tears mingling like they've been waiting to meet again.

"Okay," Jasper says like it's been decided by powers greater than us.

"Okay," I echo.

We're quiet for a while, a comfortable silence that feels like coming home after a long journey.

"So many wishes," he says, breaking the stillness.

"What do you mean?"

"I just mean, and I want to be very clear that I am not taking away from what we've also lost, but even when you aren't meaning to grant a wish, you do. Last night, for example, you granted wish number eight—my greatest wish of all."

"You've been counting?" I ask, genuinely surprised.

"Emerson," he says my name like it's sacred text, "I thought about you every single day we were apart. I wanted to know how you were, what you were doing. I wanted to call you, to say I was sorry. I reached out to your friends, and they very quietly filled me in on what you were up to. Ryder told me about his day. Billie told me about the rest. When I saw you those few times, I thought I was literally going to shatter into a million pieces. I have no idea how I held it together. I know, I know, sometimes you were doing things I might not have loved, with Nicolas for example, but I can see now it was all part of the healing process, yours and mine. So, yes, I counted."

"You've always been good at math," I say with a small smile. "You talked to Ryder? And Billie?"

"They were careful," he says quickly. "They were so proud of your wishes, but that's really all they told me. I was just glad to know anything about you. Don't be mad at them."

"I'm not mad," I say, smiling. "They've just never been good at keeping secrets. I'm intrigued."

"They love you, Em," Jasper says, his eyes serious. "You are an extraordinary human being."

Last night we were careful with each other. We kissed a little, but we were almost shy, which felt weird considering our history. I felt both completely protected and also slightly exposed, and he sensed it, I think, and didn't push. But now, well, I have the feeling that if he doesn't make love to me right this minute, I might spontaneously combust. I pull off my shirt, and he just looks at me, a slow smile spreading across his face.

"Clothes are nice," I say. "I know I spend more time than most people thinking about clothes. But right now, I don't want to have anything to do with them."

He sits up and pulls off the T-shirt he slept in, the one he had on beneath the sweater he wore last night. It's the first time I'm seeing his amazing body again. I run my hand over his shoulder and then down his chest and over his abs like I'm memorizing a map. He closes his eyes for a second, savoring the touch. When I stop moving my hand, he opens his eyes and mirrors my actions, running his hand over my shoulder and down my chest, stopping at each breast, and then down my belly. We continue like that, reacquainting ourselves with each other's bodies, slowly, carefully, lovingly. And then we're all in, each focusing on the other's pleasure with such precision it's almost scientific and also mind-blowingly satisfying.

Eventually, we need a break, and we lie here, breathless, almost all of our wishes granted—the ones we knew about and the ones we didn't even realize we had.

Chapter Twenty-Six

Six months later…

"So many wishes," I whisper.

Those words have ricocheted through my mind more times than I can count since Jasper first said them about six months ago. If I'm being honest with myself—which is something I'm trying to do more of these days—I probably murmur them at least once daily, like a prayer or a mantra. We're in bed, our favorite sanctuary, both pretending we should get up and tackle some work, but it's a special day, so maybe productivity can wait. We're contemplating the possibility. I glance down at Jasper, his palm resting protectively on my swollen belly, and I can't help but smile.

"Happy birthday, beautiful," he says, voice still husky with sleep.

"Forty-one," I say, the number hanging between us.

"Thank goodness for a new year," he says, and we both laugh, the sound mingling in the morning air. "I was thinking, let's skip the Chinese food today."

My mind drifts back to two years ago on this day—my thirty-ninth—when we stayed tangled in these same sheets, eating takeout, convinced we had everything figured out. How naïve we were. Then last year: my party at Buddakan without Jasper, how I strained to be present, to enjoy the moment. Now I realize how achingly lonely it was, despite my valiant efforts. Despite my wonderful friends who tried their best.

"Yes, let's," I agree. "How about pizza?"

"Perfect," he says, his eyes crinkling at the corners.

"Maybe we shouldn't stay in bed all day either," I suggest. "If we're going with the theme of trying not to repeat things from years past."

"Maybe," he says with exaggerated seriousness.

I laugh, and then abruptly stop. "I'm scared," I admit. The thought had been swimming beneath the surface, but I hadn't planned to voice it.

Jasper sits up immediately, his posture signaling that I have his complete attention. "Of what?"

I roll my eyes in a gesture that says *what am I not scared of?* He places his hands on my arms, anchoring me.

"I know, I know," he says. "Believe me, I know. But tell me anyway."

"Okay." I draw a deep breath and fight the familiar sting behind my eyes. "I'm scared of thinking we have it all again, of believing we're going to have this incredible family with a baby on the way, of my new fashion line taking off, of getting too comfortable, and then… well, we know how quickly everything can change."

"I do know, we know," he says thoughtfully. "And they can, but sometimes things do go as planned. Sometimes everything is okay, and we just have to hope for the best. Or at least…" He pauses, considering his words. "We have to try to believe in the best."

I nod, not entirely convinced but wanting to be.

"I think we should get out of bed and do something in this specific moment. Are you open to that? I'm starting to think birthdays in bed are too contemplative. I'm thinking we should take a long walk through the city and end up at Lombardi's for lunch. Are you in?"

"I'm in."

"Do you think he's in?" Jasper asks softly, pointing to my belly.

"He doesn't have much of a choice," I say, then soften. "But yes, I'm pretty sure he's in."

***

Later that night, I pull out my sketchbook and, instead of working on a new design, which I should be doing since I have an upcoming deadline to present my spring concepts to my amazing investors, I write a letter. The words have been orbiting my thoughts all day, as we meandered through the city, as we savored slices at Lombardi's, as we paused on a park bench to debate baby names. I need to capture these feelings on paper. Whatever happens—and please, please, please let it all be okay—I want to remember every moment. I hover my pen above the blank page, uncertain where to begin. And then suddenly, clarity strikes.

Hello Forty-One! I write.

Thank you for being here for me because you were not able to be there for Luna. But just so we're clear, I will miss her every day for the rest of my life. I'm going to keep this short, and I'm not going to look at it again until... well, until our baby is here. But birthdays are a time for wishes, right? So here are mine, though I hope it's okay to still have some, after so many have already been granted. I don't want to seem greedy.

First, I wish for a healthy, happy baby. We already know he's a boy, which, I have to admit, is a relief. Not that I don't want a girl, I do, but I worry that all I would see is Evie. So there, already, is another wish granted.

I wish (and vow) to be (mostly) fully present when Jasper wants to talk or play a song he's working on or just needs my attention. He has to sometimes — no, let me correct that, he has to often — be the most important person in the room. He deserves it, and I believe I can give it to him in a way I wasn't able to before.

I wish to keep granting wishes; little has been more satisfying to me than that. And here is my biggest wish of all, my true birthday wish. I want to take Jasper and the baby on a dream trip. The trip I never thought was possible. When the time is right, if we are able to be so lucky, I will hand Jasper a packing list. I dream about that moment. This is what it will say:

JASPER'S PACKING LIST: Clothes, toothbrush, toiletries, stroller, Pack N Play, diapers, burp cloths, Baby, Wife, Husband, Happiness...

It seems so bright, so audacious to ask for, that I quickly fold over the page and close the book. Next week we're getting married in an intimate ceremony at City Hall with Billie and Ryder as our witnesses. Afterward, we're heading back to Billie's for a simple catered meal. She offered, and it felt right; we've shared so many pivotal moments there lately. This wedding is so unlike anything I would have planned before. I had once imagined something massive, with hundreds of guests at the most prestigious venue in New York City. But I don't want that anymore, and I certainly don't need it.

A thought occurs to me, and I return to the letter. I unfold it quickly, cross out the apostrophe and S after Jasper's name and then add *and Emerson's* to the top so now it reads *JASPER AND*

EMERSON'S PACKING LIST. It belongs to both of us and, if there's anything I should take from this past year, it's that I can make my own wishes come true, at least some of them. Some, I am painfully aware, I have no control over.

Another thought surfaces, and I add: *Remember that things can't always be perfect. Remember that you will make mistakes, and that's okay. You don't have to run from them. You can face them and try to make them better. Stop trying to control everything. It is impossible, frustrating, and backfires most of the time. Instead, embrace the mess, the chaos, and the magical unknown.*

I fold the pages over and close the book. I place it in the drawer of my bedside table, keeping it closer these days since I'm using it almost daily. My fashion line, STYLE ME SATURDAY, is gaining momentum. Nicolas followed through and helped with an initial show—more public than the one in Billie's apartment, though that one will always hold a special place in my heart. And it grew from there. StyleShop has even purchased a few items for their winter collection.

I grab my phone and see one missed call from Gerald and three from Maddi, who I recently lured away from StyleShop to become my director of sales. Over coffee not long ago, she confessed she didn't love the corporate atmosphere of StyleShop as much as she'd anticipated, though she was careful not to make it sound like criticism. She said she prefers to be closer to the clothes and the people wearing them. I told her there was a spot for her on my team whenever she wanted it, half-joking. She replied, "I thought you'd never ask," not joking at all.

I can hear Jasper playing his guitar in the living room. He isn't calling for me; he knows I have work to do—I've been mentioning my deadline all day—but I know he's working on a new song for a movie, and already the melody wraps around me like a familiar embrace.

I leave my sketchbook where it is, tucked away for the night. I set my phone on the counter and abandon it there, then pad over to the couch, one hand cradling my growing belly, my legs curled beneath me, and I listen to my soon-to-be husband compose a love song that feels, somehow, like it's always existed, just waiting for him to discover it.

THE END

Acknowledgements

Two and a half years ago, *Eight Wishes* arrived in my thoughts during a season of upheaval, one of those times when life feels more like unsteady ground than solid footing.

At first, the project took shape as a list of wishes I hoped to explore with the people I love, a way to invite deeper conversations. For a while, I imagined turning those wishes into a documentary, but I soon realized I needed a quieter, more personal medium. So, I began writing a novel, uncertain where it would lead.

I wanted this story to exist without a business plan or a marketing strategy, just the simple act of creating for its own sake. *Still, doubt followed me closely: You're not a real writer. This might fail. Can you actually finish?* I filled my phone with notes taken on morning walks, fragments of dialogue scribbled after gym sessions, and ideas that surfaced in the shower. Collecting those moments was joyful; committing them to the page was harder.

Once my outline stretched past 14,000 words, there was no turning back. Over the next two years, I swung between wanting to give up and wanting to spend the rest of my life telling stories. Some days the pages felt impossible; others, they felt like home.

I wouldn't have reached the end without the patience and encouragement of Elizabeth, Amanda, Jaime, Alejandro, Tina, Allison, my mum, and all the friends and family who listened, advised, and believed in the work even when I struggled to believe in it myself. Thank you for steadying me through every late-night worry and early-morning rewrite.

I'm grateful you've chosen to spend your time with *Eight Wishes*. If the book brings you a moment of reflection, comfort, or connection, or simply keeps your coffee company on the table, I'm honored.

With thanks,
Cas

One Last Thing

Thank you for reading all the way to the end of *Eight Wishes*. I'm grateful you chose to spend your time with this story. If the book touched you, made you think, feel, or simply offered a welcome escape, would you consider leaving a short review? Even a few sentences on your preferred retailer make a genuine difference, helping other readers discover the novel and guiding me as I continue to grow as a writer.

Thank you again for your support and for sharing this journey with me.

With appreciation,
Cas

About the Author

Cas Caldicott is an award-winning entrepreneur, best-selling author, and speaker who has founded and sold five companies over the past two decades. Named 'Entrepreneur of the Year' at the American Business Awards, Cas's work has been featured on NBC, Fox, and ABC.

Eight Wishes is a debut novel, extending a lifelong commitment to human connection from scaling companies to crafting stories.